CW01654318

Stepping Out

JO HOWARD

This edition first published in paperback by
Michael Terence Publishing in 2023
www.mtp.agency

Copyright © 2023 Jo Howard

Jo Howard has asserted the right to be identified as
the author of this work in accordance with the
Copyright, Designs and Patents Act 1988

ISBN 9781800945708

No part of this publication may be reproduced, stored
in a retrieval system, or transmitted, in any form or
by any means, electronic, mechanical, photocopying,
recording or otherwise, without the prior
permission of the publisher

Cover image by
MTP under licence from www.123rf.com

Cover design
Copyright © 2023 Michael Terence Publishing

Michael Terence
Publishing

Chapter 1
London 1959

Lunchtime at the hostel was quiet as Alice unpacked her few possessions. The business of leaving home should take longer. She wondered what Dad was doing and remembered Saturdays, years ago, when he came home on leave and took her to Stamford Bridge to watch football.

She had told Spencer she could not see him this weekend, now she wished she hadn't. Dare she telephone and suggest a meeting? That would seem too forward and his mother might answer. From what Spencer had said, Alice didn't think she would like his mother but he had promised he would arrange for her to meet both his parents so he must be keen.

It would be six whole days before she saw him again. She looked round the bare room, it was now her home. She felt frightened; had she been stupid to leave Dad's flat, was this place any better? She stretched out on the bed and listened to other residents moving along the corridor, chatting to each other. She heard the occasional laugh. Any of these strangers could become friends, it was up to her. There was no point in wallowing in self-pity. She'd get some postcards, write to Spencer, say she had settled in and remind him of their date. She could also write to Mum and Gran and give them her new address. She wondered if Dad would expect her to write to him, probably not.

Earlier, she had walked to a parade of shops which the hostel warden, Miss Pritchard, had said was not far. The shops looked dusty and rundown but they would provide bare essentials. It was going to be all right; with just a few friends she would cope.

The only postcards on display in the newsagents were unappetizing local scenes; Baron's Court was unlikely to attract visitors if the cards on sale were the best they had to offer. With no stamps and the Post Office shut, she had the weekend to decide what to write.

She stared through the window of her room; what a pity there hadn't been a card with a picture of the hostel then she could have put a cross on the appropriate window and written 'I am here'.

When high-pitched screams ricocheted up the corridor; Alice rushed to her door and peered out. The screams were coming from a room two doors away. A group of girls had gathered so Alice hurried to join them.

'It's Susan again,' someone said, 'always making a fuss.'

'Spoilt rotten, attention seeking,' another girl added.

How unkind, Alice thought, as she peered into the room. The girl, who must be Susan, was crouched on the bed.

'There it is!' she yelled. 'There!'

Alice saw something moving in the corner of the room, a large spider.

Susan moved closer so Alice could see her tear-streaked face emerge from the shadows, a pretty face.

'Shall I get rid of it for you?'

'Please, oh yes do, kill it, I can't stand spiders.' Susan's hysteria made Alice feel flustered. She grabbed an empty cup from the chest of drawers and banged it, upside down, over the spider.

'I'll never be able to drink out of that again,' Susan said.

Alice decided there was no point in telling her not to be silly.

'I'll open the window if you put your hand over the cup.'

'I'm not getting off this bed until that thing has gone.'

'I don't think it's a man-eating variety.' Alice grinned, 'Have you got a piece of card?'

'What for?'

'To slide under the cup to keep the spider inside, then I'll drop it out of the window.'

Either Susan didn't have any card or she wasn't prepared to look.

'Just keep your hand on top of the cup while I go next door.'

Susan didn't move.

'If you don't the spider might sneak under the rim.'

'Don't be long,' Susan whispered.

Amazing, Alice thought, pretend you're in control and people believe you know what you're doing. It's all one big confidence trick and now I have met someone. She ran to her room, picked up a postcard and hurried back. Susan watched as Alice pushed the postcard under the cup.

'You'll be safe now.'

Alice leaned out of the window, turned the cup upside down and removed the card but nothing happened. She looked inside and saw the spider huddled in the bottom. She shook the cup and the small body, legs folded tightly to its sides, fell out. She turned and beamed at Susan, what a wonderful start, a friend already she hoped.

'I hope it lands on the grass.'

'I don't,' Susan said, 'it might come back, they always do. I hate it here.'

Alice didn't know what to say; had she made a terrible mistake?

Susan bounced off the bed and gave Alice a hug.

'Thank you so much, I'm really grateful.'

Alice felt herself blush.

'If I hurry, I'll just have time to change before I meet Tony; he is my boyfriend.'

Alice watched as Susan brushed and combed her wavy, blond hair. She was very pretty.

'I'm meeting him in town. He's twenty-six and a real dream boat.'

Alice was surprised; twenty-six seemed very grown-up for a girl as young as Susan.

'My boyfriend is nineteen.' Alice realized it was the first time she had referred to Spencer as hers.

'Well, I can certainly recommend older men,' Susan said, as she started to apply bright, blue eye shadow, 'they know so much more about life.'

Alice was fascinated. Perhaps, if she asked, Susan would help her with make-up. She waited, not sure whether to stay or leave. She didn't want to be on her own, not yet.

Susan applied scarlet lipstick, checked the effect, slipped off her dressing gown and put on a full-skirted summer dress.

'Zip me up,' she said, 'and take that cup if you want, I shan't use it. Anyway, I've got another one.' She glanced at her watch. 'I'd better go, thanks again you're a star.'

Left with no choice, Alice went back to her room where she brushed dust marks off her postcard.

Dear Spencer, she wrote,

Settled in well, my room is nice (he would never see it). All the other girls are friendly, (they will be when I get to know them). See you on Friday. I'll meet you outside the hostel at 7 p.m.

She stopped, unsure how to finish, should it be love, best wishes or nothing, just Alice? Perhaps she should write a bit more then there would only be room for her name.

She gazed out of her window and watched the trees wave forlorn farewells to summer with branches clad in leaves already changing from green to russet and bronze. Sadness gripped her. This is only the beginning, she thought, I shall be staying in tonight and I must accept it; I can read my book. She wondered what Spencer was doing, she hoped he was thinking of her.

Joan pushed food around her plate only half listening as Stanley talked to Spencer, their older son, about a new order from Germany.

'Stanley, it's lunchtime; do you always have to talk business? No one asks me what I've done, do they?'

Anger bubbled in her throat and the sickly, heavy taste of brandy made her dizzy. They were always ignoring her yet she had been someone once, a top model in Canada. Some had said she was the image of Wallis Simpson. She sighed, that was so long ago. She pushed herself to her feet and walked with heavy precision from the room. Swaying with nausea she wondered if she had been wise to drink on an empty stomach, but why shouldn't she if she felt like it? She sat on the easy chair in the hallway and closed her eyes. If she sat still, she would feel better. Words drifted in and out of her hearing and then she heard footsteps; someone was standing over her.

'She's asleep.' It was Spencer, 'Why do you put up with it, Dad?'

How dare he? If she hadn't felt so dizzy, she would have given him a piece of her mind. A tear slid down her cheek, all she wanted was her darling Malcolm at home, but it was weeks until the half-term holiday. Stanley didn't understand; he complained that she made a favourite of the boy, and said she'd ruin him. But he would always be her baby.

She listened as husband and son cleared the table. Stanley had muttered when she bought the Crown Derby dinner service, but why not have nice things? He's just tight-fisted, always ready to deprive her of some happiness.

As Joan resented cooking on Saturday evenings, she and Stanley often ate out. She had eaten little all day and now, after a nap, she was ready to be wined and dined. A hot shower and her new dress would make up for the business at lunchtime. She wondered if Stanley had decided which restaurant they would go to. If only Malcolm was here, she thought, that would make the evening perfect.

'Spencer is coming to Stockholm with me on Thursday, we will probably be away a week.'

Joan crumbled her bread and pushed the plate away. She wondered who else would be going. That tarty secretary, Gill, used to figure in dispatches rather too often, now she was never mentioned; he must think she was stupid. She took another cigarette from her case and waited for Stanley to light it, knowing he hated her smoking between courses. She exhaled and stared across the room rather than at him.

'So, I'm going to be on my own again.' Joan drained her brandy glass.

'What do you want me to do? Trade doesn't appear out of thin air.'

'Perhaps you should employ someone else to do the donkey work.'

'My dear, I don't like all this travelling any more than you do. Things are difficult with this Common Market business. If de Gaulle has his way…'

'What do I know about that?'

'Since you don't mind spending the money, we make, perhaps you should show some interest in where it comes from.'

Joan sighed and ground out her cigarette.

'Scandinavian countries may be our only chance. The other alternative is the States, that's even further away.'

'At least I could go there with you, look up some old friends.'

'Yes dear, but how long is it since you left?' He took her hand in his.

She pulled her hand away and lit another cigarette, the exhaled smoke swirled about her head. He was smiling that condescending smile that made her want to lash out. She had given up everything for him.

'And what about Malcolm? I notice he doesn't get a mention

in your master plan or is it only Spencer you're interested in?'

'Malcolm has exams, I'm sure he'll tell us his plans when he's ready. We can have a chat with him when he gets back.'

'If you hadn't insisted on sending him to that confounded boarding school we wouldn't have to wait for end-of-term holidays to speak to him.'

Joan looked at her watch, 'How long have we been waiting?' She clicked her fingers at a nearby waiter.

'Since your chef's working at half speed, I'll have another Courvoisier while I wait, make it a double.'

Joan watched the waiter give a startled glance towards Stanley who nodded.

'Let's change the subject, my dear. I've brought you out to enjoy yourself not to talk business.'

Joan stared at him and picked up her glass.

'Cheers, let's hope you have a wonderful time impressing the Swedes, both male and female.' She tipped her glass in mock salute; her lips smiled but her eyes were cold.

'Has Spencer told you about this young lady of his?'

'When has he ever confided in me?'

'Recently moved into a hostel, I believe,' Stanley said.

'Has she no parents?'

'Divorced, I think, been living with her father, difficult fellow, Spencer said.'

'Not much of a recommendation.'

'They met at Chelsea swimming baths apparently.'

'Really Stanley, what kind of girl allows herself to be picked up in the swimming baths?'

'Things aren't the same as when we were young. People meet anywhere; I think it is more natural than all this formal introduction nonsense.'

'Maybe but at least, you knew what a person's background was.'

'Surely we can trust Spencer to be sensible; we've brought him up well.'

Joan gave a dismissive shrug.

'Well, there's only one way to find out; we'll just have to meet her.'

'Oh, and will that be before or after your little jaunt to foreign parts?

Chapter 2

Alice trudged upstairs. After a week in her new job, she was exhausted. There was so much to learn and though Professor Walker seemed kind, Alice was not sure how well she would get on with the other laboratory assistants.

The Tube was packed, as always, on Friday evenings. She hated being crushed together with strangers some of whom could do with a wash. Rain poured down all the way from the station, but at least she was meeting Spencer. She was surprised to see a letter from him in her pigeonhole in the hall. She would save it until after a hot cup of tea.

Grinning with anticipation she sprinted up the last flight of stairs, threw her coat and bag on her bed and joined the gaggle of girls, outside the nearest kitchen, all waiting to use the kettle. As she stood in the queue, Alice could not stop her mind from drifting back to the dreadful afternoon when Spencer called round to see her at home. He must have known she would be alone. After all, she had told him Dad worked funny shifts at the Post Office. She had been reluctant to let him in; Dad didn't like people being there when he was working.

'But you live here for heaven's sake,' Spencer had said.

She had offered him tea and biscuits then realized there were none; Dad thought biscuits were an extravagance. She offered to go to the local shop, but Spencer had put his arms around her.

'Never mind about tea, give me a kiss.'

It had been lovely, just like in the cinema. She had gasped for air when he released her and she remembered leaning against him. It must be what Victorian ladies swooned over.

'I'd better put the kettle on, in case Dad comes in.'

She smiled at the memory of that kiss and shuffled a little nearer to the kitchen after two girls left with mugs of steaming tea.

She remembered how Spencer grabbed her hand and led her into the sitting room, sat in the nearest chair and pulled her onto his knee. He had held her in his arms and kissed her again with a gentleness that left her weak with desire. She blushed s she recalled how she'd felt at that moment.

'Got soaked walking from the station.'

Alice jumped.

'You were miles away.'

It was the girl in front who had turned to speak.

'Yes, dreadful wasn't it and the Tube was packed.'

'That's rush hour for you, settling in all right?' The girl smiled, 'I'm Maureen, my room is at the end of the corridor.'

'I'm Alice. I think you're next.'

She fingered Spencer's letter while she waited, but uncomfortable images jostled in her head. After that gentle kiss, his hand slid down to her breast. She wasn't ready for such intimacy, not yet. But his hand was so soothing, surely it couldn't be wrong. Then he rested his hand on her thigh and pushed her skirt up.

'Please don't,' she'd said, 'please.'

When he looked at her, she felt scared.

'I think we both need a cup of tea.'

She leapt off his knee and rushed to the kitchen. He had followed and watched as she put out cups and saucers. Their conversation that day had been stilted yet every eye contact was like an electric shock. Alice was unsure now if she had been shaking with fear or longing. She knew sex was where relationships ended up; if she wanted him, it was inevitable.

'Show me the rest of the flat,' he had said.

'There isn't much really.'

Spencer smiled, 'I didn't mean to frighten you, I'm sorry.'

He said it so gently, Alice smiled.

'Your turn,' Maureen said as she left the kitchen, 'it's a wonder the kettle hasn't melted. You know where to find me if you want a chat.'

'Thanks,' Alice replied. She topped up the kettle and gazed out of the window, listening to the hum of the gas stove and the chatter of the other residents.

She should have done things differently that day; she should have suggested a walk along the Embankment with Spencer.

'Come on, show me where my lady rests her weary head.'

She had laughed and led him upstairs. Her room had looked cheerless, dismal, with no carpet just cold linoleum; even on a warm day, her room felt chilly. Spencer had said nothing. Embarrassed, Alice walked to the landing.

'Dad sleeps here,' she said and opened his bedroom door."

Sunlight had streamed in on that autumn afternoon giving the room a welcoming glow. Alice had moved back, ready to go downstairs.

Spencer had rested his hands on her shoulders, 'I do love you; you know.'

She remembered blinking away tears and her heart had felt ready to explode. She opened her mouth to speak but he kissed her again.

'I promise I won't hurt you.'

Together they had sat on the edge of Dad's double bed and kissed, leaning back until they rested side by side, arms entwined.

'I promise I'll stop when you tell me to.'

Alice nodded, as he fumbled with the buttons on her blouse. Above the waist is all right, everyone knows that. But then, she was not sure how, her skirt had ridden up and she was choking.

She struggled and fought him off.

'It's wrong,' she'd sobbed.

It was still so clear. He stared at her. 'I think I'd better go.'

He left, without a backward glance.

Alice's hand was shaking as she made her cup of tea. She walked back to her room. He had only been testing her, making sure she was a nice girl. She had straightened Dad's bed clothes so carefully but, remembered how he had shouted at her when he got back from work. He had sensed that something had gone on and said she was just like her mother.

'That is why I am here,' she said to her empty hostel room, maybe one day Dad will believe what I told him.

She kicked off her wet shoes, put on her slippers and stretched out on the bed. She tore open the envelope and scanned the letter.

Dear Alice,

Sorry about Friday, I'll be back next week. Love Spencer xx

Disappointment sucked at her heart and filled her head. Her tea grew cold as she lay too heavy-limbed to move.

It was time for the evening meal. She didn't want anything; she would just stay in her room and waste away. The sound of feet walking along the corridor emphasized the evening routine. Feeding time at the zoo, it is half past five and you will be hungry. Soon the corridor was silent.

I'm alone, she thought, Dad is better off without me, Mum's got Alec and the kids and Spencer is going to Stockholm. He's bound to meet some gorgeous Swedish girl.

There was the sudden staccato tap, the tap of high-heeled shoes accompanied by knocking. Alice roused herself, it was Susan's voice.

'Yes?'

'Thank heavens,' Susan rushed in, 'I'm late and my zip's stuck.'

'Going out with Tony?'

'Of course, he's taking me to dinner, none of this hostel muck.'

Alice tugged and released the lining which was caught.

'There you are.'

'Thanks a million, can't stop, aren't you eating?'

'No, not hungry.'

Susan raised her eyebrows and left with such speed she left a vacuum behind her. Alice stood at her window. It was still raining and she watched as Susan ran up the road with her umbrella bobbing up and down like a demented daisy.

Alice sat on her bed, well, it's no good starving. She couldn't afford to miss a meal she had already paid for. She slouched down the stairs trying to decide, from the smell, what was on the menu; she hoped it was something tasty.

She joined the queue which moved, at a snail's pace, around the dining room. When at last she reached the hatch there was only shepherd's pie left. After the grey mash and even greyer mince, Alice decided enough was enough. The pudding was a sponge with lumpy custard, school dinners all over again. She managed some of the shepherd's pie which was tepid then with a heavy heart she went back to her room.

She had finished all but one of her books and would have to go to the library tomorrow, once she found out where it was. She loved reading, it was always her way to escape reality; she would be doing a lot of reading over the next few days.

Several girls in the dining room had smiled and nodded, but apart from Susan and Maureen, she had not had a conversation with anyone. Now Susan was out having a good time and somehow, she didn't feel like talking to Maureen.

She heard crying as she walked along the corridor; someone else having a rotten time. She listened outside Susan's room, but surely, she was out.

Alice wondered what to do, was it best to leave people alone in such circumstances? She decided it wasn't and knocked on Susan's door.

A muffled voice said, 'Go away.'

If Susan had not wanted anyone to know she was crying she should have been quieter about it, Alice thought, as she opened the door.

'What's the matter, are you okay?'

'There was a wail from the figure on the bed. Perhaps the other residents were right, perhaps Susan was always making a fuss about something.

'He stood me up.'

So much for older men. 'Do you want a cup of tea?'

Another wail from Susan as Alice went to the kitchen, Susan would have tea if she wanted it or not. Once she stopped crying, perhaps they could have a chat, get to know each other better. That would be nicer than staying alone in her room.

'Here you are, drink this, I've put some sugar in it, it will make you feel better.'

'Nothing will make me feel better, you don't understand. I wish I was dead.'

Alice had often wondered how film stars could cry without suffering devastation to the face. Crying always made her go a blotchy red and she ended up with swollen eyes and a streaming nose. Susan had the same problem. Alice felt quite heartened as she sat on the edge of the bed with two cups of tea. Susan snivelled and dabbed at her face.

'I waited for ages in the rain; Tony's an absolute pig. These awful blokes kept leering at me, asking if they could help. Can you believe it?' Her voice was shrill.

'Where were you meeting him?'

'Leicester Square Tube station, it was awful.'

'Were you late?'

'Only ten minutes, surely he should have waited.'

Alice didn't know. She was always early when she met Spencer and had to hide until the appointed time.

'Can't you phone him?'

'I haven't got his number; I'll have to wait until he gets in touch.' She started to cry, 'Perhaps he never will.'

'Maybe you'd be better off without him if he's like that.'

Susan's wails increased in volume.

'How long have you known him?'

'Three months.'

'I've known my boyfriend longer than that. He's had to go to Stockholm, on a business trip with his dad. We had a date for tomorrow, but now he can't make it.'

Susan sipped her tea. 'I don't even know where he works.'

That's strange, Alice thought, I know a lot more about Spencer than Susan knows about Tony.

'Where did you meet him?'

'At the Palais.'

Alice looked blank.

'You know, the Hammersmith Palais, dancing.'

Alice knew Dad would never have sanctioned dancing at the Palais.

'Haven't you ever been?'

Alice shook her head.

'Tell you what,' Susan said, 'sod these bloody men, let's go tomorrow.'

Alice opened her mouth, but then shut it again.

'Come on, it'll be fun.'

'I've nothing to wear.'

'I'll lend you something.'

Alice laughed as she stood up. She was much taller than Susan and definitely not as slim.

'Anything will do, a summer dress and a cardie, you must have something.'

'What about getting back in time?'

'Oh, never mind about that, don't push the sign across when you go out. Old Pritchard will never know that we aren't tucked up with our hot water bottles.'

'But where will we go if the door's locked?'

Susan sighed, 'Don't worry, Pat round the corner used to live here; has her own flat now, she always lets people sleep on the floor.'

It was all so easy, but what was she going to wear?

'Well, will you come?'

'Yes, I'll go and check my clothes.' That won't take long, she thought, as she returned to her room. She was going to the Palais, what an adventure.

Joan roamed from room to room with a cigarette in one hand, a brandy glass in the other. The only person she had seen since Stanley and Spencer left was the cleaning woman, hardly stimulating. If only I had a daughter, Joan thought, I would have a companion and a friend. We could have done things together, gone on shopping expeditions.

She glanced at herself in the long, hall mirror. Leaving the cigarette in her mouth, she put her glass down and smoothed her hands over her hips. Turning sideways she pulled in her stomach muscles. She turned her face to the mirror and exhaled, for a moment the swirling smoke softened her features and she looked young again.

'Stanley is damned lucky,' she said to her reflection. Her voice echoed in the black and white tiled hall to remind her of her solitude.

'I'll go into town, I deserve some new outfits,' she said and recalled the horrified looks her dressmaker's bills would always elicit from Stanley. Joan had told him once that you only got what you paid for.

Of course, Stanley in his usual cheese-paring way had pointed out it was not she who paid; he did. She recalled the occasion, years ago, when he had muttered about unnecessary extravagance and she had, with a seraphic smile, suggested the offending items be returned with a note to explain he could not afford them. She had been startled by the vehemence of his response; the breakfast crockery had bounced as his fist hit the table.

'Don't be so bloody silly, woman,' he had shouted. Since then whilst there was bad grace in his acceptance, accept he did. She smiled; it was ages since she had had a day in town.

She took her astrakhan coat from its hangar; it always made her feel special. She would browse through the fashion departments and by the time she got back most of the day would be over. She'd phone Sylvia and arrange for a discussion and fitting; that would take care of another day.

She paused; she knew she should go to see her parents, but it was such a pain. Her sister, Lillian, would look reproachful and Dad would mutter about how long it was since her last visit and why didn't she come more often. The whole business would be hateful, besides no one could accuse her and Stanley of not helping out. After all, Stanley had paid for Mum and Dad to come back to England as soon as Mum was diagnosed with M.S.

Joan checked her makeup in the mirror.

Of course, as Lillian was single it was only right, she should come too. If she'd wanted to stay in Canada, to have a life of her own, she could. It was unfortunate that mum was now bedridden which did tie Lillian to the house.

Joan touched up her lipstick.

'I have my own family to look after,' Joan said to her reflection, 'no one should expect me to take on my parents as well.' No, she decided, a visit to the aged parents could wait until Stanley was back, he was so good with them.

Joan wanted Sylvia to start on her things before he returned then it would be too late for him to make a fuss. Feeling more cheerful, she went to phone for a taxi, no point in driving to town.

Chapter 3

Thank goodness it's Saturday, Alice thought, as she woke bleary-eyed after a restless night. Her neck ached and the rollers had dug into her scalp. She wondered how girls went through such torture on a regular basis. The beer Susan had used as setting lotion had made Alice's hair stiff and sticky; the smell was frightful.

If she wanted breakfast, she'd better hurry. She dressed and attacked her hair with her brush. When she looked in the mirror, she was relieved to see it looked presentable. After breakfast, she'd go out for fresh air to get rid of the smell of beer.

When she got back to the hostel, Susan's hair had been lacquered into a fashionable French pleat. She had hung her dress on the wardrobe door. With its full skirt in deep folds below a fitted bodice, it hung like an exotic blossom. Alice saw a froth of paper nylon petticoats on the bed. White winkle-picker stilettos and a white cardigan completed the outfit.

Alice knew she could never compete with such finery. She sighed as she returned to her room to look again at what she had. There was her best blouse, pale cream, shantung silk which Dad had chosen two years ago. It was suitable for a mature lady, nice, elegant but not what teenagers wore. There were two possible skirts; she chose the fuller of the two. At least she had one decent petticoat.

'It's not fair,' she muttered, 'some girls have everything, I can't even get pretty shoes with my big feet.' Had Susan asked her as a foil, pretty girl, plain friend? Pretty girls always got the boys who never seemed to look beyond face and figure. What about personality? Still, Spencer must be more discerning than most, he liked her and still wanted to see her. What would she tell him about tonight? Perhaps she should wait to see if there was anything to tell.

After a rushed meal, they raced out of the hostel, praying that Miss Pritchard didn't see them. They caught the District Line train to Hammersmith. The carriage was full of excited girls, all with the Alma Cogan look of full skirts and nipped-in waists. Young men stood in self-conscious groups near the train doors, ostentatiously smoking and smoothing their D.A.s into place with dirty combs. Their hot eyes surveyed the talent. The atmosphere buzzed and Alice felt swept along by the excitement.

They arrived outside the Palais where there was already a chattering queue of girls. Moody-looking boys were trying to disassociate themselves from the melee, anxious to emulate James Dean. Alice remembered seeing 'East of Eden' and found Dean utterly delectable; so sad he had been killed.

Efficient doormen kept the queue moving, hustling girls into the dance hall first. Tommy Steele's 'Singing the Blues' was belting out and some couples were jiving, while others perambulated in a more tentative manner. Alice felt cold with fear, would she be able to dance well enough? It had never occurred to her that she might not know how to do it.

She looked around, but Susan was not there; she must be dancing with someone already. She'd just sit down quietly here and watch, as Susan whisked past in a cloud of petticoats and L'Aimant perfume. Alice smiled, but Susan was too engrossed to notice.

'Would you like to dance?'

Alice looked up. A short, dumpy, young man with bad acne was smiling at her. Oh dear, she was going to tower above him. As she rose from her seat the young man seemed to shrink. His smile became fixed and Alice wanted to giggle. His head barely reached her shoulder. He would never be able to steer her through the dancers although he seemed determined to try. She wondered if she should offer to lead – she had plenty of practice at school where she had always had to take the part of a man. Perhaps it would not be tactful to suggest this to a stranger.

'My name's Derek, do you come here often?'

Alice choked, so people really did say that. According to magazines, she had read in her doctor's waiting room, it was the least original opening gambit. At least she was dancing even if it was with a midget, that was better than being a wallflower all night.

'I've just moved into a hostel, at Baron's Court.'

Derek looked surprised. 'I'm still at home, me, my sister, with Mum and Dad.'

'I work at the hospital and the hostel was easier for getting to work.'

'Oh,' said Derek, 'what do you do?'

'Weigh rats.'

'What for?'

'They have their thyroids cut out.'

Alice watched Derek's face turn white.

'You don't do that do you?'

'Oh no, Professor Walker does that, he's working on diets for people who have thyroid deficiency. One of my jobs is to weigh the rats to see if they've lost weight.'

Derek nodded, content to continue using Alice as a battering ram, steering her firmly through the crowd while she looked for Susan.

'How did you know I'd be here?' Susan asked as Tony whisked her around the dance floor.

'Thought you'd probably be sulking after the other night, I can read you like a book, see. Know you like dancing so where better than here?'

'So, who was the girl you were talking to?'

'A girl from work actually, not a patch on you.'

'It was awful, just standing there at the station; I couldn't call you or anything.'

'I've told you, I had to work late.'

'Why can't I have your number then if it happens again, I can give you a call.'

'Don't give my number to anyone, doll; not allowed, company policy.'

'What about your home number then?'

He whirled her around. 'You don't want to stay here all night, do you? There's a bit of a party back at the flat. Come on, we'll have some fun.'

'Well, it's a bit awkward you see, didn't know you'd be here so I bought this girl with me, from the hostel.'

Tony sighed and then gave Susan a hug. 'Let's sneak out when she's not looking.'

About to agree, Susan caught a glimpse of Alice on the far side of the room, she was waving.

'She's seen me, I can't just leave her.'

'Go and get her then, I'll wait outside.'

'What's the matter?' Derek asked.

'I'm sorry; I was looking for my friend.'

'Would you like a drink?'

'Oh, yes please.' Her mouth was dry with anxiety rather than exertion.

They threaded their way through the crowd to a bar. Alice was impressed by the way Derek made a pathway, a bit like a terrier going down a rabbit hole. She followed, looking from side to side, but couldn't see Susan now.

'What will you have?'

'Just an orange squash, please.'

She noted the look of relief on Derek's face, perhaps girls usually asked for something stronger. Dad had always said don't be a gold-digger and Derek didn't look as though he had money to spare.

Alice felt a tap on her shoulder, it was Susan.

'Where've you been? You were over there a minute ago; I thought

I'd lost you.'

'Derek asked me to have a drink.'

'Who's Derek?'

'This bloke I've been dancing with.'

Susan was glowing. 'You'll never guess what, Tony's here, would you believe it? Wasn't his fault the other night, he had to work late. Anyway, it doesn't matter now, he's here and he's taking me to this party. Are you coming?'

Alice swallowed hard and watched as Derek, with an orange squash in one hand and half a pint of beer in the other, pushed his way through the crowd. She looked back at Susan.

'This is Derek.'

Susan ignored him. 'Tony said he'd only wait for five minutes.'

'I'm really sorry, Derek, but I'll have to go.'

He shrugged. 'You might as well drink this first, I don't want it.'

She gulped most of it down while Susan hopped from foot to foot.

'Thanks ever so much, I really am sorry.'

'Perhaps I'll see you here next week.'

'Yes, perhaps, that would be nice.' You liar, Alice thought, next week she hoped to be out with Spencer.

She raced after Susan and arrived at the entrance to see an arrogant looking man checking his watch. Susan touched his arm.

'Sorry it took so long; I couldn't find her. This is Alice.'

Tony nodded, turned and strode out of the Palais followed, at a run, by the two girls. His car was parked in a side street, a two-door saloon; Alice had to clamber into the back. Susan chatted all the way to wherever Tony was taking them, Alice felt invisible. More than anything she wanted to go back to the hostel, but she didn't think it wise to say so.

Tony parked the car and the girls waited while he locked the doors. Alice shivered although it wasn't cold, she had no idea where she was.

'It's the top floor flat.' Tony said to no one in particular.

Alice, taut with embarrassment at being, so obviously, the third that makes a crowd, walked up the stone steps. As she looked up, she could see lights. That must be where the party was although there was no noise; perhaps it wasn't that kind of party. She paused at the top of the first unlit flight of stairs. She could hear giggling and rustling below, Susan and Tony were following her up. Reassured she went up two more flights and still no noise; she felt frightened. She couldn't see how they would get back to the hostel before the doors were locked and she didn't know the girl that Susan had mentioned. She had nowhere to go but up. She climbed the last flight and stood outside the only door, an attic flat she assumed.

She pushed the door open and saw a dimly lit room with hardly any furniture. Four men were sitting around a low coffee table, playing cards. There was a beer crate on the floor and from the number of empties scattered around, most of the crate's contents had been drunk. The men looked up, surprised.

'Tony said there was a party here.'

The man with his back to her swivelled round: he eyed her up and down and smirking said, 'Yes, darling, you're it.'

Joan lay on the settee and wondered if she should have another brandy; the effort of getting up was too much, she closed her eyes. Stanley and Spencer would be back tomorrow so she would have to tidy the place; heaven only knew what the cleaning woman did.

'I'll sack her, that's what I'll do,' she said to the television, murmuring in the corner. She lit another cigarette and slumped back, watching as the smoke drifted upwards; alone always alone. Stanley kept suggesting she should take up a hobby and meet some like-minded women. There were no women in Hendon with whom she had anything in common. None of them had mixed in high society – with film stars in fact. All that was so long ago in a faraway place; she wondered if she would ever go back to the States, probably not. She drew on her cigarette and watched the column of ash quiver.

She heard a car door bang. It was close, and then there was the scrape of a key in the front door lock and Spencer's voice. Was it part of the watching campaign to return early? She knew Stanley and Spencer were always checking up on her.

'She's in there.' She, not Mother, Mummy, Mum, just she, Joan wanted to slap him for his insolence. Then Stanley was sitting beside her, he eased the cigarette from her fingers.

'Lucky you didn't burn yourself on that.'

Joan looked at him, forcing her eyes to focus. 'Why didn't you let me know you were coming back today? I'd have killed the fatted calf.'

'I phoned, but you weren't in.'

Joan giggled and closed her eyes. No, she thought, I was with Sylvia being measured.

'Come on, my darling, it's time for bed.'

She opened her eyes a fraction, shielding them from the light.

'What time is it?'

'Well past midnight.'

'Have you come to take me to bed, my handsome prince?' She

took his hand and placed it on her breast. Stanley glanced at Spencer who stood in the doorway. Joan turned to follow his gaze and caught the look of disgust on her son's face. Without a word he turned and went upstairs.

'Don't tell me baby Spencer's shocked.'

Stanley sighed. 'Come on, Joan, I'm shattered, let's just go to bed.'

Chapter 4

Alice felt faint; she had to get away but her legs wouldn't move. Tony and Susan burst into the room, she was flushed and laughing.

'I want to go home,' Alice whispered.

'Don't be silly, we've only just got here.'

Panic and rage struggled for dominance; this was a nightmare. Alice couldn't believe what was happening. Also, she needed the toilet but where was it?

One of the card players shouted, 'Want a beer, Tony?'

'Cheers, you too babe?' Alice was ignored.

Susan nodded and checked her lipstick in a small mirror.

'Where's the bathroom?' Alice whispered. Susan pointed to a door on the other side of the room while admiring her reflection. Tony continued to talk to the card players, there was much guffawing and Alice realized she was the subject of their hilarity.

She opened the door to her left, and rushed down a corridor opening doors to left and right, the first two were bedrooms, the third a bathroom. There was no lock on the door, but by now Alice was past caring. She struggled to raise her skirt, she must get out and try to find her way back to the hostel.

She heard footsteps coming down the corridor and clenched her fists, she was ready to hit anyone who came in, but the footsteps went past. She took gulping breaths and sat in the dark listening to her heart thudding, bit by bit she became calmer. Susan only cared about herself and Alice was angry for being such a fool. It would not be wise to set off on her own since she didn't know where she was.

There was no chance Tony would volunteer to drive them back to the hostel. She had no choice; she had to stay here. Perhaps one of these men would let her share a bed with Susan; they would just have to make the best of it. She straightened her skirt, took a deep breath and headed up the corridor. There was no sign of Tony or Susan. The skin on Alice's scalp prickled as the four men looked at her.

'Want a beer?'

'Alice wasn't sure which man had spoken. 'No thank you, I don't like beer.' She tried to steady her voice; she must not let them know how scared she was.

'A coffee then?' The man opposite her turned and smiled, 'I'm Mark.'

'I'd prefer tea, please.'

'O.K., tea it is.' He walked down the corridor with Alice following him. She felt like a stray dog, one kind word was all it took.

'I didn't know I was being brought here, I really ought to go back to the hostel. I don't think you are supposed to stay out overnight. I wouldn't have come if I'd known.'

She realized she was gabbling, words tumbling over themselves. She was amazed what she said was coherent. Yet the words she most wanted to say remained locked away. She was frightened, very, very frightened.

Mark glanced up as he spooned tea into a battered teapot.

'Don't worry, you can sleep in my bed; you'll be O.K.'

Alice stared at him.

As though reading her thoughts he said, 'I'll kip on the settee.'

Air whistled out of Alice's mouth and she wondered how long she had been holding her breath.

'What about the others?'

'Who, Susan and Tony? You won't see anything of them. Mind you, Tony won't be too late away, his wife might ask questions.'

Alice's mouth opened and closed again; did Susan know Tony

was married?

'No, I meant the other men, your friends, won't they mind if I stay here?'

'Nothing to do with them who sleeps in my bed, I pay my share of the rent.'

Alice nodded, 'You're very kind, do you mind if I go to bed now?'

The sooner she was asleep the sooner it would be morning and she could escape.

'Right, I'll tell the others, don't worry they'll leave you alone.'

Alice gave a quiet sob of relief and with difficulty stopped herself from throwing her arms around him. Better not, she decided, such action could be misconstrued.

'I really am grateful."

He grinned as he handed her a mug of tea. 'My room is on the left, opposite the bathroom,' he said over his shoulder as he left the kitchen.

'Sleep well.'

Alice rushed to her sanctuary, closed the door behind her and leaned against it, trying not to slosh tea over herself or the floor. How could Susan be so irresponsible? No decent girl behaved like that; no-one would want to marry her. Men only wanted virgins.

She didn't put the light on somehow the dark seemed safer. She drew the curtains to shut out the light from the street lamps and lay, fully clothed, on the bed which was under the window. The blankets and sheets had an unfamiliar masculine smell that was not unpleasant. She yawned and realized how exhausted she was. She shuffled round until she had wrapped the top blanket around her. The room seemed to be swaying, rocking her to and fro. Sounds from the street rose and fell like sounds of the sea. She slept.

Alice woke with a start; someone was trying to get into bed

with her. For a moment she couldn't remember where she was. There was an overpowering smell of beer mixed with stale tobacco. She pulled the blanket around her. She was outraged; Mark had said they would leave her alone.

'Come on, girl; move over, there's room for two. Let's have a good time, don't be shy.'

'Go away,' Alice hissed. An arm went around her and she felt herself being pulled towards whomever it was.

'Go away.'

'Oh, don't come the innocent with me. You walked in tonight as bold as brass; you were just asking for it.'

Alice realized it was the man who had had his back to her when she first entered the flat. So, he thought she was the party did he; well, she'd got news for him.

'I've told you to go away.'

He tried to kiss her; his hot breath made her want to retch. She pushed him away, but he was too strong. What had her mother always said? When threatened by a man, knee him in the crutch. It was a shame such sound advice did not take into account being molested whilst wrapped in a cocoon of a blanket. Perhaps it would have its uses; if she couldn't get out of it, he wouldn't be able to get in.

'Go away, Mark said no one would bother me.'

'Well, I'm not Mark and I'm here so let's stop buggering about.'

'I'll scream.'

He clamped his hand over her mouth and nose so hard her eyes watered. She tried to push him away with her free hand. He was so strong. She tried to bite him and he grabbed her hair.

'You do that and I'll bite you back, where it shows.'

She went limp, too shocked to fight anymore. He pulled at the blanket, the bed creaked and groaned. Perhaps someone would hear, perhaps Mark would come. The blanket was yanked off her.

This ignorant, drunken slob, this pig of an apology for a man; how dare he? She hit him as hard as she could in the face. As he rolled away from the unexpected blow, she wrestled her other arm free. She clenched her fists and rained down blows on any part of his face and shoulders not protected by his upraised forearm.

'You animal, you drunken, filthy animal, go away, leave me alone.'

She sobbed with the exertion. He grunted as he tried to fend off the blows by grabbing her arms. She realised that in the struggle her legs had come free from the blanket. With one final effort, she brought her right knee upwards. There was a loud gasp, then a thump and he was gone.

Alice lay still on the bed. Her ragged breathing was drowned by the sound of the man being sick; the sour smell of beer-drenched vomit filled the room.

'You frigging bitch,' the voice was thick with venom and pain, 'who wants to screw an ugly, evil cow like you anyway?'

Alice managed a tremulous smile, in the dark. 'Well, you did for one.'

She heard him shuffle from the room and then there was the heavy click of the bedroom door shutting. She lay in the darkness, waiting for her heartbeat to settle. She wondered if he would come back. She grabbed the honour-saving blanket and wrapped herself in it even more tightly. At last, despite her anxiety, exhaustion dragged her into a deep sleep.

Joan wandered into the kitchen. She looked pale, her eyes were puffy and her hair uncombed. She sat down with a thump as though not in full control of her legs. She lit a cigarette while Stanley poured her a cup of coffee.

'Morning Mother,' Spencer said.

She didn't reply.

'I've brought you a little something.'

Spencer rose from the table and left the room; silence began to swell.

'Trip went well, had some quite good news,' Stanley said. 'There's talk about an alternative to this Common Market nonsense.'

Joan sighed; business, always business.

'A European Free Trade Association', there were hints that it might be set up soon, in Stockholm. That would help things.'

Spencer returned and placed a package on the table. Joan put her cigarette down and removed the wrapping paper to reveal a blue box. Her hands were shaking and she wondered if Stanley had noticed. She opened the box and pulled out the tissue-wrapped gift. It was a small glass bowl, delicately etched with a tracery of leaves.

'I thought it would look nice on your dressing table.'

'Thank you, very nice." She could muster little enthusiasm as Spencer only gave presents when he wanted something. She saw him give Stanley a quizzical look.

'I'll give Alice a ring, let her know I'm back,' Spencer said.

Mark knocked then walked into the bedroom. The girl was still asleep; she looked like an Egyptian mummy, cocooned in a blanket. The smell of sick was overpowering. He leaned across the bed to open the window. Alice jumped and opened her eyes very wide.

'You look like a startled rabbit and do you usually wear your shoes in bed?' Mark laughed, 'Don't worry; I'm just opening the window to get rid of the smell.'

'Where's the other man?

'Who Jim?'

'I don't know his name but he came in here in the middle of the night, he attacked me, it was awful. I gave him my knee, in his crutch and then he was sick. I'm sorry, has he made a mess of your carpet? Let me clean it up.'

Mark grinned, 'I wondered why Jim looked dog-rough, nothing to do with the night of unbridled passion he hinted at.'

Alice gasped, 'Certainly not.'

'You leave this for Jim to clear up later. Do you want some breakfast?'

Alice nodded. Mark watched as she unwrapped herself.

'I don't believe it, not a single item of clothing removed. What a most determined girl you are.'

She grinned at him and her eyes sparkled. A most attractive, determined girl, Mark thought.

'Breakfast, what a good idea,' she said, 'I'm ravenous.'

They sat in the kitchen eating toast and chatting, it was so easy. Jim did not appear and neither did Susan or Tony. Although it was Saturday and Alice didn't have to go to work, she did have to go back to the hostel. She had already missed breakfast without notifying the canteen, she and Susan would have to brazen it out together.

'Have you seen Susan yet?'

'She left last night; said she'd see you back at the hostel.'

Alice was horrified. If Susan stayed with her friend, she would have gone back to the hostel in time for breakfast. Susan had left without her, what a rotten trick.

'Thank you for being so kind.'

'Can I see you again?'

Alice hesitated, he was nice and she liked him, but what about Spencer?

'Have you already got a boyfriend?'

'Well, sort of but we're not engaged or anything.'

'Would you like to see me, just as a friend?' He smiled a most appealing smile. Alice thought for a moment, why shouldn't I have a friend who happened to be a man?

'I'll take you out to lunch one Saturday, how's that?'

'O.K. that would be nice.'

'I'm busy next Saturday, how about in a fortnight? After all, you've slept in my bed, you might as well let me buy you a meal.' He winked and Alice blushed.

'Do you know the Strand Palace Hotel? They have a Salad Bowl Restaurant and you can help yourself to what you want. You can use the Tube; I'll meet you at 1 p.m. We aren't on the phone so I'll just wait for you to arrive.'

Alice felt wonderful, after the horrors of last night the world now seemed a nicer place. 'I'll be there.'

'If you change your mind, I'll understand, but I hope you'll come.'

'If I don't sort myself out and get back to the hostel, you'll be able to take me to the restaurant yourself. So where am I exactly?'

'Fulham.'

'Oh, I need to get to Baron's Court.

'I'll walk you to the station; you can catch the train to Earl's Court then change.'

'That's fine, no need to walk me to the station, I'm a big girl now.' That was just how she felt, a big grown-up girl, who made her own decisions.

'Can I see you downstairs then?'

'Don't worry, I won't run off with the family silver.'

He tapped her on the bottom as they walked out of the flat.

'Behave yourself, just because you put Jim in his place doesn't mean you can get uppity.'

She grinned; this was fun. She stopped at the front door, uncertain what to do. Should she give him a hug?

'Go to the end of the road then take the first left, on to the end. That's the main road, the station's about a hundred yards on the right.'

'Thanks for everything.'

'By the way, you still haven't told me your name?'

'Alice, Alice Ward, see you.'

'See you in a fortnight.'

He put his hands on her shoulders and kissed her on the cheek. It felt nice. She strode down the road then turned and waved. Mark was leaning against the door frame watching her.

Chapter 5

The note in Alice's pigeon hole said Miss Pritchard wanted to see her. Alice took a deep breath, walked to the office door and knocked.

'Come in.'

'Did you want to see me, Miss Pritchard?'

The hostel warden removed her glasses and looked at Alice for a moment.

'Did you forget to indicate on the board that you would be out last night?'

Alice hung her head; this was like being back at school.

'No, I didn't forget, I'm sorry.'

'Although I feel responsible for my girls, I am not in the habit of checking up on them. However, I have had a phone call this morning.'

'Oh.'

'A young man called, Spencer Martin, your boyfriend I understand.'

'Yes.' Delight was quickly replaced by anxiety and guilt. He must have come back earlier than planned and would want to know where she had been.

'The world can be a very dangerous place; young girls do not always realize how dangerous.' Miss Pritchard paused. 'My system is for your protection; I presume you were out all night.'

Alice nodded.

'What you do with your life is your business but, as a courtesy, I wish to be informed if you are going to be away overnight. Supposing, heaven forbid, there had been a fire. Firemen could have risked their lives searching for you whilst you were safe, elsewhere.'

Alice felt guilt press down on her head like a rock.

'Sometimes girls come here with the idea that they will be able to do what they like. Sometimes they do foolish things and live to regret it. I'm sure your father would not want you to fall into that category and neither would I.'

A gentle rebuke, Alice thought, but more effective than Dad's hectoring approach. After what had happened last night Alice wanted to cry; every word Miss Pritchard said was true. She had been foolish to trust someone who thought only of herself. Susan fitted into the dubious category Miss Pritchard had been talking about. Alice had got away with it this time but might not do so again.

'I really am very sorry; I didn't mean to stay out; I couldn't help it.' Alice's voice wobbled.

'Are you alright?'

'Yes,' Alice whispered.

'Just be careful who you associate with. Now you had better phone your boyfriend, he sounded quite anxious.'

Susan was in the kitchen talking to Maureen when Alice reached the third floor. They were engrossed in an animated discussion of the pleasure to be had dancing at the Palais, at least Susan was. Maureen had never been there. Perhaps she would make a more suitable friend, Alice thought. Then she heard her name mentioned.

'You should have seen the weed Alice picked up, small, spotty, looked a complete drip.'

Alice bristled with rage, how dare Susan be so dismissive, at least Derek had behaved like a gentleman. Alice rushed into the kitchen, Maureen smiled and Susan turned round.

'Oh, hello, had a good time?'

Alice had expected some contrition, an apology, some sign of regret.

'No, I didn't actually but a fat lot you care.' She realized she had raised her voice and Maureen looked nervous.

'I'll see you two later,' she said and scuttled away.

Susan turned back to the sink where she was washing underwear. Alice grabbed Susan's shoulder and spun her round.

'How could you leave me like that? What a rotten trick, how could you?'

Susan shrugged.

'Anyway, where did you go? And why didn't you wait for me this morning? Don't you care about anyone but yourself?'

'Look I only suggested you come with me because you look so damned miserable all the time. I was doing you a favour; don't worry I shan't do that again.'

She turned back to the sink and continued rinsing her clothes.

'You did me a favour!'

'There's no need to shout, I'm not deaf.'

'Who was it that stood you up, the gorgeous Tony wasn't it?'

'No, it wasn't like that, he had to work late.'

'I don't believe it, that's what he wants you to think.'

Susan turned. Alice noticed a slight frown wrinkling Susan's brow as though Alice had verbalized something she didn't want to believe.

'Anyway, what's all the fuss about, you're okay, aren't you?'

'No thanks to you. I was nearly raped last night, but don't you give it another thought.'

'How was I supposed to know?' Susan stood with her hands on her hips.

'And that isn't all you don't know,' Alice paused, 'he's married.'

Colour drained from Susan's face. 'Who is?'

The words were whispered as though she already knew the answer.

'Tony is.'

'How do you know?'

'Mark told me. He's one of the men in the flat, but of course, you probably know that since I expect, you make a habit of staying out. Anyway, Mark's nice; he let me sleep in his room. And before you ask, he slept on the settee.'

Susan swayed and clung to the sink.

'What's the matter?'

'I'm pregnant.'

Alice put her hand to her mouth, the words hung in the air.

'Are you sure?'

'I've missed two periods already.'

'What will you do?'

'That's why I was so desperate to see him again. I wanted to tell him but I just couldn't.' Susan started to cry.

Unlike previous outbursts Alice had witnessed, these were genuine tears of grief and fear. Alice held out her arms, not sure whether or not to hold Susan, to offer physical comfort. Susan slumped into her arms.

'But he'll have to know.'

Susan shook her head. 'There's no point, I'll just have to get rid of it.'

'How?' Alice shivered, her scalp tingled with horror at the casual way Susan suggested the destruction of her own flesh and blood.

'There are ways, what does it matter, what does anything matter? I thought he'd marry me.'

Alice recalled all the veiled warnings her Gran had mouthed, oh so quietly, about girls who got themselves into trouble. So, this was it, this was terrible trouble. Alice took a deep breath to steady herself. She relived the events of last night. Had that revolting Jim had his way she could have found herself in the same position in a few months' time. It didn't bear thinking of.

'Can't you tell your parents?'

'They're too busy, always too busy. I'm just a nuisance, in the way. I don't think they ever wanted a family; too selfish I suppose, they just want each other. They give me money, pat me on the head and tell me to be a good girl. I don't think they've ever really cared.'

She's as lonely as I am, Alice thought. She has more money, but now she is pregnant. Alice no longer felt anger, just relief. Money or no money she would not want to change places with Susan.

'Let's have a cup of tea,' Alice said, unsure if her presence was a help or a hindrance. She had to phone Spencer, but now was not a tactful time to do it. Susan sobbed, her whole body shook as Alice held her and patted her back.

Joan was silent during the short drive home. The visit to her parents had been unsettling.

'You're miles away, my dear.'

'I hope Lillian isn't going to do anything rash,' Joan said.

'What do you mean?'

'She hasn't seen hide nor hair of this Harry for years. She'd better be careful.'

Stanley said nothing.

'I know you will think I'm being selfish, but I don't want my sister to make a mistake.'

'Lillian has always struck me as pretty sensible and she does a great job with your parents.'

'Yes exactly, and it would be a shame if things had to change.'

'I don't think you need worry about that yet. Anyway, let's forget about it now, I want us to have a relaxing evening together. We'll tackle any problems when they arise. By the way has Spencer said anything about this girl of his coming over.'

'No.'

'I know he wants us to meet her.'

'The girl he met at the swimming baths?"

'Yes, I think so.

Alice dialled Spencer's number. She had her fingers crossed, hoping that he and not one of his parents would answer. She was in luck.

'Where have you been?' Spencer asked.

'I went to the Palais with a girl from the hostel.'

'So, what are you doing tonight, gadding off somewhere or shall we meet?'

'Oh, let's meet, but don't forget I have to be back by half-past ten.'

'That doesn't give us much scope; we wouldn't get out of the cinema unless we went in the afternoon. Are any pubs near you? We could go for a drink I suppose.'

Alice sensed his lack of enthusiasm, but dared not flout hostel rules again.

'You could meet me outside the hostel, what would be a good time?'

'If you've got to be back so early, we'd better meet at half past six.'

'Lovely, I'm sure we'll find a nice pub somewhere.'

'Let's hope so.'

Alice's feeling of anxiety persisted, but at least she was seeing him. Perhaps he was just tired after the business trip. She would ask him about it, and show lots of interest; that was what girlfriends were supposed to do. As she walked upstairs, she reflected on the morning's events. How would Susan get rid of the baby?

The streets of Baron's Court were dingy and rundown but they did find a reasonable pub not far from the hostel. Alice felt nervous. She had not frequented pubs often and the frosted glass, which stopped people from looking in suggested such places must be dodgy. Spencer came back from the bar with a soft drink for her and a pint of beer for himself.

'So, what's with the dancing?'

'Should she tell him everything, all about Jim, but then what? Should

Mark be mentioned? She thought it might not be wise.

'It was just an evening out, nothing special, but we were too late to get back before the door was locked. We stayed with some friends of Susan's, that's the girl I went with.'

'So, you can stay out.'

'Yes, but we should have let Miss Pritchard know and we didn't. She was very nice about it, but I must not do it again. Anyway, what about Stockholm, was it nice?'

Spencer was reluctant to say much, he claimed it was a bit boring really. Alice was surprised, she could hardly wait to get a passport, surely travel couldn't be that bad.

'Was it just business meetings all the time?'

'Sort of, but Dad arranged a guide to show me some of the sights, a girl called Berthe.'

'Oh, a beautiful blonde, I suppose.'

'She was O.K.'

Spencer pulled a small package out of his pocket.

'A little something,' he said.

It was a small painted, wooden horse that had been decorated with a pattern of flowers.

'How lovely,' Alice said, 'I shall call him Alfie and put him on my chest of drawers.'

Spencer glanced at his watch. 'Suppose we could take a stroll back. At least at this time I will have no trouble getting the Tube back home.'

'Have you spoken to your parents yet?'

'It's tricky with Mum, but Dad said he'd have a word, don't worry I haven't forgotten.'

They walked back arm in arm. The soft evening light muted the stark brickwork of the cramped terraced houses and their feet echoed in the quiet streets. He kissed her at the hostel gates but Alice felt uneasy as she went up to her room.

Chapter 6

Barbara Anderson checked her hair and make-up; it would have to do. She heard a knock at the front door, it would be Gordon and Anne, taking her to Jeffrey Ward's flat. She recalled his embarrassment when he admitted it was council property, not his own. She had told him that she too rented her flat and was perfectly happy with the arrangement. Mr Jeffrey Ward was very conscious of his image, it would be interesting to see where he lived. Barbara had been tempted to quiz her friends about him, but then decided to make her own judgment.

When they arrived, the door opened so swiftly that Barbara wondered if Jeffrey had been watching from the window. They were welcomed, with exuberant courtesy, to a small flat. It was cosy, with good solid utility furniture. Barbara was surprised to see a tablecloth laid out on the floor with cushions spread around. Jeffrey seemed nervous.

'What the bloody hell is this Jeff, we could have brought our own chairs; you only had to ask.' Gordon grinned as he spoke.

Barbara suspected Jeffrey took a lot of teasing from Gordon and probably didn't like it.

'I thought we'd have a picnic, like Arabs in the desert.'

He switched on a reading lamp and turned off the central light.

'That's better,' he said, 'I would have used candles but I forgot to get some, anyway wax always makes such a mess.'

'We won't be able to see what we're eating,' Anne said.

'Might be as well,' Gordon replied.

Barbara watched Jeffrey and noticed his face flush. Not much of a sense of humour there then.

'I'll get you a drink,' he said.

Barbara wondered if he was always so nervous, 'Can I help?'

'Certainly not, you're my guests. Now come on Anne, a glass of wine, I've got white, you too Barbara?' He rushed from the room. 'Beer for you, Gordon,' he called, from the safety of his kitchen.

'I didn't expect this,' Anne said, 'wouldn't have worn such a tight skirt.'

'If we're supposed to be Arabs, perhaps he's tracked down some sheep's eyes.'

Anne gasped, 'Gordon, you aren't serious, are you?'

'Of course, he isn't, come on, love; roll your skirt up and sprawl provocatively, like me. Make the poor man relax a bit.' Barbara settled herself on the cushions and smiled. 'This will be fun.'

Jeffrey returned with brimming glasses. He seemed relieved to see the women seated.

'I can easily get the table out if you would prefer it, won't take a minute.'

'Nonsense,' Barbara said, 'it's the most original dinner party I've ever been to.'

Jeffrey smiled.

'A drink, my man.' Barbara clicked her fingers and Jeffrey laughed

'Food's nearly ready, I didn't want to do anything fancy so I hope bangers and mash is all right with everyone.'

'No sheep's eyes, old chap, what a disappointment.'

'Gordon, that's enough, I'm relieved.' Anne said.

'Cheers,' said Barbara raising her glass.

'There's lemon meringue pie and cheese and biscuits afterwards. Will they be acceptable?'

There were murmurs of approval and Barbara watched the tension in Jeffrey's face lessen; how awful to be so anxious all the time.

Alice sat with Susan on her bed.

'You'll have to tell him,' Alice said, 'he's just as responsible as you are.'

Susan chewed her lip, clasped and unclasped her hands.

'How can I get in touch with him?'

'Why not go to the flat and see if Mark can pass on a message.'

Susan thought for a moment. 'Will you come with me?'

'I can't, I'm seeing Spencer. It was difficult enough explaining why I wasn't in when he phoned. I can't alter the arrangements now.'

The look on Susan's face warned Alice not to add that she would soon be meeting Spencer's parents.

'Go today, you can't just do nothing; you never know, things might work out.'

Susan got off her bed and reached for her jacket.

'Good luck; let me know how it goes. I'd better be off too.'

The two girls faced each other, both apprehensive about the coming evening, but their reasons could not be more different. She patted Susan on the shoulder and left.

Joan and Stanley were watching the early evening news. Joan was unconcerned by this meeting with Spencer's girlfriend, what troubled her was that her beloved Malcolm, home from school, had chosen to spend the evening with some of his friends. Joan was hurt.

'Anything I can do in the kitchen?' Stanley asked.

Joan glanced at him; he didn't usually offer to assist her.

'No, everything's fine. You seem very anxious to impress this girl; shouldn't she be setting out to impress us?'

Stanley shrugged, 'I just want Spencer to be proud of us.'

Joan raised an eyebrow and poured herself another sherry before strolling into the kitchen. She heard the front door opening and then Spencer's voice. She walked back into the hall. She had assumed Alice would be small, blonde and pretty. She was, therefore, surprised to see a tall girl with short, dark hair being ushered in. She seemed shy, gauche and certainly not pretty in a conventional sense. Joan wondered what the attraction was.

Stanley came into the hall and after stilted introductions, Joan left Stanley to offer drinks while she checked on the meal. With some prompting from Spencer, Alice talked about her job and the hostel. Joan stirred the gravy and wondered what kind of parents allowed their daughter to leave home for such a dreadful place.

Pauses in the conversation lengthened until Stanley suggested Spencer should show Alice the garden. Once they were outside, Joan joined Stanley at the French window.

'Rather an unprepossessing girl, don't you think?'

Stanley shrugged, 'Maybe, but she's got a brain, you don't work in a laboratory without some scientific knowledge.'

'Do you think it's her brain Spencer's attracted to?'

'I've no idea, but I like her straightforwardness, even if she hasn't got your poise and self-confidence.' He put his arm around her. 'The girl's nice, I prefer someone like her to some sophisticated little piece with a shallow personality.'

'So, if a girl's got poise and self-confidence, like me I think you said, she's bound to be shallow.'

'Look, love, I know you're upset that Malcolm isn't here this evening, but please don't let's argue. Don't spoil things.'

'Well, all I can say is she could have made more of an effort.' Joan turned and went back to the kitchen, Stanley followed her.

'It doesn't make you feel old, does it, having your son interested in a young woman?'

Joan stirred the gravy with vigour. 'Don't be so silly.'

'Just think, you could have a lot of fun helping that young lady make something of herself. She could learn a lot from you.'

Joan wondered what was he suggesting, was Alice to be a daughter substitute? Of course, he was right; there was plenty of room for improvement. Joan pulled away from Stanley and stared at him.

'Isn't that what her mother should be doing?'

'I get the feeling she has little contact with either of her parents, why else is she living in a hostel?'

Joan continued to stir the gravy. With Stanley away so much it might be nice to have some female companionship.

'If Spencer is serious about this girl, shouldn't we meet her parents anyway?'

'I think it is early days for that, they are both very young.' Stanley sniffed the air. 'I think this meal is just about ready if the aroma is anything to go by. Shall I call the young lovers in, I think they're still in the garden.'

'Lovers! I hope you are joking; I don't fancy being a grandmother yet.'

Susan rang the doorbell again, still no reply, a wasted journey with nothing sorted. What on Earth was she going to do? She stepped back onto the pavement and looked up, absolutely no sign of life. She turned and walked slowly back to the station. Once on the main road, she became caught up in the early evening crowd of couples and groups of people. There were all on their way somewhere, to have a good time, Saturday night fun.

Such fun would be impossible for her once the pregnancy became obvious. She must do something. Deep in thought, she took little notice of the people approaching her, and almost bumped into them. It was Tony with a woman, could this be his wife. Mark was with them.

The woman was pretty and she smiled at Susan who was unable to move. She saw panic in Tony's eyes. The crowd surged around them; Susan was in the way. For a split second, she wanted to point a finger at Tony and scream to the world 'I'm carrying his bastard'. That would wipe the smile off his wife's face. Mark grasped Susan's arm.

'Susan, how nice to see you, what are you doing in this neck of the woods?'

Susan opened her mouth, but no words came. Her brain whirred. She wanted to lash out, to hurt Tony as he had hurt her, but what good would that do? She must clutch the lifeline Mark had thrown her. She must hide her feelings as Tony's unborn child was hidden.

'I was supposed to meet a friend, but she didn't turn up.'

'Oh, what a shame,' the pretty woman said. She looked from Tony to Mark.

'How about spending the evening with us, if these two don't mind? I'm Maggie, by the way, and this is my husband, Tony. Mark you already know.'

Susan wanted to laugh, to throw back her head and laugh until her tears flowed.

'Yes, why not,' said Mark, 'we are just going to have a bit of supper and a drink at my flat. You'd be welcome.'

Tony said nothing and avoided eye contact with Susan. Had she become invisible? They strolled back the way she had come. Should she try to have a word with Tony tonight, but how? Mark linked her arm through his. She wondered if he had guessed the reason she was there. Alice was right, he was nice and he was doing his best to help. If she had no chance to speak to Tony, she would leave a message with Mark.

She watched Tony and Maggie out of the corner of her eyes and knew, without a doubt, that Tony would never leave her. Why should he? He had a pretty wife who seemed to adore him and a willing mistress, wasn't that every man's dream? What a fool she had been. She thought about the off-hand way she had talked to Alice about getting rid of the baby. She had spoken as she did because she never believed that was how it would end. Now she knew. There would be no happy ending, this tiny life must be dragged from her and the sooner the better.

As they walked down the road Susan tried to join in the conversation, she must present no threat. She sensed that if she were not careful Tony would disappear from her life without a qualm. She must get his help or turn to her parents; that was the last thing she wanted to do.

They clumped up the three flights of uncarpeted stairs. The other men who shared the flat were out, presumably on a normal Saturday night booze-up. Mark put on some music.

'Make yourselves at home. I'll rustle up some grub and a drink, give us a hand will you, Susan?'

Once in the kitchen, he shut the door.

'I assume it wasn't a coincidence for you to be near here.'

Susan shook her head, 'I've got to speak to Tony.'

'I don't think tonight's the night.'

'It's vital, please.' Susan's eyes filled with tears.

'Be careful, he can be a hard-faced sod when pushed.'

'If I can't speak to him tonight, will you give him a message for me?'

Mark nodded. 'It doesn't take an Einstein to work out your problem. Now put on a brave face, we have supper to prepare.'

Susan tried to be natural but it was impossible, everything she said sounded artificial, contrived or downright stupid. She knew she was drinking too much but what did that matter? Perhaps it would solve the problem. She knew alcohol wasn't good for pregnant women and she had heard that gin and hot baths were used to induce miscarriage. She couldn't manage those right now, but perhaps too much wine would do the trick.

She looked at her watch; she would have to go soon otherwise she would be locked out. Of course, there was always Pat, around the corner, she was a good sort. If necessary, she could always sleep there again, on the floor, good old Pat, yes that was what she would do. Just hang on a bit longer. She had been to the toilet twice, surely Maggie would have to go soon; she must have the bladder of a camel. She'd be bound to go before she and Tony left. Just hang on a bit longer.

The room seemed to be moving from side to side. Perhaps she should eat a bit more, to soak up the booze. She felt sick. No, more food was not a good idea. She looked at her companions and didn't know whether to laugh or cry. Maggie was chatting away without a care in the world and Tony hung on her every word. The adoring, faithful, model husband, what a hypocrite. What a sod he was. Perhaps she had had a lucky escape, at least she would have once she got rid of his baby.

She felt a rush of shame, women were supposed to cherish babies not murder them; what else could she do? He'll find someone, leave a trail of broken hearts and shattered dreams and none of it would touch him. He'll go home tonight to a nice house and a nice wife because she was nice. Would Maggie ever know, or would she remain secure in married respectability?

Susan sat up very straight. Maggie should know; she was a decent woman who deserved better. She should be told what her husband had been getting up to. It was Susan's duty to save this nice woman from a selfish, deceitful man; she'd be grateful in the end. It was her duty, one woman to another. Susan's mouth was full of words, hateful, spiteful words all jostling to get out but, as she opened her mouth to speak, Maggie stood up.

'I think it's time we made a move, darling. I'll just go to the bathroom.'

'Down the corridor, third on the right,' Mark said.

Once Maggie had left the room there was silence. Tony half-turned away from Susan so she couldn't see his face. He started to speak to Mark, his voice low. Susan leaned across and almost fell off her chair. She grabbed his shirt sleeve.

'I've got to talk to you, please; I've got to see you, it's urgent.'

He looked at her with distaste and pulled his arm away.

'I'm pregnant, don't you understand?' She swallowed hard; the nausea was getting worse.

'What's that to do with me?'

'You're the father.'

She heard the sound of the toilet flushing. Tony leaned towards her. His bright, blue eyes that had once made her tremble were hard and angry.

'Prove it,' he hissed.

Just then Maggie walked back into the room.

Chapter 7

Barbara undressed slowly, easing her skirt past her overfilled stomach. Jeffrey believed in making sure his guests didn't go hungry. He was such a prickly man, and she wondered if huge portions were his way of expressing his feelings. There was no doubt that Jeffrey was physically attractive and a charming host, if somewhat eccentric. Did she like him enough to continue with a friendship? She wasn't sure.

She enjoyed her life, solitude held no fears, the library work engrossed her and she loved her flat. Did she want anything to upset that? Jeffrey was intriguing, but was that contrived? She had sorted out the question of his being an unmarried father, a silly expression to invite enquiry. She sensed the pain his divorce had caused. Still, there was his daughter, Alice, to consider; perhaps he didn't realise how lucky he was.

She cleaned her teeth, washed her face and looking in the bathroom mirror said, 'Now, my girl, regard it as a challenge, ask him over for a meal.'

She slid into bed and, as always, lifted the silver framed picture from her bedside table and kissed the image. 'Goodnight, my darling.'

Stanley was already in bed when Joan entered the bedroom.

'That meal was excellent, as always,' Stanley said, 'well done, my dear.'

Joan sat at the dressing table and creamed her face. She could see Stanley's reflection in her mirror. His dark hair had thinned to a shiny, single layer when he combed it carefully into place each morning. He had the well-padded look of a successful businessman. They were both going downhill.

'Quite came out of herself after a glass of wine, didn't she.'

Joan frowned, 'I still think Spencer could do better.'

'Good heavens, I don't suppose he intends to marry her. She's just a girlfriend; it may not last five minutes. How many boyfriends did you have before you met me?'

'Not enough.'

'Ouch, that's below the belt.'

'She looked so dowdy.'

'Now come on, Joan, she explained that her wage, at the hospital, was poor.'

'So why doesn't she get financial support from her parents?'

'I don't know.'

'It all sounds a bit odd to me.' She removed her dressing gown and got into bed. They were propped up on pillows, side by side, sipping their nightcaps. Physically we are together, Joan thought, but our emotions are worlds apart. She heard a noise downstairs and sat up straight.

'Quick, that's the key in the lock, Spencer's back.' Joan emptied her whisky glass in one swallow, turned off her light and lay down.

'Goodnight.'

Stanley sighed, 'I don't know what all the rush is about.'

'I don't want Spencer to think we've been waiting up for him.'

She watched as he drained his glass and switched off his light. She felt his arm move across her body and moved away from him; she wasn't in the mood for that. Stanley turned and hunched his back towards her. It was the end of another unsettling day.

Clearly, her beloved Malcolm preferred his friends to her and Spencer had picked up a waif and stray. She stared at the ceiling; the hum of traffic was soothing and the pattern of lights from passing cars had a hypnotic effect. Sleep wrapped itself around her and she sighed.

Mark escorted Maggie and Tony downstairs; on his return, he realized Susan was in the bathroom. He listened, with resignation, to the sounds of Susan emptying her stomach. This flat seems destined to smell of other people's vomit. He started to clear plates and glasses. He'd let her get it over with, no girl wanted an audience in such circumstances. He carried the dirty crockery through to the kitchen and started on the washing up. He realized the noises from the bathroom had stopped.

'Susan,' he shouted, 'would a cup of black coffee help?' No reply. He shrugged his shoulders and continued clearing things away. After a while he was aware of movement behind him, Susan stood in the doorway, her face a dingy green.

'Do you feel as awful as you look?'

Susan nodded.

'For heaven's sake, sit down before you fall down. Shall I call you a taxi?'

'Please.'

'Won't you be locked out of the hostel by now?'

'It's all right; I can stay with a friend who lives nearby.'

Mark felt relief, get her a taxi; it would be his good deed for the day.

'I've got to speak to Tony about…' Her voice trailed away.

'What will you do? He'll never leave Maggie.'

Susan began to cry. Dear God, Mark thought, this good deed was turning into a full-scale mercy mission.

'I'll have to speak to him; I just don't know what to do. He'll have to help me, after all, it is his no matter what he says.'

'Listen, Susan, take it from me you are unlikely to see Tony again, not after tonight. He wouldn't dare take the risk.'

Susan began to wail and moan. He put his hand on her shoulder.

'Crying isn't going to help; do you want me to speak to him?'

'Please, yes please, I would be so grateful.'

Mark felt irritated by the whole thing; it wasn't his problem so how come he had landed in the thick of it?

'Alice said you were nice.' Susan gave a watery smile.

Alice, he hoped she didn't behave like this; histrionics he could do without.

Susan's face crumpled, 'She didn't say she was going out with you too; she's already got one boyfriend.'

'I know.' Spoilt, it was Susan's trouble, used to getting her own way. With luck, this business with Tony should cure her of that.

'Come on, it's time to get you a taxi. The others will be back soon; you wouldn't want them to see you like this would you?'

At such a blatant appeal to her vanity Susan stood, patted her hair into some semblance of order and smoothed her clothes.

Mark grinned at her. 'That's better. Now I'll give Tony a ring in a day or two, take him for a beer. I'll do what I can but I'm promising nothing. What will you do if he won't help?'

She whimpered, 'Go to my parents, they'll go mad. They'll never forgive me.'

'You'll just have to trust me to come up with something, won't you?' He hustled her out of the house, tired of the whole business.

'We'll walk up to the main road and see if there are any taxis about.'

As they started down the stairs, they heard the front door bang. That was followed by raucous laughter and a crash, it suggested someone had fallen up the stairs. The noise got louder as Susan and Mark went down the first flight. As they turned for the next flight, they saw Jim and the other flat-mates on their way up.

'Well, what have we here, poaching Tony's property?'

'Shut up, Jim,' Mark said.

'Oh, dear me,' Jim held up his hands in mock horror, 'what will the great lover, Tony, say when he finds his little chick has strayed?'

'For Christ's sake, Jim, piss off. You are not even slightly funny.'

'Pardon me, your honour,' Jim turned to the others, 'the great and mighty

Saint Mark strikes again.' He bowed low, wobbled and fell over. 'Pardon us miserable sinners.' He turned to Susan, 'Let me guess, lover boy has stood you up but Uncle Mark has kissed you better.'

Mark took a swing at Jim and caught him on the chin. 'That's for scaring the daylight out of Alice the other night.'

Jim didn't answer; he was slumped on the stairs.

Susan started to cry. Mark grabbed her hand and dragged her downstairs.

'You really are a prize prick, Jim,' Mark shouted as they ran down the last flight of stairs.

Maybe,' Jim replied, 'but at least I've got one.'

Mark and Susan left the house to the sound of drunken laughter.

They didn't wait long for a taxi and Susan slept until the driver shouted at her. Then the taxi pulled away leaving Susan standing under a defunct street lamp. The fare had taken the last of her money and she had no idea how she would manage for the rest of the month. That was not her main problem at the moment. The immediate question was where was she going to sleep? She shivered.

The night was cold and after being so sick she felt light-headed. She looked at the house where Pat lived on the second floor. All was in darkness. She hesitated, reluctant to ring the bell. Her belief in herself had been badly shaken. She felt terrible shame at the way she had behaved with Tony. Meeting Maggie had been a shock; she was so nice and didn't deserve to have such a treacherous man for a husband. If he could treat his wife so badly, he would, without a qualm, deny all responsibility for the child Susan was carrying.

She sat on the top step and leaned against the front door. She wrapped her arms tightly around her body, hugging what warmth there was to her body. She needed time to think, to sort out what she was going to do. Ever since she realized she was pregnant she had assumed Tony would marry her. No more boring jobs as a shop assistant, she would be a wife and mother in a nice house with a loving husband. It was incredible that she could have been so naïve. Of course, there would be no wedding, no happy ever after, no Tony.

In fact, would she have wanted to go on with Tony now she knew what he was like? How many lies had he told Maggie? How had he managed to get out in the evenings? A lie, his whole relationship with that nice woman was based on lies. Susan shivered again. What was she going to do? The question had gone round and round in her head like a gramophone needle stuck in a groove, round and round until her head ached. She was eighteen and her life should be beginning, if she had this baby everything would change for ever.

What would Mum and Dad say? She remembered the dreadful rows she had with them both, particularly Mum. What had she said to them when she stomped out? She'd show she didn't need them. She'd manage on her own; all they'd wanted to do was stop her having fun. They were jealous because they were old and she was young. She had screamed it at them. It was then that Susan saw a look of deep hurt on her mother's face. They would have the last laugh now; who would be first to say I told you so?

Fun was what she had wanted but now, sitting in the dark, she knew she wanted to go home. She must sort out the problem of the baby first; her parents must never know. She got herself into this mess; she must get herself out of it. She sighed and leaned her head against the rough wooden door. A wave of peace washed over her and looking up at the clear, night sky the millions of stars, like pinpricks in dark velvet, made her feel very small.

Perhaps once she had got rid of the baby, she would be able to make a fresh start. She marvelled at how once the decision was made, mental turmoil vanished.

'I may not know how I'm going to do it," she whispered to herself, 'but at least I know what I'm going to do.'

She put her hand to her mouth, shocked to have spoken her thoughts out loud. All she had to sort out now was whether or not to rouse Pat. There was no alternative. She stood and, with stiff legs, walked down the steps to look again at Pat's window. No chance she would be awake now if she hadn't been earlier. Perhaps she had gone out for the evening or, worse still was stopping out overnight.

'Hello, girlie.'

The voice made Susan jump. A large man was meandering down the street. The absence of street lighting outside Pat's house made it difficult to judge the appearance and mood of the stranger. The light further away outlined his shape and cast a long, menacing shadow. Susan felt a tremor of anxiety, should she stand her ground or run? If she ran, where would she run to? She did not relish waking Miss Pritchard at this time of night.

'What's the matter, girlie, nowhere to sleep?'

'Go away.'

'Now don't be like that, I'm only being friendly.'

'Leave me alone.'

Now he was beside her and the smell of beer almost knocked her over. She felt sweat break out on her forehead and upper lip even though she was shivering. After all, she'd been through tonight, this was too much.

'I'll look after you, dearie, come home with me. A nice girl like you should be tucked up in bed. He put his arm around her shoulders, but she knocked his arm away with a clenched fist.

'Don't you understand? Leave me alone, just leave me alone.' She could hear the panic in her voice and wondered if she should scream and maybe get help from the occupants of one of the silent, dark houses. The man looked puzzled as he swayed in his heavy work boots.

'Want a fag, girlie? I only want to be friendly, have a fag.'

Susan could stand no more. She turned and ran up the three steps and jammed her finger on Pat's bell push. The man stood watching her. With an unsteady hand, he got a cigarette from a crumpled packet and after several attempts managed to light it. Susan turned her back to the man, hoping if she didn't look at him, he would leave her alone.

She listened to the shrill insistent note of the bell as it echoed in the hallway. Please God, she sobbed, let Pat be at home. She sensed rather than heard the man come closer. Another sob caught in her throat, please answer the door. Just as she thought she would have to run for it she heard the window above her being thrown open.

'What the hell's going on? Who is it?'

It was Pat's boyfriend, John. Relief made Susan's knees tremble.

'It's Susan I'm so sorry to wake you up, please let me in.'

'For Christ's sake,' John said and the window was slammed down.

The man behind Susan went back, with hesitant feet, down the steps and shuffled off along the road. When John opened the door Susan fell into his arms.

Chapter 8

Sunshine streamed through Alice's window. She lay in bed watching the clouds and reliving the previous evening which hadn't been as dreadful as she had feared. Mr Martin had been kind and made her feel welcome. Mrs Martin was a different kettle of fish; Alice had sensed an unspoken hostility. Spencer had warned her how difficult his mother was and hinted at a problem. Alice wondered if it was drink. After her experiences with step-father Alec, she was sensitive to what alcohol could do, drunken behaviour frightened her, it made people unpredictable.

She looked at her watch, once again she would have to hurry or miss breakfast. She felt happy because Spencer had said if it was a fine day, he would call for her. They would go for a walk, what a nice way to spend a Sunday afternoon. She rose, put on her dressing gown and checked the bathrooms, both were occupied. That was the trouble with living with so many girls. At the sound of footsteps, she turned to see Susan shuffling up the corridor. Alice was shocked; Susan had aged years overnight, the vibrant, pretty girl was dishevelled and there was heaviness in her step that was not caused just by lack of sleep.

'Are you okay?'

'I've just got back, I stayed at Pat's place.'

'Oh,' Alice heard a bolt slide back and a girl emerged from the nearest bathroom.

'I must have a wash or I shall be late for breakfast, have you eaten?'

Susan nodded. 'Are you going out today?'

'Spencer said he'd call for me later, why?'

'Will you come to my room after you've had breakfast?'

Alice nodded although she didn't really want to become too involved in Susan's problems. As she ate her cereals and toast, she listened to the chatter of the girls, crowding the dining room, apparently without a care in the world. When she returned to Susan's room the girl was slumped on her bed.

'I met Tony's wife last night.'

Alice gasped. 'You didn't go to his house, did you?'

'No, I went to Mark's, as we agreed. I didn't know he had invited Tony and Maggie to visit him. I met them when I was on my way back here after I couldn't get an answer at the flat.'

'What in the street?'

'Yes, I made some excuse, but Tony's wife suggested I spend the evening with them. She's really kind. When I had a chance I told Tony about the baby,' Susan faltered, 'he told me to prove it was his.'

Alice took Susan's hand, 'I'm so sorry.'

'I'll have to have an abortion, that's all there is to it.'

'But how, it's illegal isn't it?'

'Mark said he would speak to Tony, get some money and find out what I have to do.'

'How much will it cost?'

'More than I've got, I spent the rest of this month's money on a taxi, last night.'

'I wish I could help, but I can only just manage myself.'

Susan gave a weak smile and squeezed Alice's hand. 'I suppose I could always tell my parents.'

Alice watched as Susan struggled to hold back tears. Suddenly she leapt to her feet, 'I'm going to be sick,' and she raced from the room.

Morning sickness, Alice thought, the baby is making its presence felt, this tiny speck of life would soon be disposed of.

Susan returned ashen-faced and shivering.

'Would some water help?'

'Please,' Susan said, 'you were right about one thing, Mark is nice. He asked me to remind you of your date.'

Alice blushed. Would Susan think Spencer was being deceived? She hurried to get the water. There were so many things Alice wanted to ask as the two girls sat side by side on Susan's bed. It was obvious that Susan's immediate future would be traumatic; Alice did not want to make matters worse.

'Is there anything I can do?'

'Not really, but thanks anyway.'

Alice stood up, 'I'm sorry, but I've got to go.'

Susan smiled. 'Thanks, I'm sorry too, but it is my own fault, I know that now; make sure you don't do the same.'

Mark had a restless night. Once he had got Susan into a taxi, he was faced with the drunken outbursts of his flatmates. Finally, they staggered off to bed, leaving the flat in chaos. He was sick of the whole business. He wasn't a prude but he seemed to spend far too much of his time clearing up after other people. A vague unease and discontent had dogged his thoughts for months and now began to crystallize. He did not like living in London, it was too impersonal, too big. He was a Mancunian born and bred and that was where his roots were.

When he moved down to the Big Smoke two years ago a group of friends came with him, all intent on making their fortunes. He had smiled at their naivety. One by one they had fallen by the wayside and returned to their families. Now only he was left.

As his friends had gone home, they had been replaced by young men who had answered the cards he had placed in local shop windows. He had nothing in common with any of them, least of all Jim. Mark felt engulfed by homesickness, he was a city boy, but London wasn't his city.

It was a year since Dad died and Mark had offered to return to Manchester, but Mum insisted he must get on with his life, she would manage. It seemed ironic that he, not his mother, felt lost and lonely, in a crowd, the worst loneliness of all. He decided to get up and have breakfast before the drinkers roused themselves. He went into the kitchen which was littered with mugs, plates and saucers full of dog ends. At least the sun was shining and the clear bright light echoed the clarity of his thoughts. He would ask for a transfer to Manchester.

During his time at Rainham's Estate Agents, the firm had done well. There had been talk recently of opening one or two new branches in the regions. He was sure the North West was being considered, it could be Manchester or maybe Liverpool. He would speak to his boss on Monday. He felt light-headed, the decision was made and it felt as though a boulder had rolled off his back; to go home was the right decision. Unlike his old mates, he wasn't going back with his tail between his legs. He was going back with a job, a job with prospects in an area he knew. It was the logical thing to do and his mother would be delighted.

He looked at the debris around him and laughed, he would clear it, but it would be for the last time. He wrinkled his nose at a pungent smell, a mixture of stale beer and B.O. He stacked the dirty crockery and admitted to himself how irritated he was by his flatmates' filthy habits.

Now, at last, the end was in sight. He put the kettle on the stove and whilst he waited for it to boil started on the washing up. What must he do before he left London? He felt a tremor of anxiety. It was all very well for him to make up his mind, but suppose the boss doesn't agree.

'Sod it," he said, "I'm going anyway, feeling as I do this morning, it must be the right decision.'

'Bad sign talking to yourself.' Jim lounged in the doorway.

'Only person here who can give a sensible answer.'

'Charming.' Jim wandered off muttering about sanctimonious

sods who should stay where they belong, in the sticks.

Jim's comment reinforced Mark's resolve. Then he remembered Susan and the promise he had made; he'd call Tony on Tuesday. He leaned against the sink and gazed out of the window, how had he got involved and what was he going to say? It was none of his business. Tony could tell him to push off, but a promise was a promise; he could only do his best. The whole squalid business with Tony and Susan was an example of all he disliked about London.

Of course, the same thing happened in Manchester, but he'd never been aware of it. Maybe that was the difference, in Manchester he had lived with his parents in a decent, residential area. Here he was a tenant in a rented property with a high turnover of occupants. People had no roots, no standards, and no responsibility; they were ships that passed in the night making passing contact before going on their way.

The next problem was Alice; he could not contact her. Did she live in the hostel with Susan or was she a friend from somewhere else? He couldn't remember what she had said. They had joked and talked nonsense and it had all been so natural and relaxed. The date must go ahead as planned; he really wanted to see Alice again.

If he did go to Manchester, no, when he went to Manchester they could keep in touch, write to each other. If they hit it off, she could always visit. He stopped. This was day-dreaming; he mustn't get carried away because it all might come to nothing.

Spencer and Alice sat on the grass and watched couples and families strolling around the park, enjoying the warm sunshine.

'Dad's taken Mum to the Dorchester for lunch, a treat for all the cooking she did yesterday.' He leaned back and stroked Alice's arm.

Isn't that what housewives were supposed to do, Alice wondered, particularly when they didn't go out to work. It didn't seem wise to say so.

'Didn't you want to go?'

'Not really, all you can get out of her at the moment is Malcolm this and Malcolm that. I'm sick of it. He's all right, but the way Mum goes on you'd think the sun shone out of his bottom.'

Alice looked at him and wondered if it was jealousy speaking.

'What's he like, your brother, do you look alike?'

'No, he's more like Dad; I'm the one who takes after Mum's family.'

Strange, Alice thought and let her mind drift. It was an irony that Mrs. Martin appeared to worship the son who looked like the husband she didn't seem to get on with. Yet Dad and I don't get on because I remind him of the wife he divorced. The difference was the Martins were still married. Perhaps Malcolm reminded her of her husband when he was younger, when they did get on. Relationships were a minefield.

'But what's he like as a person?'

'Oh, I don't know, he's just my little brother.'

'Will I meet him?'

'I expect so; he's coming home at the end of the week. That's what rattled Mum. Her precious boy decided to spend the first week of his holiday with one of his boarding school chums. She expected him to come rushing home to her.'

The bitterness in Spencer's remark was clear. Alice watched his expression and wondered if he was the one who needed his mother's devotion. He did resent Malcolm. Perhaps Mrs Martin felt she could afford to be less careful with her treatment of Spencer. Maybe she knew he craved her love and attention; it was Malcolm she wasn't sure of.

With a sudden movement, Spencer stood and stretching out his hand helped Alice to her feet.

'Let's walk.' The subject of Malcolm was now closed. 'Dad wants me to go to Stockholm soon.'

'For a visit?'

'No, to stop.'

Alice's heart lurched. 'How long for?'

'Not long, I don't suppose.' He squeezed her hand. 'I'll have to get some orders first,' he paused, 'I don't think I'm cut out to be a salesman.'

He looked at her and smiled. 'You're a nice kid,' he said, 'come on, we'll have an ice cream before I take you back.'

Alice wasn't sure she wanted to be a nice kid; it reminded her of when Dad came home on leave and took her to the zoo. The day always ended with ice cream or sticky cakes and then, like today, she was taken back to wherever she lived at the time.

Joan phoned her parents' phone number; it was so much easier than seeing them. She couldn't bear the cloying atmosphere of ill health. She had often wondered if Multiple Sclerosis was hereditary, but had never dared ask. Supposing she ended up bedridden, reliant on others for everything; she must not think like that. Lillian answered the call.

'Dad and I were just talking about you, wondered when you were coming around.'

Joan gripped the receiver, how she hated disapproval from her kid sister.

'I may not have a job but I do have a family you know.'

There was a moment's silence.

'Mum's not too good today, had a bad night and I can't get her to eat much.'

'Have you called the doctor?'

'Not yet.'

'Look Lillian, why do you think we pay for Mum to have a private doctor?'

'Yes, I know but maybe it isn't the doctor she wants to see.'

Joan sighed. 'Any news on the boyfriend front?'

'Who, Harry?'

'How many boyfriends are there?'

'He's coming over.'

'Oh.' Joan tried to control her feelings of unease. 'Where will he stop?'

'Here. Dad's been great; he's offered to sleep on the put-you-up downstairs so Harry can have Mum and Dad's room.'

'Be careful.'

'Why?'

'Just be careful, don't encourage him too much, too soon.'

'Don't worry, Joan, he's only a friend, I am allowed to have friends you know.'

'Yes, well, tell Mum and Dad we'll try to get round soon.'

Alice walked through the hostel hallway just as Miss Pritchard came out of her office.

'I'm glad I've seen you,' Miss Pritchard said, 'your father has been on the phone.'

'Is something wrong?'

'No, I don't think so; he was just calling to see how you'd settled in.'

Alice smiled.

'I think he was calling from a call box. Anyway, he was cut off before I could tell him much.'

'He doesn't have a phone; says he doesn't think anyone should be able to interrupt what he's doing.'

Miss Pritchard laughed. 'Sounds like a good idea.'

'Did he want to speak to me?'

'Don't think so, just checking you were all right and you are alright, aren't you?'

'Yes, thank you, Miss Pritchard.'

Alice turned to walk up to her room. She was all right, but what about Susan, she wondered if she should tell Miss Pritchard.'

Chapter 9

Although Mark and Tony had joined Rainham's Estate Agents at the same time they had been sent to different London offices once they completed their induction. Mark dialled Tony's number still unsure of what he would say, only sure that the longer he left it the more difficult it would be.

'It's Mark, fancy a pint after work?'

There was a pause. Mark wondered if Tony would refuse; he was scared after what happened on Saturday.

'Don't know, I told Maggie I'd be home early.'

'Don't tell me she's got you on a tight rein.'

Another pause; Tony always kicked against the slightest suggestion that he might be henpecked or 'under the thumb'.

'You're on, what time, where?'

Mark grimaced; he'd done it again, if he'd kept my mouth shut, he could have told Susan it was no good and in a couple of weeks he'd be off to Manchester.

'Six o'clock at the 'Crown and Anchor'.'

'Right, see you there then, bye.'

Mark put the phone down. Now he just had to plan how best to approach the delicate subject of Susan and the baby. Best be direct, no beating about the bush. He looked at his watch, two hours to go. He really must get down to work; there were lots of loose ends to tie up before his transfer.

He had seen the manager yesterday and Mr. Baker had said he would contact Head Office to check how plans for the North West were going. He thought Mark was an ideal candidate for relocation although he would be missed in London. It had all been too easy. Mark wondered if life was mapped out, and it only goes wrong if you kick against the master plan.

Head Office had approved his request, pleased to be saving the resettlement allowance as Mark would be able to live with his mother. It had been decided he could go as soon as he had completed any outstanding work. It had been as simple as that.

His mother had been delighted by the news and was, by now, almost certainly in the throes of redecorating his room. He was going home, but not as a failure like the rest of the gang.

Joan rushed about in a state of frenzy. Malcolm had called to say he was arriving on Wednesday, tomorrow. He hadn't said why he'd changed his plans and Joan didn't care. Her heart swelled with delight; her darling boy would soon be here. She had called her cleaning lady, Mrs Cartwright, to get her to come today. There had been no reply, the woman was useless.

Joan would tell Stanley to go back to the agency and demand a replacement.

There was no alternative; Joan must clean Malcolm's room herself. She stripped the barely used sheets from the bed, smoothed the sheets and placed two hot water bottles between them. Everything must be aired. She dusted, polished and vacuumed the carpet with an enthusiasm she hadn't felt for years.

Leaning against the window sill, she could smile with deep satisfaction at the results of her labours; all that was needed now was a vase of flowers. She could go to the florists or get something from the garden. If she called on, the florist she could pop into the off-licence and replace the bottle of brandy she had taken from Stanley's stock. She hesitated. No, she would be strong, she would not drink today. She wanted to look her best when she greeted Malcolm tomorrow. She turned and glancing down she saw several deep red roses in the garden, just right for cutting. They would be perfect.

She wondered if she should phone Stanley and give him the good news, no not yet, she wanted to keep it to herself for a little longer. She hummed quietly under her breath as she arranged the roses in her best cut glass vase. She took them upstairs and placed the vase on the window sill. The velvety, red petals glowed as though illuminated from within, red roses, a symbol of love, how appropriate. Above all others, she loved her son, Malcolm.

She wandered around the empty house not sure what to do next. This was her life, always looking for something to do. She'd go to Stanley's office; he can take her out to dinner. She showered and changed into clothes suitable for a managing director's wife. She scribbled a note for Spencer; he would have to get his own meal tonight. She called a taxi. Stanley could settle the fare at the other end, she paused, perhaps she should pay herself if she was expecting to be taken out. He was always complaining about her extravagance and there was no point in spoiling the evening for the sake of a few pounds.

Stanley was at his desk signing letters for that evening's post when Joan walked in. His secretary, Gill, was standing beside him, her hand resting on his shoulder. The speed with which Gill removed that hand told Joan everything. The ensuing silence, which could only have lasted a few seconds, seemed to expand to fill all available space leaving no room to breathe.

In a quiet voice, Stanley said, 'That will be all, Gill, see they are posted tonight.'

As Gill walked past Joan, the air crackled. The office door was closed with a sigh and Joan felt a great weight crushing her chest. How long had she suspected this? Had she known all along, but refused to acknowledge it? She had never looked at another man; she had all the men she wanted, Malcolm, Stanley and of course Spencer.

Stanley smiled at her and she wondered how he could be so calm.

'This is a nice surprise, my dear.'

She wanted to hit him, to wipe that inane and hypocritical smile from his smug face. She wanted to hurt him, scratch at his face and make him bleed as she was bleeding inside.

Stanley continued in a quiet, calm voice, 'You look very smart, my dear, been somewhere nice?'

How dare he behave as though nothing had happened; how could he deny the evidence of her own eyes? Gill only had a hand on his shoulder but it was more, so much more than that. They had been too close. People only get that close if they have or want to have a physical relationship. Everyone knew that. How often had he taken this woman away on business trips? He had said less and less about his trips away from home, but then he would, wouldn't he, if Gill was his mistress. Did Spencer know what was going on? That was more than likely which made the whole sordid business worse.

Stanley didn't get up from behind his desk.

'I came to give you some good news; there's no point now, you've spoilt everything.'

She could hear the shrill note in her voice but didn't care.

'Are you going to share this good news?'

'Don't you dare take me for a fool, Stanley. I've suspected for a long time that something was going on. Don't you dare deny it.' She noticed that the finger she was pointing at him was shaking, but this time it was not caused by alcohol. She gasped for breath as Stanley walked towards her.

'I have never wanted to hurt you, you know that.'

He tried to put his arms around her; she moved away. He leaned back against his desk and smiled, but she could see wariness in his eyes and she was glad; his nonchalance was a cover. She stared at him willing him to look away, to lower his eyes in shame.

'If I've done anything to upset you, I'm sorry. Let me take you out and we can talk, you still haven't given me your good news.'

He's humouring me, she thought, as though I'm a wayward child. Yet she felt the tension diminish. She wanted to cling to the terrible rage, it shut out the hurt. If she stopped feeling angry, she might cry. She sensed that was what Stanley wanted then he would be able to comfort her and everything would go back to normal. She hated his capacity for conciliation. Why wouldn't he fight back? Why wouldn't he shout and scream as she did? That was the aphrodisiac she needed, perhaps then her long-dormant desire would reawaken.

Stanley had always been a gentleman. She wondered if he was a gentleman with Gill or, was she his 'bit of rough'? Just the thought of him in bed with another woman made her want to scream. Did Gill talk about this sordid affair to the others in the office?

'You are having an affair with that woman, aren't you?'

Joan watched and wondered if he was going to try to wriggle out of it.

'Yes, my dear, I would not insult your intelligence by denying it.'

His words hung in the air between them before sinking like stones into a thick and clotted silence. Without a word, Joan turned on her heel and left the office.

When Mark arrived at the pub Tony was already at the bar ordering a pint. Mark stood in the doorway and watched his friend for a moment. The arrogant man with the world in general and women in particular, at his feet, had vanished; he looked nervous.

'Want a pint?'

Mark nodded and looked for a quiet table.

'We can sit over there.'

They sat side by side, facing the room. Mark was glad they did not have to look at each other during what was going to be a tricky conversation. He took a deep breath.

'I expect you realise why I wanted to see you.'

'Susan?'

'She's in a hell of a state.'

Tony did not reply or look at him.

'What are you going to do, Tony? She's determined to get rid of the baby, but has no idea how.'

'What does she expect me to do?'

'Oh, come on man, it takes two.'

'What does she want, money?'

'Probably, but she needs to know who to go to. I don't think Mummy and Daddy would welcome her back in her present condition.'

'What makes you think I know anyone who will do the necessary?'

'Do you?'

'I might.'

'For God's sake, don't play silly buggers.'

'How soon does she need to know?'

'The sooner the better…'

'I need to make a couple of phone calls.'

'I'll wait here then.' Mark felt sure if arrangements were not made tonight, they never would be. While he sipped his beer, he wondered again how he had become embroiled in all this. After fifteen minutes he wondered if Tony had done the frightened rabbit act.

When he did return, he was the old confident Tony again.

'Had a couple of calls to make, took ages, first phone box was out of order.'

'Well?'

'This is the number she has to ring, the woman who answers will make all the arrangements. Knows some bloke, claims he's a doctor, probably been struck off for doing this sort of thing. But Susan should be all right, he must know what he's doing, it costs seventy-five pounds.'

Mark stared at Tony who finally, with great reluctance, faced him.

'One of my mates got this girl into trouble, see.'

Mark said nothing.

'I suddenly remembered.'

'This has happened before, hasn't it?'

Tony took a large swig of his beer and nodded.

'I know it's none of my business, but don't you think it's time you learned your lesson?'

'Don't you ever make mistakes?'

'Yes Tony, but I try not to make the same mistake twice.'

Tony looked away and drew on his cigarette.

'Has she got any money?'

'Not seventy-five pounds she hasn't.'

'I can give her thirty out of my account, but that's all. Most of our money goes into a joint account.'

'And Maggie might ask questions.'

Mark had a sour taste in his mouth. He had planned to tell Tony about his transfer, he wouldn't bother now; he just wanted to get away. It was all so sordid and it was obvious that Tony had no intentions of having further contact with Susan. That was best for the poor kid even if she couldn't see that now.

'Give me the cheque for thirty pounds now, I'll cash it and give Susan the money. Goodness knows where she will get the rest.'

Tony made no comment, but wrote the cheque with indecent haste, and downed the rest of his pint in one swallow.

'Must go, promised Maggie I wouldn't be late.'

'How the hell does that woman put up with you?'

Tony didn't reply but rose and without a backward glance threaded his way through the, now crowded, pub to disappear out of the door. Mark sighed; Susan would have no further contact with her baby's father.

There's a call for you, Susan, I transferred it to the booth in the hall.'

'Thank you, Miss Pritchard,' she said and raced downstairs. For a wild moment she thought it might be Tony, but in her heart, she knew it wasn't.

'Hello'

'Susan, it's Mark, I've just seen Tony.'

'Oh thanks, I'm so grateful, what did he say?'

Mark paused, no point in dressing it up. Tony was making a small financial gesture in order to disassociate himself from a problem he didn't want to acknowledge.

'He's given me a phone number for you to ring and thirty pounds towards the cost. You still want to go ahead with it?'

Susan had known this was how it would be yet the harsh reality of Tony's callousness still stabbed at her heart. What a fool she had been.

'Thirty pounds, how much does it cost then?'

'Seventy-five.'

Susan gasped, where on earth would she get the rest?

'Are you still there?'

'I've got no money, what can I do?'

Mark sighed, the whole mess was going deeper and deeper.

'Look, I can manage twenty if that would help.'

Susan felt her thoughts go into free fall and words tumbled into space, incoherent, disjointed.

'Of course, it would help, but how can I ever repay you? I'll just have to ask my parents for the rest.'

'Will you tell them why?'

'No, I couldn't possibly do that. I'll think of something, I know, I've had my purse stolen. I'll tell them I'm broke. Yes, that's it, I'll call them tonight.'

'When do you want me to bring the money and telephone number round? Be quick, I'm out of change for the phone.'

'Can you come tonight? I've got to get this sorted before I lose my nerve; I haven't got pencil or paper with me.'

'O.K.'

'Do you know where the hostel is?'

'Yes, Baron's Court, near the station.'

Susan hoped Mark heard her say thank you before the line went dead.

She stood for a moment and watched as fellow residents moved through the hallway, chatting and laughing. What would they think of her if they knew?

She took several deep breaths and tried to sort out what she would say before she rang her parents' number. She needed twenty-five but still had to get through the rest of the month. Better ask for forty pounds, that should be enough. She dialled their number and crossed her fingers, hoping they would be in. She listened to the ringing tone and prayed.

'9842, Eric Johnson speaking.'

'Dad, it's Susan.'

There was a pause. 'This is unexpected, how are you?'

'I'm okay, sorry I haven't rung recently, you and Mum all right?'

'Yes, do you want to speak to her?'

He'd always left things to Mum whenever he could. He'd never seemed too keen to converse with her, his only child. Susan had often wondered if he had wanted a son, but that wasn't her fault.

'No, er yes, in a minute. It's just that an awful thing has happened. You see I've had my purse stolen. I'd been to the bank and I had all the money for the rest of the month, forty pounds. I don't know what to do.' She paused and leaned her forehead against the cool glass of the booth.

'I see.' There was a pause.

'You still there, Dad?'

'Yes. It's just that we haven't heard from you for close on six months. Have you any idea how that's been for your Mum?'

Susan gritted her teeth, always the lecture. If they were so concerned, why hadn't they called her? They knew where she was.

'I'm sorry, Dad.'

'And now, when you do deign to ring, it's because you want something.'

'I wouldn't ask if I could manage and I will pay you back.'

'I've heard that before and if you could have managed, would you have rung?'

'Yes, I would, but you know how things are.'

'No, Susan, I don't; you could be dead for all we knew. Have you reported the theft to the police?'

Susan hadn't thought of that. 'No, because I can't be sure exactly where I lost it.'

'That's no reason, could it be one of the girls in the hostel, you never know?'

'I'm sure it isn't one of them, but I'll report it tomorrow.'

She clenched her fist and waited, was he going to send the money or not?

'How do you want it; will a cheque do?'

Susan felt faint with relief. 'Would you send cash, Dad, you see I'm absolutely broke, I haven't even got the fare to get to work. It would be safe if you sent it by registered post. I can probably borrow my bus fares until it arrives.'

'Right, cash it is, I'll sort it tomorrow, you should get it by Thursday. Now you'd better have a word with your mother, she's been sick with worry about you.'

'Thanks, Dad.'

Barbara gazed out of the window and chewed her pen. The pale blue writing paper lay before her, untouched. It shouldn't be so hard to write a note of thanks to Jeffrey. He seemed to have enjoyed her company on Saturday evening and now was the time to do something positive. She started to write and thanked him for a delightful evening and wondered if she could return his hospitality soon. Was he doing anything this coming Saturday? Would he like to come for a meal?

She was intrigued to see how he responded. Joan had said that Jeffrey was fond of flirting with women but only when there were others present. Barbara wondered if the idea of an evening alone with her would prove to be too daunting. Both her address and telephone number were at the top of the page, he could write or call; she wondered which he would do.

Susan hoped she had enough change, although, it probably wouldn't be a long call. She dialled the number Mark had given her. She had overcome one hurdle this evening. Mum had been quite pleasant and commiserated with her over her loss, of course Dad would send the money. Just this one call then she could go upstairs and have a hot bath, as hot as she could stand it. Maybe nature would sort the problem, but she was sure she should drink gin as well. That was out of the question.

She listened to the ringing tone. Just as she was about to replace the receiver a woman answered. She gave no number and Susan was terrified she might not be speaking to the right person.

'Is that 6264?'

'Yes.' Not a voice to encourage confidence.

'I've been given your number by a friend. Can you help me?'

'How?'

This was awful. 'My name's Susan Joh…

'No names, I don't want no names.'

'I'm in trouble, I've got seventy-five pounds; that is what it costs isn't it?

Please can you help, I've got to get rid of it.'

'Where did you get this number?'

'I told you; a friend gave it to me.'

'So, what exactly do you want?'

Susan leaned nearer the wall aware of movement outside the booth. Girls were walking past; they must not hear what she was saying. She fed her last coins into the slot. Perspiration was running down her face, she wanted to scream and make the nightmare end. She hissed into the receiver, 'I want an abortion.'

'You said you'd got the money.'

'Yes, I will have by Thursday.'

'Okay, Thursday evening, seven o'clock, 52 Larkhall Lane. It's off Wandsworth Road, Stockwell.'

Susan scribbled the address down.

'Make sure you come alone, anyone with you and the deal's off.'

Yes,' she replied, but the phone line was already dead. With trembling hands, she replaced the receiver; there was no going back now.

Chapter 10

Joan had avoided speaking to Stanley since her visit to the office. She had concentrated all her time and energy on Malcolm. She was surprised her boy had made no comment on the obvious atmosphere; he had changed and seemed distant. She realised with sorrow that he was growing up and soon he would not need her. Even her efforts to make his room perfect had largely passed without comment. Of course, he had removed the flowers and put them on the hall window sill. What had he said?

'Come off it, Ma, I'm not a pansy.'

She laughed and claimed it had been the cleaning woman's idea, but she had been shocked.

What was she to do about Stanley? Coming back from his office she had been determined to divorce him, take him for every penny he had. How dare he? And, with a common little madam like Gill, she was a jumped-up nobody who had ideas above her station. But Joan could not ignore her own humble origins. Mum and Dad had been ordinary working folk with few aspirations and less money.

What had her sister, Lillian, achieved? She had managed a lowly office job with few prospects, not unlike Gill. Of course, Lillian was tied to Mum and Dad now, but if she had really wanted to make something of herself, she could have.

Now there was this wretched man, Harry somebody or other. Joan felt sure that his arrival would have a far from a beneficial effect on her life. It was so unfair. She had brought up her family and now just when she and Stanley should have some time and money to do whatever they liked it was all going wrong.

She sensed a new determination in Lillian. She wasn't so young anymore; did she think this was her last chance to grab a husband? Joan thought of all the glamorous men she had dated before Stanley. Of course, she had been a stunning young woman, everyone said so. She opened the drawer under the wardrobe and looked again at the many photographs taken all those years ago when she was young. She could have had any man. Now when she glanced into the mirror the clear light of morning told no lies. Years of drinking and smoking had left their smudged finger prints on her face.

If I divorce him, who will I have? Her reflection stared back at her. She acknowledged that her relationship with Spencer was uneasy; he was resentful and always sided with his father. What of Malcolm? He would leave her; the signs were there. Already he had mentioned some stupid idea of going into the army. I will be alone, she mouthed silently. The very thought seemed to bounce from wall to wall and back into her head. She shuddered. If she divorced Stanley, he would still have Gill; if it was what he really wanted, the fool.

Once she was alone the way would be clear for Lillian to go off with this Harry fellow leaving Mum and Dad to her, the older sister; Joan felt her eyes fill. None of this was her fault. Lillian was the caring one, always had been. Joan knew she could not cope with her elderly parents; she had other talents. I'm a good cook, and a good hostess, I know how to entertain. I can cope with all Stanley's business contacts, put them at their ease. Lillian could never do that.

Joan rested her chin on her hands and said to her reflection, 'I can't be a geriatric nurse and that's all there is to it so divorce is out, there is too much to lose.'

She gave a little smile to herself as she added, 'But things will have to change, Stanley will not be allowed to get away with it.'

Today was Thursday; Malcolm was going back to boarding school on Sunday. It could wait until then; she needed more time to think. She looked at her watch, mid-day and more than time for Malcolm to get up. He won't be able to lie abed in the army. She decided she would point that out to him, maybe the thought of such rigors would make him decide on a different career, one that didn't take him away from her. She hurried downstairs to make him a coffee. She would sit on his bed while he drank it and chat like they had done when he was younger.

Susan walked down an unfamiliar street. Although it was still light on this pleasant, late summer evening, Larkhall Lane had a forbidding exterior emphasized by the absence of children playing or in fact the evidence of any life at all. Some of the houses were boarded up and the windows of the rest stared at her, sightless and dead. That was it, the street seemed dead and all that remained was a decayed carcass. Litter had been blown into untidy heaps by capricious winds, rain had reduced those heaps to sodden lumps, festering growths which no one had attempted to remove. Some windows bore scant signs of any previous occupation. Shredded lace curtains hung like nicotine-stained seaweed, soot encrusted plants of indeterminate variety clung to life in a few tiny, walled, front gardens.

Susan was frightened, very frightened. Alice had offered to come with her but Susan explained that was impossible. She checked again the number on the scrap of paper Mark had given her. Number fifty-two was over the road. Her footsteps sounded too loud as they echoed across the grimy street. She heard a door bang behind her but did not dare look around. Perhaps squatters had moved into some of the empty properties. She didn't want to see who it was; it might be some dirty old tramp hoping to snatch her handbag. There would be no abortion without the money.

She stood outside fifty-two, trembling too much to knock on the door. Take deep breaths, calm down, it's going to be all right. She could hear footsteps coming nearer. They were quick, light steps, not a man's; she glanced back. A hatchet-faced woman was coming towards her. She was dressed in a shabby, nondescript coat which had once been black, but now had a greenish tinge to it. She wore an old-fashioned cloche-type hat, pulled well down. Her eyes were in shadow. A large, bulging shopping bag hung from her arm, she had a key in one hand. Although in a hurry her eyes darted up and down the street as though she feared being seen or followed.

'Quick, out of the way,' the woman said.

Susan realised it was the voice she had heard on the phone and now this shabby woman fumbled with the key, pushed open the paint-peeling door and hustled Susan inside. She must live in this awful street, Susan thought, she's been waiting and watching for me to arrive.

'Go through to the back, there isn't much time. Doctor will be here any minute; we've got to get ready.'

The narrow hallway smelt of damp and decay; it was gloomy after the bright light outside. Susan stumbled against an ancient bicycle, minus one wheel, which leaned against the wall.

'Ssh, don't make a noise.'

Since the evidence of her own eyes suggested that most, if not all, of the inhabitants of Larkhall Lane, had long since escaped to something better, she could see little point in worrying about noise. Under the circumstances, Susan's decided, it was in her best interests to do exactly as she was told. She said nothing.

The woman led her through to a room at the back of the house. It was empty with newspaper stuck to the windows. What light there was came from a window in what, Susan assumed, was a scullery. She was surprised. Where would the doctor do what had to be done? There was no bed, no anything. The woman was pulling wedges of newspapers from her bag and spreading them on the bare, splintered floorboards. The middle of the floor was covered with large, dark stains. The room smelt strange, it was a smell that reminded Susan of a butcher's shop, but it was overlaid by the sharp stench of cat pee.

The woman ignored Susan and removing neither hat nor coat continued to spread newspapers on the floor. Once satisfied she produced a small bar of soap and a bit of clean towel. These she took through to the scullery which, Susan could see, held an ancient, filthy sink and one corroded cold-water tap.

Susan felt hysterical laughter bubble in her throat, she wanted to run away. This was a nightmare; anything would be better than this. For a split second, she wondered if she could have the baby after all; Mum and Dad wouldn't turn her away, would they? She stood paralysed with fear and dread, she wanted the toilet but didn't dare ask.

She jumped as the door to the hallway opened. There had been no noise of the front door being opened or closed, the man just appeared. He was short and dumpy. The first thing Susan noticed, because of his silent entrance, was his abnormally small feet. They were like a child's; Twinkle-toes, that's how I shall think of him, a little fat man with a child's feet. She needed something to help her cling to reality and the certainty that the whole business would soon be over.

The shoes, like the rest of his clothes, indicated money. Without a word he removed his hat, grey raincoat and the jacket of a dark blue pinstripe suit all of which he hung behind the door. Susan wondered why she was taking so much note of a man she would never see again; at least it stopped her thinking about anything else.

The man seemed anxious and breathed heavily as he rolled up the sleeves of his pristine white shirt. Perspiration shone on his brow as he loosened his tie and stroked into place the thin strands of hair that didn't disguise his pink, naked crown. He walked through to the scullery where the woman waited. The gush of water drowned the sound of their muffled conversation. Susan stood not knowing what she was supposed to do.

The woman came in, 'Get yourself ready, doctor hasn't got all night.'

'I need to go to the toilet.'

The woman gave an exasperated tut. 'Be quick, upstairs, first on the left, don't flush it.'

Susan raced upstairs as quietly as she could; her breath came in short gasps. The toilet was unspeakable; Susan felt her stomach clench at the nauseating, foul smell. In addition to faeces and urine which almost filled the toilet bowl, there was blood and vomit everywhere. She clung to the door frame and willed herself not to faint. She could not use that toilet, but she had to go somewhere.

A voice hissed up the stairs, 'Hurry up.'

Susan tiptoed into the backroom, beyond the toilet. It was empty except for a pile of rubbish in one corner. With a whimper of relief, she pulled down her knickers and squatted. No sooner had she emptied her bladder than she was running downstairs pulling her clothes straight as she went. They were waiting for her.

'Give me the money first.'

Susan was startled by the man's voice; it was light and high like a woman. She fumbled in her bag for the envelope and handed it over. Her hands trembled. He took the money and, with expertise, counted out the notes. He nodded to the woman, then peeled off five pounds and gave them to her. He stuffed the rest into his trouser pocket.

'Lie down,' the woman said.

Susan glanced around the room, 'Where?'

'On the floor, girl, for God's sake, do you want to get rid of it or not?'

Susan noticed a clean piece of sheeting on top of the newspapers. She hesitated, wondering if that was for her, but while she watched, the man lower himself with care onto the protective plastic. Of course, she thought, he must not get his good suit besmirched by newsprint. What did she matter? She must lie like a lump of meat; she was of no importance now.

'Take your knickers off, pull your skirt up and bend your knees.' His hands on her knees pulled them apart and with no warning, he thrust his fingers into her vagina with such force it made her gasp.

'How many periods have you missed?'

'Two.'

He pressed on her abdomen and grunted with satisfaction.

Susan assumed he was pleased to verify the pregnancy was no further advanced than she claimed.

'Right, I'll do what I have to do to start things off. That's the end of my job, understand?' Nodding to the woman, 'She'll clear up the mess and see you out. You should start to bleed within twenty-four hours. Any problems go to your own doctor.'

Susan nodded. Tears blurred her vision and she could not speak.

'Do not, under any circumstances, say anything about this place, understand. And the next time you decide to indulge in an adult activity behave like an adult and protect yourself.'

The menace in his voice combined with his total lack of sympathy felt like a slap and Susan, now terrified, wept great, shuddering, silent sobs. She dared not make a noise in case they walked out and left her.

'This will hurt but I can't do anything about that. Don't make a noise.'

Susan stared at the ceiling while he fumbled with something wrapped in a piece of cloth. The ceiling sagged in the middle and was festooned with cracks like an old man's face. Bits of plaster were missing showing wooden laths that resembled the ribs of a prehistoric animal. The single, flyblown light bulb was moved by some undetectable current of air as it hung from a frayed central flex.

Susan concentrated on the bulb, focusing all her attention on that; she would not think about what he was going to do. She clenched her fists. Already she was drenched with sweat even though she was icy cold. She felt pressure on her abdomen again and a violent thrusting as something thin and cold and sharp was pushed into her womb. Searing, excruciating pain radiated outwards and reached to her fingertips. A hand clamped down on her mouth.

She tried to raise her knees, to curl into the foetal position, to expel this instrument of torture from the secret, the innermost part of her body. She couldn't move. His knees were pressed against her thighs while his hand was pumping backwards and forwards, twisting, thrusting, dragging her flesh, tearing her.

Suddenly the pain was gone and Susan watched what was happening with detachment. Nothing mattered. The woman kept one hand on Susan's mouth; the other held her shoulder down. Susan struggled no more. She watched the man, as he squatted like some obscene toad, gripping her legs, holding them down and apart. Why was there no pain?

She felt warm and her eyelids drooped. She was floating away from this scene of torment. This was not her lying on the floor, an empty shell, a bleeding carcass. It was like a silent movie. Everything seemed distant, disconnected. She wondered if she were dying. Would her parents mourn their loss?

She sensed rather than felt the woman's hand release its grip. Susan did not move. The tears on her cheeks were dry now; she could cry no more. Far away she heard the woman say something, she sounded worried. Susan felt herself being shaken, gently at first. The man must have stopped what he was doing because Susan felt the slender, sharp instrument being withdrawn. She exhaled in a long, drawn-out sigh.

The man leaned over her; she felt his breath on her cheek. He slapped her face hard; the shock made her jump. He slapped her again. She moaned aware once more of this terrible pain in her abdomen. She was on fire; sharp daggers of pain stabbed at her again and again.

'She's all right now,' the man said as he mopped his brow. 'That was a close thing.'

He struggled to his feet, with rings of sweat under his arms which tarnished his immaculate shirt. He grabbed the piece of towel from the woman and Susan watched as he dragged the knitting needle through a fold of the material to remove the blood.

Susan did not have the strength to do anything but clench her fists and teeth to keep the screams inside. Wave after wave of pain washed over her. She could not move even to pull her skirt down to cover herself. She lay like a puppet that relied on others to control its movements. Logical, coherent thought was obliterated by pain.

The man was getting ready to leave; he had his money and now another successful consultation was concluded he would not give her another thought, without a word he was gone. The woman had started to gather the newspapers, rolling and folding them to put in her bag.

'Get up, you can't stay here.'

Susan struggled to sit up but overcome by dizziness she fell back.

'Get up quick, get dressed, have you got a towel?'

Susan looked at her, confused, a towel? Why would she want to wash here, in this hell hole?

'A towel, in case you start to bleed before you get home.'

'No, no I didn't think.'

'No, you didn't think, if you had you wouldn't be here.'

The woman groped in her bag for a moment and pulled out a large sanitary towel. She grabbed Susan's shoulders from behind and forced her upright.

'You've got five minutes to sort yourself out then you're out of here, see.'

Susan most certainly did see. She struggled to stand, picked up her knickers and, leaning against the wall, put them on. She felt a thin trickle of blood creep down the inside of her thigh. Her vision was blurred by tears as she dabbed at the blood on her leg with the sanitary towel and then pushed it into place in her knickers. She tried again to stand upright but was doubled up with stomach cramps. With a great effort she gritted her teeth and with heavy breaths forced her shoulders back until they touched the wall behind her.

The woman continued clearing the papers. Then she hurried into the scullery to retrieve the soap which she wrapped in the bloody piece of towel. After a final check that everything was now how she had found it, she grabbed Susan's arm.

'Off you go now, straight home, have a hot bath and go to bed, not a word to anyone mind. I've never seen you before.'

Susan nodded; there was nothing to say. She lurched her way down the hallway and out into bright sunshine. The woman did not follow, probably waiting until Susan had walked to the bottom of the road, turned the corner and was out of sight.

Alice felt dreadful; her throat was getting worse. She had staggered into work ashen-faced and shivering. Both Professor Walker and Doctor Anderson had been concerned. Even Suzanne, the laboratory assistant, had been sympathetic, made a fuss of her and brought her several cups of tea during a day that seemed endless. When Alice left that evening, she had been told not to come in the next day unless she felt better. She was not any better, in fact, she was worse. She alternated between a high fever and a chilling cold that made her shiver.

She must be running a temperature. Although she had offered to go with Susan to the abortionist, she was thankful the offer had been refused. Alice hoped a good night's sleep would help, but it hadn't. She was supposed to be going over to Golders Green to meet the wonderful Malcolm on Friday. Then on Saturday, she was having lunch with Mark at the Strand Palace.

She had agonised over how she would explain this to Spencer but it had been easy. She said she was having lunch with a friend. He hadn't queried it. At the time she hadn't known whether to be glad or sorry that he wanted no more information. Did that mean he wasn't bothered or did he just assume it would be a girlfriend?

At this rate it wouldn't matter; all she wanted to do was go to bed. Perhaps a hot bath would help. As she lay soaking in water as hot as she could bear and wondered how Susan was getting on.

How long did these things take? She didn't know. How could a doctor do it anyway; she thought abortion was illegal. Susan had said it was being done by a doctor so she was bound to be all right. The steam seemed to be easing Alice's throat. I'll have a hot drink and early night with fingers crossed I'm bound to be fine in the morning.

Susan walked up the road from the station, every step jolted her insides. She knew she was bleeding; she felt weak and the pains were like daggers. She stopped every few steps to get her breath and wait for the next dragging contraction to pass. Not far now, only a hundred yards or so then she'd be safe. She thought about her parents as she clung to some railings. Thank God they would never know. She only had to get back to the hostel and then have a hot bath and go to bed, that was what the awful woman had said.

She let herself in and staggered up the steps, each one was agonising and she rested on every landing. She was relieved no one was about. Each careful step got her nearer to safety. As she reached the door of her room Alice came out of the bathroom. She looked flushed. Susan hoped she hadn't taken all the hot water.

Alice stared at Susan. 'Are you okay?'

Susan nodded. 'I've just got to wait now.'

'Can I do anything?'

'Run me a bath, will you, then I'm going to bed.'

Alice nodded, too shocked by Susan's grey face to speak.

Susan went into her room, undressed and got into her dressing gown. She was alarmed by the amount of blood she had already lost. The towel was saturated. Perhaps that was a good sign; it would all be over quicker. She checked her supply of sanitary towels, there should be enough. She'd ask Alice to let her have a few extras, just in case. Alice knocked at the door.

'The bath's running. Are you sure you can manage?'

Susan nodded and started to weep. Alice put her arms around the girl's shaking shoulders and held her.

'You'll soon feel better, the worst is over now.'

'It was dreadful, Alice, just dreadful. I wanted to die it was so awful.'

'Ssh, don't cry, you'll feel better after a bath and a good night's sleep.'

Chapter 11

Barbara enjoyed cooking. Much of the enjoyment came from planning the menu and choosing the ingredients. She believed the amount of care put into a meal indicated the depth of feeling a cook had for those who would eat it. Although what Jeffrey had given them last week had been simple Barbara detected an overwhelming need for him to give. Here, she thought, was a man in an emotional desert. Yet was it not true that after only a little rain a desert could become an ocean of flowers, flowers that came from seeds lying dormant for who knew how long. Perhaps, like a desert, Jeffrey too would blossom with a little encouragement.

She carried the heavy bags upstairs to her flat. Striking the right balance was important; too complicated a menu would embarrass him, too simple and she would not have an opportunity to show off her culinary skills. It was a shame she had work tomorrow. The library was always busy on a Saturday and it was her turn to go in. She would have to do a lot of the preparation this evening; make the pate and the coq au vin. Tomorrow there would just need to prepare vegetables and fruit salad. She kicked off her shoes and put the kettle on.

Relaxing on the large, comfortable settee she looked around and wondered what Jeffrey would make of it. This main room was light and airy with floor-to-ceiling muslin curtains which shut out the, less than inspiring, view of the row of terraced houses opposite. The heavy curtains which protected her from the outside world, when she sought solitude, were a rich golden brown. In fact, she had purposely chosen earth colours, ochre and gold that made the room feel warm even on the coldest day.

The cream-coloured walls were covered with an eclectic collection of pictures, prints and photographs. Although there was a central light, she seldom used it. She thought a few table lamps gave a more intimate atmosphere. Pools of light glowed on the handmade, embroidered cushions she had taken delight in designing. She loved this room more than any other because it was hers. She had chosen everything with care and thought and the end result was an enduring pleasure to her eyes.

She stood up, stretched and went into her bedroom. Once changed into jeans and a blouse she could start cooking. She hummed to herself. Like the living room, this too had been furnished with care, but it emphasized her solitary state. No man had left his socks and underpants in a heap on the pale pink carpet. There was no electric shaver or aftershave on the dressing table. The large, double, mahogany wardrobe had been part of her parents' trousseau; it was more than enough for her clothes. All that remained as proof that she had once been a wife and mother was the photograph of Andrew when he was a baby.

This was the room in which she had, over the years, been able to mourn her loss. It was here that she had cried until no more tears would come. This room had witnessed not only her grief but also her anger at the unfairness of life. It had been a sanctuary and repository for all the negative feelings that, if not contained within these four walls, would have destroyed her.

She sometimes wondered if she should leave the flat. Perhaps now the ghost of the past had been laid she could start again. Barbara wondered if she was running away from the past. She was relieved happy memories were beginning to superimpose themselves on any still able to cause her pain. She had found a measure of happiness.

After Andrew's death, her world had been nothing but grief and pain. She had clung to what the young minister had said after the funeral. 'God never gives you more than you can cope with.' At the time she had wanted to rail against a god who could be so cruel, but in the end, it gave her strength. The difficult part had been to develop strategies that enabled her to cope. She did not want to blot out everything because then she would lose precious memories of her only child.

It was the physical pain that was so hard to deal with. Now after so many years, she could think about him and not cry. He would have been ten if he lived and have dirty knees and pockets full of rubbish to treasure. She picked up his photograph in its silver frame and kissed it. Now she thought, I must get into the kitchen and do some cooking.

Susan struggled out of the bath. The water was an ominous pink; the bleeding was getting worse. She put two sanitary towels inside a clean pair of knickers. The pain in her abdomen expanded until it enveloped her, obliterating thought. She was not a person anymore; she was a deep, grinding, cramping agony, it had no beginning and no end. It invaded every bone, every muscle and every cell of her body.

She swayed and, frightened she might fall, clung to the edge of the bath. She felt dizzy as the next pain radiated from her womb. She bit her lip and whimpered as she stood with her head down, her arms rigid, her hands still clutching the bath. Just a little longer, she thought, then there will be a minute release as the pain eases a fraction before the next one comes. She was panting with the exertion of remaining upright and retaining the cries that jostled in her throat.

I've got to get out of here and into bed, have a hot bath and go to bed that was what the woman had said. Susan repeated it under her breath like a mantra, do as she told me and she would be all right. She shuffled hand over hand to the end of the bath and pulled out the plug. Perspiration was running down her face and dripped off the end of her nose. Any movement was agonising. I can't stay here, I can't stay here, I must go to bed; I must do as I am told. She could hear a voice muttering and wondered if it was hers.

She had no strength to dry herself. Just pulling her nightdress on took the last of her energy; without warning her knees gave way and she slid down the wall. It felt cold and damp with condensation. She didn't care. The night dress was stuck to her back, but what did it matter? What did anything matter? She sat, head back, leaning against the wall. She became aware of a warm, wet feeling between her legs; blood now stained her clean knickers.

She was tired, so very tired; I've got to get to bed, that was what the woman said, go to bed. She struggled onto all fours and used the edge of the bath to lever herself upright. With one hand she managed to drag her nightdress down far enough to cover evidence of her disgrace and stupidity. No one must see her, not like this.

The pain was so bad she could not stand upright. She grabbed her towel and slid back the bolt on the door, careful not to make any noise. No sound came from the corridor. She turned the doorknob and eased open the door. Glancing up and down she was relieved that no-one was about. She would make a dash for it, although the thought of further movement made her head spin. The bleeding was getting worse. She would be found in the morning, like a stuck pig, alabaster white. She would be an empty shell, all blood drained away.

Step by painful step she sidled the few yards to her room using the wall for support. She closed the door behind her and mopped her face. Mustn't sit down, she thought, got to go to bed, got to bed and everything will be all right. She longed for a hot water bottle to place on her pulsating abdomen, anything to get relief from the agony. She knew she didn't have the strength to walk to the kitchen and boil the kettle, she would manage without; further movement was impossible.

She managed to lift the covers enough to crawl into bed. She knew she should get some new sanitary towels; these were soaked already. She couldn't do it. She was just able to reach the bath towel which lay in a crumpled heap by the bed. With great care, so she didn't fall, she reached out to grab the towel and drag it into bed. She bunched and wedged it between her legs; that would have to do.

Although she tried to relax, her abdominal muscles were clenched like bands of iron. Tighter and tighter they squeezed and camped sending their arrows of pain in all directions. I will lie perfectly still, she thought, I'm in bed now and I've done as I was told. I'm going to be all right; that's what the woman said.

Alice tossed and turned. The sheets felt damp and chilly; the beneficial effects of the hot bath had long since worn off. Her throat was on fire, when she swallowed it felt as if she were swallowing broken glass. She shivered even though perspiration rolled off her, and her pyjamas were drenched. She wondered if it was worth putting on a clean pair but she would still have to lie in this damp, cold bed.

She pulled her dressing gown over the blankets; if only she didn't feel so cold. Yet at the same time, she seemed to be burning up; she must be really ill. She looked at her watch; the luminous numbers glowed, ten past two. She recalled her grandmother telling her how important it was to keep her fluid levels up if she had a fever. She wondered if she had the energy to get up, perhaps a cup of tea would ease her throat. She was shivering as she tip-toed to the kitchen.

On her way past Susan's room, she thought she heard a noise. Perhaps Susan was dreaming. After what had happened to her this evening it was more likely the poor thing was having a nightmare.

While she stood waiting for the kettle to boil Alice thought about the coming weekend. Friday evening, this evening she corrected herself; she was going to the Martins', to meet Malcolm. Saturday she was going into town to have lunch with Mark. There's no reason why she shouldn't have a friend who happens to be a man, she told herself, not for the first time. What is more important is whether she was going to be well enough to see anyone. Standing, for what seemed an eternity, made her realise how ghastly she felt. With a sickening premonition, she thought it was inevitable she would be spending the weekend in the hostel, in bed.

She tip-toed back along the corridor, once again there was a noise coming from Susan's room. She paused and wondered if she should go in, maybe Susan was not well. She tapped on the door.

'Susan, what's the matter?'

'Help me.'

Alice opened the door. At first, she could see nothing then gradually made out a dark shape on the floor.

'Have you fallen out of bed?'

'Get help, I'm bleeding to death.'

Alice felt a spasm of terror. 'Close your eyes, I'll have to put the light on.'

She had forgotten there was a cup of hot tea in her hand; jumping back with shock at the scene before her, sent scalding tea sloshing everywhere. She yelped with pain, put the cup on the floor and knelt beside Susan.

'What's happened?' She looked at the bed, there was blood everywhere. The sheets were drenched and so was Susan who lay ashen-faced on the floor.

'I was trying to get help,' she whispered, 'but I can't stand up. Get Miss Pritchard.'

The room looked like the aftermath of a massacre; it reminded Alice of the reports she had seen on the television after the Mau-Mau troubles in Kenya. Looking around her, Alice marvelled that anyone could lose so much blood and remain alive.

'Just lie still.' Alice grabbed a blanket and draped it over Susan's limp body.

'I'll go for Miss Pritchard.'

She ran down the corridor ignoring the noise her slippers made; this was a matter of life or death. She banged on Miss Pritchard's door and gasped for breath while she waited for a reply. She banged again.

'Miss Pritchard, please wake up, Susan's dying. Get an ambulance.'

Her teeth were chattering and she was shivering. She could not be sure if it was shock, fear, fever or the chill night air. The door opened and Miss Pritchard stood in her dressing gown, composed as though such intrusions to her night's sleep were a regular occurrence. She spoke in her usual quiet, calm voice.

'Now tell me again, what's the matter?'

Alice took a deep breath and swallowed hard, wincing at the jagged pain in her throat.

'It's Susan, she's bleeding to death. I got up to make a hot drink and I heard her. It's awful, I've never seen so much blood.'

Miss Pritchard looked surprised.

'I'm not exaggerating. Something happened to Susan this evening, I can't tell you what, but I think that's why she's bleeding so much now.'

'Let's go to see how she is shall we?'

'I don't want her to die, Miss…'

Of course not, but we don't want to call out an ambulance unless it is necessary.'

'There's blood everywhere, Miss…'

She raced upstairs in front of Miss Pritchard. Her chest ached with the exertion and her limbs just ached. This won't help me get better, she thought, but that was uncharitable, Susan needed help.

She rushed into Susan's room followed by Miss Pritchard. Nothing much had changed except that Susan was even paler. Her breathing was shallow and noisy, her skin was translucent. One look was enough and Miss Pritchard turned on her heel.

'Stay here with her, Alice, while I dial 999.'

Alice listened to the rapid tap, tap, tap of the woman's receding footsteps. It was not the sound of running feet but Alice knew that Miss Pritchard was moving at considerable speed.

Now that action was being taken by someone else Alice realised just how ill she felt. She was icy cold sitting on the hard linoleum-covered floor, her head ached and her throat was raw. This whole business seemed more and more unreal. Susan groaned and moved a little, at least she's still alive, Alice thought and squeezed her hand.

'Miss Pritchard's gone for the ambulance; it will soon be here. They'll look after you.' She brushed hair back from Susan's face and tried to smile encouragement.

Susan groaned. 'Don't let her tell my parents.'

Alice felt as though she was floating. Only the touch of Susan's cold hand stopped her from drifting away, far, far away. There's no way she could go to work. She glanced at Susan's alarm clock, two thirty, it was only twenty minutes since she woke up, she could not believe it, so much had happened.

At first, Alice sensed rather than heard activity downstairs. Then a few minutes later she heard heavy footsteps climbing the last flight of stairs after which everything was a blur. The room was filled to overflowing by two burly, hearty men in ambulance men's uniforms. They were oblivious to the hour and the fact that the rest of the world was sleeping. Alice stood out of the way by the window. Her body ached for warmth and her need to lie down was overwhelming.

Susan was lifted onto a stretcher and wrapped in a thick red blanket. Alice watched and wondered if ambulance blankets were deliberately red to disguise blood loss which would alarm badly hurt patients. She realised she was swaying as she watched the activity. Miss Pritchard looked so calm as she supervised Susan's departure.

She smiled at Alice. 'I'll be back in a minute.'

Alice stood, now alone, and looked round the room that had been defiled by so much blood. It was like that scene from 'Macbeth' she and the rest of her class had watched long ago. What had Lady Macbeth said about King Duncan? Alice mouthed the words, 'who would have thought the old man had so much blood in him…' Duncan had died, would Susan die?

A deep weariness made Alice's head droop as she leaned against the wall; her legs did not want to support her. Should she go to bed and leave the carnage for someone else to clear up? How dreadful that this tiny speck of humanity had been wrenched into extinction. Would anyone grieve for this child that would never be?

The world was full of sorrow, a sorrow which now washed over Alice till she seemed to be drowning. Then tears came and the pain of them wrung her heart. She cried for what had gone before, for what was yet to come, for herself, for Susan and for the death that had occurred in this room. It was then that Miss Pritchard returned and taking Alice's arm led her back to her room.

'You have had a dreadful shock this evening, my dear. Thanks for your prompt action. I'm sure Susan will be all right but she has a lot to thank you for. It could have ended in tragedy. I'm going to make you a cup of hot sweet tea then I must contact Susan's parents.'

'Oh, please don't do that. Susan really doesn't want them to know about this.'

'I do realise what has happened you know, Alice. I have no choice but to inform her parents.'

Alice tried to speak but what was the point? The matter was out of her hands now; she knew she could do no more. She leaned back on the damp pillows. Her head was swimming, her throat was so sore she could only croak.

'My cup's in Susan's room somewhere.'

Miss Pritchard leaned over and placed a cool hand on Alice's forehead.

'I don't think you are very well; in fact, I am sure you are running a temperature.'

Alice nodded and tears came again, why was it always worse when people were kind?

'I'll get you your tea and I suggest you stay in bed tomorrow.'

Alice nodded, she craved sleep and then maybe she would feel better in the morning.

Chapter 12

Joan was in the kitchen preparing the evening meal when Spencer returned, after his first day working for Stanley. She turned from the stove as he slumped onto a chair.

'What's the matter with you?'

He sighed. 'What a drag. The whole day's been awful, I've trudged up and down Oxford Street all day trying to interest buyers.'

Joan pulled a face. Of course, Spencer was bound to be annoyed at not having much success; he'd had it easy all his young life, not like when she was his age.

'What did you expect; a book full of orders on your first day?'

'You just don't understand, Mum. I thought I'd cracked it when Jaeger's gave me something. It was only small, but it was better than nothing. I went back to tell Dad and guess what, he'd had a phone call to cancel the order. It was the only one I got all day.'

Joan turned back to the stove to hide her smile; it was about time Spencer grew up. She continued stirring the sauce she was making

'Oh, by the way, I had a call from the hostel, the warden or someone. Alice's ill, she's running a temperature apparently.'

Spencer groaned. 'Has she seen a doctor?'

'How should I know?'

'Well, she should, shouldn't she?'

'That's not for me to decide.'

'Will she be coming over then?'

'I doubt it.'

'I suppose I'd better ring the hostel and see how she is.'

Joan listened as Spencer made the call. He didn't seem too bothered perhaps the events of an unsuccessful day were on his mind. She tried to imagine what it would be like stuck in a hostel on her own when she wasn't well, poor girl.

Spencer came back into the kitchen.

'Spoke to someone called Miss Pritchard, I think she's in charge. She said Alice was running a very high temperature and if she's no better tomorrow they'll get the local doctor to call.'

'So, who's going to look after her?'

Spencer shrugged.

'Do you want us to get her over here?'

Spencer looked surprised. 'Don't you mind, with Malcolm here as well?'

Joan put down the wooden spoon she was holding. 'I am used to caring for the sick you know. I just thought it would be better if Alice wasn't left all alone.'

'She can't be too good if they're calling in the doctor.'

Joan thought for a moment. Alice could be a useful additional responsibility. They were all supposed to be going round to her parents on Sunday. Lillian had insisted she would cook a meal for them all. This would give Joan a good excuse to get out of it.

'I'm sure your young lady could do with some home cooking.'

'That would be great, Mum. I'm really grateful.'

'It'll save you having to take her back tonight, won't it?'

Spencer's face became flushed; she had hit the mark there.

'I'd better call the hostel and tell them to put her in a taxi.'

'Thanks, Mum.' He put his arm around her and gave a quick kiss on her offered cheek.

Joan dialled the hostel and listened as the phone rang with a hollow, echoing sound and Joan imagined the gloomy, institutional corridors. Alice would be better here. Maybe she now had the chance to get to know the girl; she could be a useful ally.

'Baron's Court Hostel, Miss Pritchard speaking.'

'Hello, I'm Mrs Martin, Spencer's mother. I'm calling about Alice Ward, I think it would be better if she came to us as I understand she is unwell. Would it be possible for you to put her in a taxi, please?'

'That is very kind, we do our best to care for the residents. I am sure she will recover quicker if she is with your family.'

Once arrangements were made, Joan returned to the kitchen.

'She's on her way and I've got a meal to cook.'

'What can I do, Mum?'

'I'll need to check the spare room, to make sure the bed is aired.'

'I can do that; shall I put the electric blanket on?'

'Umm,' Joan nodded and watched as he left the room. Was he really fond of the girl, she wondered, or just trying to please her?

He always seemed to be in league with Stanley, always so keen to check up on her and report back to dear Daddy. She sipped her sherry. It was her first glass, delicious, but never needed in the same way when Malcolm was at home. At home, that was a joke, using the place like a hotel, that was what all parents said.

She spread the whipped cream over the fruit and encrusted the surface with demerara sugar. Under the grill the granules melted and bubbled to form a thick, molten crust, Malcolm's favourite.

Spencer clattered down the stairs. 'The room looks fine, Mum. I'm going for a shower, what time are we eating?'

'In about an hour but I'll have to get Alice settled first. I think I'll phone Doctor Goodwin; perhaps he should come over.'

'Thanks again, Mum.' He paused and she waited for him to speak, but he turned and went upstairs.

Alice was shivering and again, the room seemed to be swaying; she was going to fall out of bed. She had been dreaming, dreaming of oceans of blood. She was drowning in a thick, clotted morass. She fought for air as the snake came towards her. The snake of childhood nightmares was trying to force itself into her mouth. She thrashed at the covers that were suffocating her and managed to half sit, half slump against the wall. Her heart thumped and her nightdress stuck to her, sodden and limp.

She heard a gentle tap on the door and Miss Pritchard walked in. She sat on the edge of the bed and took Alice's hand.

'You look very flushed, my dear.'

She rested her other hand on Alice's forehead; it was burning hot.

'Spencer and his mother have been on the phone. He and his parents want you to go to their house, they want to look after you. But are you well enough to travel?'

Tears streamed down Alice's face. She felt so ill how would she get herself over to Golders Green?

'Now looking at you, I'm not sure you should go on your own. I'd take you there myself but the rest of the staff are off duty. I can't leave the hostel.'

'I'll be all right. I'll have a wash and pack some things. I'll manage.' She gave a watery smile and sat up. Her head swam but she must make the effort. Miss Pritchard helped her out of bed.

'Now you tell me where everything is and I'll pack. You have a wash it will make you feel better.'

Alice tottered to the bathroom and wondered if this was how it would feel when she was very old. There was no strength in her and she seemed to be moving in slow motion. The bathroom was miles away and when she got there the taps resisted her attempts to turn them on. She shivered. Her bones ached and she gritted her teeth then tried the taps again. Success, she splashed her face and for a moment felt revived.

She peeled the drenched nightdress from her clammy skin – like a snake sloughing off a redundant outer layer. She splashed her body with water and made a half-hearted attempt to dry herself. She rinsed her mouth but the foul whiff of infection remained. She looked in the mirror and was shocked. She looked dreadful, what would Spencer think? She felt too ill to care and longed to lie down until her body sorted itself out. She walked back to her room.

'I've packed for a few days and put out something for you to wear now. You must keep warm. Get dressed while I call a taxi.'

Alice slumped on the bed, so weak it was scary. She had had bad throats before, but nothing like this. As she dressed, she thought about Spencer and his family; it was nice of them to take her in. She thought back over the years of her childhood; it hadn't been easy. With Dad in the army, even though he had custody of her, life had been disjointed.

There had been so many homes, but only because people had been paid to have her. Now here was a family who wanted her to go to them because she wasn't well. Her constant longing to be part of a family brought tears to her eyes; she hated feeling so alone.

She wondered who had suggested she should go over; she hoped it was Spencer. She thought it was more likely to be Mr. Martin; he seemed such a nice man. She wished she didn't feel so wary of Joan; there was something frightening about her. She must have agreed to the arrangement, since it was unlikely, she would do anything she didn't want to do.

Alice blew her nose, wiped her eyes and, feeling a little better, stood up to finish dressing. She checked her bag; everything had been folded, with nothing, Alice could think of, missing. What a kind woman Miss Pritchard was; she heard the brisk footsteps coming along the corridor.

'Taxi's here.' Miss Pritchard took Alice's bag and shepherded her out of the room, downstairs and into the taxi.

'Now take care of yourself, I'm sure you will soon be feeling better. I've explained to the driver that you are not well, just give him the address and you'll be there in no time.'

She smiled and left. Alice did as she was told, sank back in her seat and slept.

Susan lay still; the pains had receded to a point where they were just a dull ache. The anaesthetic had left her feeling groggy and when she came round, she had been violently sick. Now the drip had been taken from her arm she assumed that her blood level was back to normal. She was in a side ward. It was a pleasant room with pale yellow walls and floral curtains. She had wondered, when she first opened her eyes, if they were expecting her to die.

There seemed little chance of that now. However, she felt like a rag doll which had lost most of its stuffing. Last night had been different. She had wanted death then, had yearned for an end to the agony. That combined with the horror and shame at what she had done made death appealing. Today, as she looked out of the window, there was hope. The sun shone and she could see people walking in the grounds. The past is dead and gone but I am not.

She had vague memories of her parents being with her last night, but it was all so confusing. She wondered how they would be feeling and how much they had been told. Her relationship with them had been so full of anger and resentment. She was surprised by a great desire to make amends, to start again, to stop fighting and be at peace with these two people who made her. Perhaps I'm beginning to grow up, she thought. She smiled to herself; she thought she was so grown up, but it was all an illusion. She closed her eyes and relished the sensation of peace.

She was floating on a sea of sleep when she heard footsteps. Eric and Sarah Johnson walked into her room. Susan opened her eyes and smiled at her parents. Her mother placed a bunch of flowers by the bed and bent to kiss Susan's forehead. Her father pulled a chair to the other side of the bed and sat down.

'Hello Mum, Dad, I'm feeling so much better.'

'Are you well enough to talk?' Eric asked.

'Not too much yet, dear.' Sarah said.

Susan looked from one to the other.

'We thought we'd lost you.' Sarah dabbed her eyes and clutched Susan's hand.

'We talked to Doctor Stirling; he was the surgeon who patched you up.'

Susan picked up a note of censure in her father's voice.

'I'm so sorry. I didn't want you to find out, I was stupid. I know that now.'

'You lost three pints of blood; it was a close call. Thank God you were found when you were, the transfusion you had saved your life.' Eric cleared his throat and looked away. At that moment Susan realised the thing her dad was best at was, hiding his feelings.

'You could have told us you know.' Sarah stroked Susan's hand.

'What that I was pregnant? I don't think so. What would the neighbours have said?'

Sarah wept into her handkerchief.

Doctor Stirling said he thought something had been done to make you lose the baby. Is that right?'

'Oh, Dad I did it for the best. I didn't know this was how it would end.'

'Who was it?'

'I don't know; a friend gave me an address, that's all. I went there and this man started things, I was told he was a doctor, I thought it would be all right.'

Sarah gasped. 'A man, some strange man claiming to be a doctor?'

'Yes, Mum, that's how these things are done.'

'This friend; was he the one who…'

'No, Dad he wasn't the one responsible; he just wanted to help me out.'

'The police should be told before some other poor girl is butchered.'

'I can't, Dad. Please don't ask me.'

'That's enough now,' Sarah said, 'We should think about what's really important and that's getting you fit and well again. We want you back; can we persuade you to come home?'

Susan sighed. 'Oh yes, please. I promise things will be different.'

Eric smiled for the first time. 'We'll do our best to patch things up; there have been mistakes all around.'

Stanley walked into the kitchen, rubbed his hands together and sniffed

'By Jove, something smells good, my dear.'

Joan knew what he was doing; the pattern never changed. Whenever she gave him the silent treatment, he would conduct one-sided conversations that didn't require a reply. To anyone else all seemed normal but not to her. He hopes I'll get tired of it in the end. In the past, his crimes had been nebulous, insubstantial compared with this business of Gill. He must realise, Joan reasoned, that this was going to cause a major upheaval. But she would broach the subject when she was good and ready.

'I expect Alice will be here soon, it will be splendid for her to have such a feast. Don't suppose this is what she's used to.'

Joan continued washing up pots, pans and bowls.

Spencer shouted from the living room. 'Hasn't mum told you, Alice's ill. They're sending her over in a taxi. Mum said she'd be better off here.'

'What a kind thought, it's good of you to take on extra when Malcolm's home.'

Washing up water dripped from her rubber gloves as she turned.

'Yes, Stanley, it is good of me. I've done my best, but then I always do. And a fat lot of thanks I get for it. I haven't just been a good wife and mother; I have always entertained your business colleagues and wives, undoubtedly enhancing your career at the expense of my own.'

She paused. She could feel the adrenalin pumping if only he would reply in kind, but they never had blazing rows. Stanley was always the peacemaker.

'Yes dear, I have always appreciated what you have done for me.' He moved closer and placed his hand on Joan's arm. She moved away.

'In fact, Bergmann and his wife are coming over from Stockholm soon and I am relying on you to do your usual wonderful job as a hostess.'

'Oh really, thanks for letting me know.'

'There hasn't been much opportunity over the past few days.'

Joan glared at him. 'And whose fault's that?'

'Mine, darling, mine, I know and I'm sorry. We'll discuss arrangements some other time.'

The front door opened with a rush. 'Hi Mum, hi Dad, I'm not late, am I?'

It had always been Malcolm's exuberance that delighted Joan. Here was her baby whose vitality made her shiver with pride and anticipation of all the wonderful things he was bound to achieve.

She knew her pride in his very existence, this wondrous fruit of her womb, glossed over any possible flaw in his character or ability, but she didn't care. He was her joy now and always. He was the son she had really wanted and she walked towards him her arms held wide.

'Of course, you are not late, my darling.' She kissed him on the cheek, but out of the corner of her eye saw him roll his eyes at Stanley.

At this moment the taxi arrived with Alice. Joan opened the front door while Stanley explained to Malcolm. Spencer went out to help Alice from the taxi and encouraged her to lean on his arm

'Sorry I'm such a sight,' she croaked.

She walked slowly to the house and was shaking with exhaustion by the time she had been eased upstairs to the spare bedroom.

'I think the doctor should see her,' Stanley said. 'I'll call him now.'

Doctor Goodwin soon arrived and after a thorough examination diagnosed a severe case of tonsillitis. Antibiotics, bed rest and plenty of fluids were prescribed. Spencer was dispatched to get the prescription dispensed, Stanley made a large jug of barley water and Doctor Goodwin departed leaving instructions that he should be called if matters didn't improve.

Joan caught Malcolm in the kitchen dipping his finger in the hollandaise sauce. She tapped his fingers.

'Naughty boy,' she said and smiled.

Upstairs, Alice lay still. The bed was like a cloud and her fevered body sank into it so she had no sensation of weight. She was floating, adrift on a calm sea, being rocked to sleep. She had drunk two glasses of the delicious barley water and taken the first dose of antibiotics two hours ago. The buzz of conversation from downstairs ebbed and flowed in and out of her consciousness like a friendly swarm of bees who would do her no harm. Spencer had popped his head round the door to check she had everything she needed. She had smiled, delighted by his concern.

The nightmarish terrors she had experienced, only hours before, had now receded and Alice could recognise them for what they were, the imaginings of a fevered mind. She was very concerned for Susan and would call Miss Pritchard for news, once she felt better. There was nothing she needed to do now but rest, let go and drift. She was with people who cared for her. She was lucky. There had been Miss Pritchard and now the Martins.

If your family didn't care there could always be others. Nice people like Mark, suddenly she was wide awake. What about Mark? Today was Friday and she was supposed to be meeting him tomorrow; what could she do? He'd be waiting for her at 1 p.m. at the Strand Palace. Could she ring the place and leave a message? What was his other name? He hadn't told her. Her head ached again, there was nothing she could do; she would just have to leave it. Perhaps she would be well enough to go tomorrow if she slept well tonight, but instinct told her Joan would never agree to that.

Chapter 13

When Alice woke the sun was shining. She swallowed gently; her throat felt much better. She stretched, yawned and sat up. There were the noises of people moving about. It was amazing that she felt so much better after last night. She glanced at her watch, half past ten, what would Dad have said at such laziness? She shuddered as she remembered the countless mornings when Dad got up at the crack of dawn and expected her to do the same. She wondered how he was; she wanted to contact him, but he always made things so difficult.

After the business with Spencer, it had been almost impossible to have a civil conversation. Perhaps she should write, but he never wrote to her. At least Mum did keep in touch, after a fashion. She knew she would have to pay her a visit soon. That would be difficult, but in a different way from Dad. Alec was all right as far as step-fathers went, it was his and Mum's kids that made things awkward, Anthony and Jane had never accepted her.

Families were a problem, particularly parents, even Spencer with all the trappings of prosperity had a mother to make your heart sink. She leaned back on the pillows, there must be some happy families somewhere, perhaps she would start one herself one day. The idea of being a matriarch overseeing this imaginary, delightful, large and happy family made her smile; it was nice to daydream.

Meanwhile what about Mark and the lunchtime meeting? She slipped on her dressing gown and went in search of the bathroom. She was confronted by Joan with a breakfast tray.

'What are you doing out of bed?'

'I needed the toilet.'

'Straight back to bed afterwards.'

Spencer was coming upstairs and pulled a face at Alice. She assumed he was warning her that any argument would be futile.

She smiled and hoped her appearance was less cadaver-like than it had been the previous evening.

Once again, she was spellbound by his astonishing good looks with his golden hair and blue eyes. He had a slow-moving, languid grace that suggested confidence. What does he see in me, Alice had often wondered? I rush about like a headless chicken, I have no poise and I'm not pretty yet he likes me.

She locked the bathroom door. Her legs were still inclined to wobble but she thought she would survive. She washed her face and hands, dampened her hair which was a disaster. It stuck to her head at the sides but stood upright on top. 'I look like Stan Laurel,' she said to her reflection. Futile attempts to flatten and tidy it were abandoned; she would have to wash it.

She wondered if Joan would sanction such reckless activity.

She went back to her room and got into bed. Joan placed the tray on her lap; there was fruit juice, boiled egg, toast and coffee.

'You look better this morning; did you sleep well?'

'Yes, thank you, I feel tons better.'

'You must stay in bed today and maybe get up for a little while tomorrow.'

Alice's heart sank; this was not going to be easy. She swallowed hard, the lump in her throat was there, but this time it was not caused by tonsillitis. What about Mark? Dad had always said it was wrong, selfish and irresponsible to let people down; she was going to let Mark down and there didn't seem to be anything she could do about it.

'It's a bit difficult, Mrs Martin.' Although she had been told to call Spencer's parents Joan and Stanley somehow, she could not bring herself to do it.

'There's nothing difficult about it; you're a friend of Spencer's.'

Alice noticed with dismay that she was a friend and not the girlfriend, a subtle but significant distinction, she thought.

'We can't have you being ill on your own; you must stay with us until you are completely better.'

'It's very kind of you but I really am so much better and you see I had arranged to meet a friend.' She paused. 'I can't get in touch to cancel the arrangement.'

Alice watched as Joan swelled with indignation. 'You see I don't like to let people down.'

She stopped. It was pointless, Joan's expression made that very clear.

'No, I'm sure you don't want to let people down so you should not even think of letting us down. We have taken you in because we are concerned for your welfare. We paid a consultation fee to our private doctor. If you leave this house to keep an arrangement with a friend and so put your health at risk you will not come here again. You can make your apologies next time you see this person; any true friend will understand.'

That was it, Alice felt as though she had run headlong into a brick wall.

'I'm sorry,' she whispered, 'I don't want to be a nuisance.'

'You won't be as long as you do as you are told.' Joan gave a tight smile and left.

Alice sighed and smacked her teaspoon down hard on her boiled egg. Spencer poked his head round the door. 'How's the invalid?'

'Tons better, thanks, you don't want an egg, do you? This is soft-boiled and I just can't eat them like that.'

Spencer plonked himself on the bed making the tray lurch.

'Shall I ask Mum to do you another?'

'Oh no, don't do that, toast will be fine.'

He raised his eyebrows. 'Crossed swords with my old lady, have you?'

Alice wondered how Joan would react to being referred to like that.

'Sort of,' Alice squirmed. She felt disloyal to Spencer, what would he think if he knew she had arranged to meet someone else, even if it was innocent?

'I just thought I was well enough to get up.'

'Whatever you do, don't try to stop Mother when she's got her Florence Nightingale cap on. She loves it. Nothing like a captive patient to get her going; watch out or she'll have you in bed for a week.'

'But I've got to go to work on Monday.'

'I wouldn't bank on it, don't let her phone your boss. He'll think you are about to peg out with typhoid and order a wreath.'

Alice giggled; he really was lovely. As he leaned forward his hands brushed her breasts before he rested his arms on her shoulders.

'Give me a kiss you bug-ridden brute.'

She tingled as she leaned towards him and their lips met.

'Just you wait until you are better.'

Her heart thumped and she could feel colour swamp her neck and face.

'Eat your breakfast, I'll explain to Mum about the egg.'

He closed the door and left her in a state of confusion.

Mark had shaved with extra care and had his hair trimmed; he would still be in plenty of time. He walked to the Tube Station in bright sunlight, it was a beautiful day. He felt inner peace, life was sorting itself out rather well. Confirmation of his transfer had come through and he would be moving north, to Manchester, in two weeks. He had told Jim et al that they would need another flatmate, and very satisfying that had been. Let Jim do the donkey work in future.

This meeting with Alice would decide whether they should see each other again. She seemed such a nice girl. Of course, since he was moving away it would not be ideal, but if they hit it off, he could arrange to see her again before he left London. He wondered if he was placing too much importance on this date. Wasn't there supposed to be chemistry between people, evident from the start? He'd thought that about dear Denise. She had blown into his life like a tornado and left it with equally dramatic effect once she had achieved the desired level of chaos and heartache. Time will tell, he thought, meanwhile the sun is shining, I've got a date with a nice girl, what more can a bloke ask for? He whistled under his breath. If things went really well perhaps, she would want to move north too. He shook his head in disbelief at his own capacity for romance. Perhaps that was what he was ready for now, a new romance.

On the platform, the noise grew and a rush of air announced the imminent arrival of his train. Unlike during the week, it was almost empty; no strap hanging today. As he was so early, he decided to get off at the Embankment and walk the rest of the way, cutting through Villiers Street and up the Strand. The streets were busy with tourists and youngsters in town for the day.

He reached the Strand Palace at twelve forty, stood to one side of the main entrance and lit a cigarette. He enjoyed people-watching and speculated on the lives of the crowd walking past. What were they like, where were they going, were they happy? He felt relaxed and more content with life than he had for many months. It was only now the heartache was diminishing that he realised how much Denise had hurt him.

He glanced at his watch, one o'clock, Alice would be here soon. He started to look above the heads of people hoping to get a glimpse of her.

Which way would she come? She was unlikely to have walked as far as he had. Charing Cross was her nearest stop and then, like him, she would come up the Strand. No sign of her. He would have predicted she was the sort to arrive on time. He checked his watch again, she was late. He felt a tremor of disappointment, perhaps she was waiting inside. He walked into the foyer and upstairs to the Salad Bowl restaurant. It was very busy but there was no sign of her. This is stupid, he thought, she's stood me up.

He went downstairs again; he'd wait until half past, then that was it. He lit another cigarette. He was just a fool and was bloody sick of it. Women let you down every time, can't trust any of them, he pulled hard on his cigarette. But Alice had seemed different; they were the worst, the ones who led you on.

He paused, unwilling to accept that his judgement could be so faulty. Supposing something had happened, she wouldn't have been able to let him know, would she? He heard a clock somewhere above the sound of the traffic; it was chiming the half hour. He hesitated, no point in waiting any longer, but somehow, he would try to find out where she lived.

Joan was making coffee in the kitchen; she had asked Malcolm to help her carry it through. She could hear the buzz of conversation between Stanley and Spencer in the living room. Alice was asleep upstairs. Joan was pleased to have exerted her authority over the girl, Malcolm might use the house like a hotel; Alice would not. With all the extra work of making meals suitable for an invalid, Joan felt she had pulled out all the stops and Alice had better realise it. She placed a plate of petit fours on the tray.

'Take it through now will you, darling.'

Joan followed Malcolm through and caught the end of what Spencer was saying.

'… I've tried I really have.'

Stanley looked up from his paper.

'When I was your age, my lad I was out every day for months, in all weathers. Woolux was in its infancy them.'

'Yes, but Dad.'

'You should listen to your father, Spencer; you've only been with the firm for five minutes.

'Mum, you don't understand. I'm just no good at selling, I have tried.'

'So, what do you think you would be good at?' Stanley folded his paper

'I don't know.'

'Your trouble is you have no fire in your belly; you've never had to struggle.'

'What do you think it was like for me in Canada?' Joan said as she poured coffee.

'Oh, it's the united front now is it, that makes a change,' Spencer said.

'Don't speak to your mother like that. She's worked hard to make things nice for you.' Stanley stared at Malcolm, 'For you both, so don't you sit smirking.'

'But selling is a special skill, everyone knows that.'

'Listen, lad.' Stanley leaned forward. 'I wore my feet ragged traipsing from shop to shop. It didn't do me any harm.'

'Why can't I work in the office?'

'Because if you want the people you employ to respect you, you have to show you can do the same as them. I assume you do still want to be in the business.' Stanley stared at Spencer for several seconds, waiting.

'Yes, of course, but not as a salesman.'

Stanley sighed. 'Things are changing. It's the young who dictate fashion now. I need younger salesmen and I want my son to be one of them. We must adjust or die.'

'And you wouldn't like that would you Spencer? The trouble is you've had too much.' Joan sipped her coffee. It was time Spencer learned some home truths.

'But if I'm no good at selling, I could do more harm than good.'

'I'll send you round with Johnny Wilson; he can sell ice to Eskimos.'

'That reminds me,' Joan said, 'when is Bergman coming over?'

'Next week, with his wife.'

'I see. You aren't expecting them to stay here, are you?'

'Of course not, but I will need to entertain them and…' He smiled at her and Joan glared back at him. She wondered if that was how he beguiled that slut, Gill? She would have to be got rid of, there was no doubt about that. Joan got up and collected the crockery before striding from the room. Stanley followed her.

'Shut the door,' she said. 'You and I are going to have a very serious talk because I have had enough. I am not prepared to upset Malcolm as heaven knows we see little enough of him. So, it will have to wait until tomorrow evening. But I warn you things are going to change.' She turned to the sink and with considerable vigour started on the washing up.

Malcolm ambled into the kitchen. 'Is it right, we are going to Granddad and Grandma's tomorrow.'

'Yes, your Aunt Lillian is putting on a meal,' Stanley said.

'Don't know why we can't have it here.' Joan said.

'Because you know your Mum wouldn't be able to come. Lillian wants us all together.'

'I'll get the late afternoon train then.' Malcolm said. 'If I pack and leave my stuff in the car boot, can you drop me at the station, Dad?'

'Certainly, I suppose you'll be glad to be back with your mates.'

Malcolm grinned and slouched out of the room.

Joan bristled, at the same time, a pang of fear made her shiver. 'I won't be able to make the meal at Mum and Dad's,' she said.

'Why not?' Stanley asked.

'Well in case you've forgotten there's Alice to consider.'

'But she says she feels so much better, surely by tomorrow she will be well enough to go back to the hostel.'

'There's no guarantee and if she is well enough how is she going to get back? I thought she could either stay here for an extra day or I would take her back myself.'

'Shouldn't I do that? Your Mum and Dad will be sorry if you aren't there.'

'They aren't fussed about me.'

'Let's wait until tomorrow, shall we?'

Chapter 14

The table was set, the candles ready to light. A bunch of anemones, bought on her way home now sat in the middle of the table, in a pottery vase Barbara had made years before, at evening class. The rich purples, blues and reds of the blooms were reflected in the crystal wine glasses placed on an immaculate white tablecloth. Matching napkins were folded simply; she was anxious not to overwhelm Jeffrey with too much grandeur.

Everything in the kitchen was under control as Barbara mixed herself a small gin and tonic. She glanced at her watch; he would be on time, to the minute; he was that type. She was about to sit down when the doorbell rang; she smiled and hurried downstairs.

Jeffrey did not speak as he looked around Barbara's living room. She watched his face and wondered if he felt as uneasy as he looked. He fumbled in the pockets of what Barbara assumed had been his army trench coat. Did he need to cling to his identity as a military man, did it give him confidence? He produced a bottle of wine and a box of chocolates which he offered with a small bow and a click of his brown-brogue shoes. Barbara smiled and gave a mock curtsey.

'Thank you, kind sir; white wine, that's good, we are having chicken.

I'll put it in the fridge. Now what will you have to drink? Sherry or gin and tonic?'

He paused and Barbara realised she should have bought some beer; he was bound to feel that beer was a real man's drink.

'Sherry would be fine, not too sweet.'

Tension crackled between them and Barbara remembered what Gordon and Anne had said after their evening at Jeffrey's flat. Perhaps he was scared of women. Barbara ushered him to the sofa.

'Food won't be long; I hope you are hungry.'

'If it tastes as good as it smells I'm in for a treat.'

'I confess I love cooking, it's the one creative thing about being a housewife.'

'I hope you haven't spent too much time on all this.'

'Why? Aren't you worth it?'

He looked at her and she realised he wasn't sure if she was serious or making fun of him.

'You'll have to decide, at the end of the evening,' he said.

There was a pause and they looked at each other.

'I'm not very good at small talk.' Jeffrey said.

Barbara pulled a face, 'No neither am I; so, let's get down to business, tell me about you.'

'I work for the Post Office. Since my mother died, I've lived alone in that dreary flat. There's not much else to tell.'

'Nonsense, what about when you were a child? Where were you brought up, do you have brothers or sisters?'

He held up his hands. 'I surrender. Gordon didn't warn me to expect the third degree; have you thought of being an interrogation officer? I could give you a good reference.'

She laughed. 'Sorry but I am interested.'

'O.K. I grew up in Camden Town, not a particularly nice part of north London. I have an older sister and my parents are dead. Actually, I did have three older brothers, but they all died as babies.'

Barbara shivered; the ghost of her own child swirled in her head and clouded her thoughts. 'How tragic, it was so common then, so much suffering.'

'I suppose so and it must have knocked the stuffing out of Mum and Dad. They never talked about it but I found the memorial cards for each of the babies, after Mum died.'

They sipped their drinks in silence, each reflecting on the tragedy of life.

'What about your sister, what is she like?'

Jeffrey paused. 'I don't know what she's like now, we lost contact.'

Barbara raised her eyebrows. 'That's sad.'

'Not seen her since before Mum was hospitalised; that's seven years ago.'

Barbara waited.

'You see I phoned her. Told her Mum was dying, she was so frail by that time, like a little bird, struggling for every breath.' He stopped and looked away.

Barbara patted his hand. 'It's the role reversal that is so hard to cope with. They care for us when we are small then as they become vulnerable, we care for them.'

Jeffrey snorted. 'Connie never came to visit, never one to put herself out, she just couldn't be bothered. I wanted nothing to do with her after that.'

Barbara realised that people who crossed Jeffrey or who didn't live up to his standards did so at their peril. 'That was her loss,' she said.

Jeffrey sat back. 'What about you? It's my turn to do the questioning.'

'Oh, very boring, I was an only child and I lived in suburban bliss in genteel Bromley. I came to London and qualified as a librarian. Went back often to see my parents.

'I envy you that; the army gives few opportunities for family visits. I wish I'd seen more of my parents as they got older.'

'Mum died three years ago, cancer. Dad coped for a bit but he had a stroke last year. It was a blessing he did not live long after that; he hated being an invalid. I'm glad he was spared the living death that some poor souls have to endure for months and sometimes years. I had better go and check the food, you wouldn't want burnt offerings.'

She felt him watching her as she walked to the kitchen. Assured that all was well, she returned with a basket of Melba toast and pate.

'Grub's up, grab a chair.'

She lit the candles which made the curls of deep yellow butter glisten. Jeffrey sat down and draped the large, white damask napkin across his knees. He looked across at her and smiled.

'Cheers,' she said as she raised the remains of her gin and tonic.

'Cheers, this looks truly wonderful.'

The train journey was uneventful and Mark had watched as the hectic jostle of cramped terraced houses melted into a more spacious suburbia with its neat semis and well-tended gardens. At last, there was open country. Mark sighed and leaned back in his seat wondering if this was what he had missed.

He recalled the times he had spent living in Greenfield, one of Saddleworth's villages. Mum and Dad had rented a weaver's cottage on the main street, but soon after, Dad decided they would buy outright even though the price was five hundred pounds, a princely sum after the war.

Then Dad trained to be an engineer and worked at Fletcher's Mill where they still manufactured cigarette papers.

It had been an idyllic childhood with the grandeur of the West Riding hills sheltering the village from the excesses of Yorkshire's winter weather. Mark smiled. He and Tommy Barraclough had roamed the fields and spent glorious days building dams in Chew Brook, which ran through the village.

Hot summer days had bronzed their skins and they had

pretended to be Red Indians on the warpath. Mark wondered what Tommy was doing now, the last news he had heard was that his friend had gone into the army, the Cheshire regiment.

When Mark was twelve, Dad had taught him to shoot and on many a crisp morning the pair of them had gone out to tackle the thousands of rabbits in the area. It had all changed when Dad decided to move nearer to Oldham. He had wanted the best for his family and a neat semi-detached house in Chadderton was their next home. Going up in the world had led to a small car too. Mark was at the local grammar school and Mum had a job managing the clothing department in Oldham's Co-op

Perhaps it had been his teenage years in Chadderton that persuaded him to go to London to make his fortune. Mum and Dad had encouraged him, but he had sometimes seen a wistful look in his mother's eyes that suggested a degree of reluctance to have her only child leave the area. She never said so and now her son and heir would return, to his roots. He was going to get on with his life away from the choking fumes and frantic noise and bustle of the Metropolis.

The other passengers were dozing or reading their papers as Mark stood up. He needed to stretch his legs and left the compartment to go to the buffet car. Yet again he wondered what had happened to Alice. He chided himself for dwelling on an insignificant episode with someone he had met once. He had been so sure she would turn up even if it was only to tell him she did not want to have lunch with him. He felt sure she was a decent girl who would not have left him in the lurch.

He leaned against the corridor window and stared out, trying to recall her face. It was the eyes that he remembered, so green – like the green of trees reflected in still pools. He shrugged.

'Don't be daft,' he muttered and swayed his way to the buffet car.

'Can I help you, Sir?' A spotty-faced youth in a British Rail jacket asked as Mark looked at the unappetising selection of sandwiches on display. Everything said about British Rail food was true, he thought.

'A cheese sandwich and a cup of tea, please,' he said. He bit into the sandwich which was as dry as it looked; it would be good to have some of Mum's cooking.

Alice was allowed to join the Martin family for an evening meal after all, once she had a warm bath, washed her hair and dressed. She was alarmed by the weakness she felt after one day in bed and wondered how people recovering from protracted illness managed to get fit again. She wished she felt more comfortable in this house. There was such a strong undercurrent of antagonism surely the Martins must be aware of it too or had it gone on so long that they ignored it? She felt apprehensive as she walked downstairs, not only was there Joan to face, but she would also meet Malcolm.

Of course, Joan was putting the final touches to what would be the last meal the family would have together for several months.

'Is there anything I can do?'

Joan looked both surprised and pleased, neither Spencer nor Malcolm often made such an offer.

'Thank you, dear. Would you carry the plates through, and tell the men their meal is ready?'

Alice smiled, the 'dear' felt nice, perhaps Joan had a softer side. Having done as she was told she waited until everyone was seated and then slid into the vacant place indicated by Stanley.

'Good to see you looking so much better,' Stanley said. 'This is my younger son, Malcolm.' He added, 'Malcolm this is Alice, a friend of Spencer's.'

Alice felt Spencer's leg press against hers and she blushed.

'Pleased to meet you,' she said to a young man who was the image of his father.

Joan pushed the laden trolley with its huge joint of beef and several vegetable dishes into the dining room. Alice watched as

Stanley carved the meat while Joan transferred the other dishes from trolley to table. It reminded Alice of Grandmother Cardew's house.

Although her memories were clouded, by the years, she did recall the grandeur and elegance of that house and all that was in it. Alice realised with shock, despite all the finery and expense which was evident in the Martin's house, the grandeur and elegance, the birth right of the well-bred, was missing. Grandmother had often scathingly referred to the 'nouveau riches' and Alice knew now what she had meant. She felt less apprehensive as she looked at Joan, perhaps she too felt insecure. Perhaps all the bluster was a contrived carapace designed to protect and deflect any attack.

'Alice kindly offered to help.' Joan looked around the table as her remark fell like a stone into a pool of silence. She watched as ripples of discomfort spread. Alice stared at her plate. To be praised to the detriment of the rest of the family embarrassed her. She wondered if that had been Joan's intention.

Stanley and Spencer exchanged glances and Malcolm laughed.

'Come off it, Ma, you just love being the queen bee, lording it or should it be queening it in the kitchen. Anyway, that's a woman's place everyone knows that.'

Alice watched as a huge grin appeared on Malcolm's face which encompassed the whole table and rested on his mother. The atmosphere relaxed at once. Joan chuckled with delight and sat down. For Alice it felt like staring into the crater of an active volcano.

'You mustn't let Ma bully you.' Malcolm grinned at her. 'Her bark's worse than her bite.

Alice had no idea how to respond without upsetting the more harmonious atmosphere which Malcolm had created. She felt herself blush and nodded.

'You are definitely looking better now,' Stanley said, 'but how do you feel?'

'Much better thank you, it is so kind of you to take me in like this and care for me.' She turned to Joan. 'I must have made so much extra work for you.'

Joan looked pleased.

'I think I shall be well enough to go to work on Monday so I had better think about getting back to the hostel.'

'We'll see.' Joan said.

'What's the hostel like?' Malcolm asked.

'Not bad, a bit Spartan, nothing like as comfortable or luxurious as here, of course.' Alice sensed the increased level of conviviality. Lots of compliments, flattery and sycophancy seemed to be the answer.

'Can't be much fun shut up with a load of women,' Malcolm speculated.

'Some people wouldn't mind, I don't suppose.' Joan said. She watched as Stanley registered the remark. He was like a fish on a line, just when he thinks he can swim away she jerked the line taut. Tomorrow, when they were on their own, it was going to be interesting.

Chapter 15

There was little conversation as Joan drove through town on Sunday afternoon. Alice had said she would be happy to go back to the hostel on the Tube, particularly as the whole family had been invited to dine with Joan's parents but Joan would have none of it.

'My son will be going to Stockholm soon to gain experience before he takes up a post with Woolux.'

Alice felt her chest contract with alarm. 'I expect he will enjoy that. I hope I will be able to travel one day. My father travelled a lot when he was in the army. He said it was exciting.'

'You should get as much experience as you can before you meet Mr Right.' Joan looked at Alice and smiled briefly. The message was both given and received. In her view, Alice was not Mrs Right. She looked down at the directions to the hostel; she had worked it out using the Martins' A-Z and decided to say nothing.

'I should have done more before I married Stanley.'

'What would you have liked to have done?' Alice suspected that after

Malcolm, Joan was Joan's favourite topic of conversation.

'I was a model, you know.'

'Yes, Spencer told me. That must have been wonderful.'

'But soon after I met Stanley, we decided to get married; he made a public announcement. Well. that was the end of my freedom. He had to go back to England and I was left high and dry. No decent young Canadian would try to date an engaged woman. That was that and I was stuck at home for months on end. I did have my work, but it started to dry up and there didn't seem much point in trying anything else, not if I was coming to England. I could have been the Jean Shrimpton of my day.'

Alice watched Joan from the corner of her eye as she told her tale of lost opportunity and thwarted ambition. If Spencer wanted to announce an engagement, she thought, at least I would belong to someone who really wanted me. The sunlight of a beautiful autumn day caught the down-turned mouth and the lines of dissatisfaction carved into Joan's face.

'Could you not develop a hobby or interest now, something that you would enjoy, that would give you satisfaction?'

There was a lengthy pause during which Alice realised how stupid she had been. Joan would never be one to take advice from a teenager. She felt her skin prickle with apprehension.

'My husband would never agree to my doing something that suggested he was not a good provider and I must always be available to act as companion and hostess to the wives of his business colleagues. That is what is expected of a managing director's wife.'

Not only did Joan assume Alice was too young to know what was expected of a managing director's wife; she never would. The final instructions were given, Alice closed the A-Z and sat in silence until she could see the hostel.

'It's the big building on the left.'

Joan stopped the car and switched off the engine.

'Thank you very much, Mrs Martin, you have looked after me so well. I do appreciate it.'

Joan smiled. 'Do you like living here?

'It's O.K. but it's not like having a proper home.'

'What do your parents think?'

'I'm not sure. I think Dad was happy to see me becoming independent and I've not lived with Mum for some time so it doesn't make any difference to her.'

'Don't you see either of them?'

'Not often.'

This was awful, like being a fly on a pin. Alice wanted to get away but she mustn't upset Joan, she was Spencer's mother, must keep her happy.

'Don't you mind?'

'Pardon?'

'Not seeing them.'

'I didn't spend much time with them when I was little so I'm used to them not being around.'

'I see. You'll be all right now, won't you? I'd better get back. I want to see Malcolm before he goes.'

She switched the engine on and put the car in gear. Alice picked up her bag, closed the car door gently and waved as Joan pulled away from the kerb.

Mark sat on the top of Indian's Head, the distinctive crag that looked down over Greenfield valley. He knew he was out of condition; life in London had made him soft. As he looked down at the fields and meadows, he knew he had made the right decision. He wondered if Mum missed the countryside as he had. Perhaps he should buy a little cottage in one of the Saddleworth villages then he could go walking whenever he wanted, straight out of the front door and away. He poured another cup of coffee from his thermos and listened to a solitude that was broken only by the chirruping of birds.

He had spent the previous evening with his mother, reminiscing and catching up on news of the people Mark had grown up with. His mate Tommy Barraclough had left the army and moved to Norwich. Mum said he was courting a girl there. Mr and Mrs Barraclough still lived in Chadderton; Mark would go to see them and get Tommy's new address.

Mark told his Mum about Alice. He wondered if she would think he was being silly. She didn't. He had been surprised by what she said.

'You know it is possible to fall in love at first sight, I did with your dad. If you really think this girl is special, you'd better track her down.'

Mark bit into the apple Mum had put in with his sandwiches. It was easy to say track her down but how? He didn't know her surname, he did not know if she lived at the hostel or if she was just someone Susan had met at the Palais. Perhaps Susan was the answer. He knew she did live at the hostel so he could contact her. A first decision had been made, he thought, as he repacked his rucksack. That's what he would do.

By the time Joan got to her parents' house the meal was over. That was as she had hoped. Walking in on them had shocked her; they all seemed so damned cheerful. She kissed her parents and talked about Alice, but the mood had been shattered simply because she arrived. Once again, she felt she was the outsider, after all she had done.

Stanley left almost at once to take Malcolm to the station and she told Spencer to stay with his grandparents for a while. Now, back home, she was ready. She stood in front of the French windows where she could see her reflection and that of anyone who came into the room. She heard the key in the lock and waited.

Stanley walked into the room glanced at her and slumped into a chair. He looked tired. She felt adrenalin flow through her, she felt alive and vibrant. Gill must leave the Woolux company, of that she was certain.

She turned and stubbed out her cigarette in the overflowing ashtray.

'You do realise this can't go on.'

'What can't go on?'

Joan lit another cigarette and exhaled noisily. 'This business with your bloody secretary cum bed mate.'

She watched as he closed his eyes. 'I'm not stupid.'

'No, my dear, you're not.' He struggled to his feet. 'Where are the aspirins?'

'In the medicine cupboard.' She stared at him, his face was grey and she wondered if she might be pushing him too far. Men of his age had heart attacks; he was overweight, he drank too much wine and smoked too many cigars.

He looked better when he returned, was it just an act to avoid a scene?

'Has it never occurred to you to ask why I might have leaned a little on Gill, as a colleague and a friend?'

'I presume you just fancied a bit of rough but didn't fancy kerb-crawling to get it. You men are all the same. A tarty piece with a tight sweater can lead you by the balls like a bull with a ring through its nose.'

'That is totally unfair. Gill is a good secretary and a decent woman.'

Joan's face flushed. 'You bastard, how dare you sit there and defend that woman to me in my own home.'

Stanley sat forward and tried to speak.

'I know you've been screwing her, you admitted it. Even if you hadn't, I'm not blind. If you don't get rid of her, I'll show your staff a thing or two. I'll go down there when you least expect it and I'll tear her bloody hair out.'

'For Christ's sake, Joan.'

'Looks as though butter wouldn't melt in her mouth. Yes, Mrs Martin, no, Mrs Martin, he's busy in a meeting, Mrs Martin. Shall I ask him to call you as soon as he's free and all the time laughing behind my back. How many other people know? Tell me that. I will not be made a fool of, not by a cheap little trollop like her.'

Joan realised she was a shrieking banshee, but what did she care she felt alive for the first time in ages. She gave a sharp gasp of pain as the cigarette clamped between her fingers burned her. She threw the dog end towards the ashtray on the coffee table, missed and watched as it rolled onto the carpet.

Stanley leapt to his feet, scooped it up and crushed it out in the ashtray. He straightened up and they stood inches apart.

'I have had enough of this, Joan. Living with you is like walking on eggshells.'

He stepped nearer and the expression on his face made Joan pause even though she was tingling with excitement. She had his full attention for once. Then she stepped back, suddenly frightened. What if he left her? She only wanted to be the centre of his world was that so terrible?

'So why should I look at someone else? Why would I? Oh yes, the grand hostess, Lady Bountiful, you are so bloody gracious. How often have I been told how lucky I am to have such a wonderful wife? If they only knew what you are really like.'

He paused turned on his heel and left the room.

Panic clogged Joan's throat as she ran to the door, ears straining, mind willing him not to walk out, praying that she would not hear the click of the front door closing behind him. It was all going wrong; somehow, he was different. She heard him returning and moved to the centre of the room. He held a brandy glass in each hand, both a third full.

'I presume you will join me in a drink.' He handed her a glass. 'I've never known you refuse.'

She glared at him. The moment's panic disappeared as though it had never been. Of course, he would never leave, not this beautiful home and all that went with it. He could not bear to make himself a laughing stock and that is what he would be, just another middle-aged fool running off with his secretary. It was the action of a man in the throes of a mid-life crisis; how laughable, how pathetic.

She took a large mouthful of brandy, holding it on her tongue to feel the warmth spread around her mouth. She swallowed slowly breathing in the heavy vapours with a sigh.

'So, it's my fault you can't keep your flies done up, is it?'

Stanley opened his mouth to speak.

'I've been a bloody good wife to you and well you know it. Look around you, see the evidence with your own eyes.'

'At a price, Joan. Yes, you choose nice things, but who pays?'

'Look at your two sons, they weren't found under a gooseberry bush.'

'Yes, two sons as different as chalk and cheese and by God, you've made it obvious that Spencer means nothing to you.'

'Are you surprised? How would you like it if I got Malcolm to spy on you? He'd have had a pretty tale to tell, wouldn't he?'

'For heaven's sake, Joan, what do you think it's like for me not knowing what state you are going to be in when I am trying to make an impression on business colleagues?'

'Is it obligatory for men in the woollen garment trade to have the sparkle, wit and social repartee of a three-toed sloth? Or do you hand-pick them for my benefit?'

'Materialism, possessions and fucking status, that just about sums you up. What about love? Where's the tenderness? I come in after a God-awful day and believe me, I do have God-awful days. Only to find you in one of your moods and off we go again.'

Joan backed away. The whole thing was getting out of control. She was the one who had been badly treated, she was the wronged wife. What right did Stanley have to start complaining?

'Do you know I can't remember the last time you put your arms around me and kissed me with any show of warmth?'

'Well, we both know where you went for a show of warmth.'

'I can't remember the last time you made advances to me, actually instigated making love. In fact, when you have condescended to allow me between your legs, I have felt as welcome as a dose of the clap!'

Joan gasped as the colour drained from her face and with shaking hands she placed the brandy glass on the coffee table.

'How dare you, how dare you use that foul language to me. Is it what Gill likes? My background may have been lowly compared with yours but that doesn't give you the right to abuse me like this.'

She stepped towards him and raising her arm brought it crashing down on his cheek. His head snapped back; he grabbed her wrist so tightly, she cried out. He jerked her towards him and thrust his face into hers. His eyes glittered as he emphasised every word as though speaking to an idiot.

'You are a fucking bitch.'

Joan tried to free her hand but he held her tighter.

'Yes, I will use that word.'

She raised her free hand, but he grabbed it and forced her to face him.

'In fact, I will go so far as to say that if there had been more fucking in our marriage we might not be in our present situation.'

She whimpered as his grip on her tightened. It should not be happening; this was not how she had planned it.

'You are so full of what you want.'

Joan closed her eyes to shut out Stanley's face, terrible in his rage.

'It never crosses your mind to think of anyone else, least of all me.'

'But…'

'Shut up woman and listen. I'll correct what I just said.'

'So, you should, I never thought I'd be a battered wife.'

'Don't tempt me. Where was I, oh yes, you do think of someone else, Malcolm. The poor bloody kid can't cope with your endless adoration.'

'He loves me, you're just jealous.'

'You are an embarrassment to him. You are choking him, driving him away.'

Joan sobbed. 'Never.'

'Listen you'd better believe me. You…are…driving…him …away.'

With each word Joan felt her arms being jerked downwards until she was half kneeling, half slumped against him. Finally, he let go of her wrists. She'd be bruised in the morning, that will be something to show the police.

She realised that Stanley was now sitting down. She watched him take a large mouthful of brandy. And he complained about her drinking. She could hear his teeth rattle against the cut-glass brandy balloon. She mopped at her eyes with her handkerchief. Now she was terrified, was this was the end of everything? Stanley had never been like this.

'What are we going to do?' She whispered. She realised with surprise that she was crying. 'What are we going to do?' She felt like a small child crying in the dark.

'I don't know,' Stanley said, 'I just don't know.'

She knelt in front of him and watched as he leaned back and closed his eyes.

'I didn't mean to hurt you Joan, I never have. All I know is that this will happen again and again and I haven't got the stamina anymore.'

'No!'

'We agree about nothing. Ours is a dance of death, the death of our relationship.'

'No!' Joan clutched at Stanley's knees. It frightened her when he had fought back, she had never expected it. She leaned against his legs and let the tears continue unchecked.

'All I ever wanted was you, but you always had something else, work, clients' deals. I was nothing, just the little woman left at home to wash nappies and cook meals.' She choked back a sob. 'Even when the children were born, where were you?' She felt swamped by sorrow. She had always done her best and now this, another woman.

She felt Stanley's hand rest on her head and then gently stroke her hair.

'I thought I'd given you everything you wanted,' he said.

'I just wanted you. Then Spencer came along so quickly and I was ill all the time I carried him. Your life went on as usual, but I was just Spencer's mother.'

Joan flexed her knees and tried to alter her position.

'You can't be very comfortable on the floor.' He looked at his watch.

'It's quite late; perhaps we should go to bed.'

Joan looked up and as their eyes met, she nodded. Stanley stood and helped her to her feet. Together they went upstairs, but they undressed, as usual, with their backs to each other.

Joan felt sad; this was how things were, but she had hated what pregnancy did to her body, both during and after. She wondered if Stanley had thought she was rejecting him when what she really felt was shame at the sagging flesh that had once been so firm.

She jumped when she felt his hands on her shoulders. He turned her around and their naked bodies touched as he put his hands on her shoulders.

'When did we last make love?'

She wanted to scream at him 'You will have done more recently…' Instinct kept her teeth clenched to stop angry words from escaping. He led her to the bed and throwing back the covers helped her slide between cool sheets. She leaned across to turn out the bedside light.

'No, leave it on,' he said.

They had invariably made love in the dark and she didn't want him to see how little she felt, it had always been so messy, sweaty and utterly undignified. At least in the dark, you didn't have to look as though you were enjoying it.

She lay back on the pillows and waited. He kissed her tenderly and let his hand move lightly, stroking her breasts, then her stomach crisscrossed as it was with stretch marks. She longed to pull covers over her imperfections.

In her modelling days, her stomach had been as flat as a board. Who would look at it now? His hand slid down her thigh, first on the outside then across and up towards her groin; it was pleasant. Was this what he did to Gill? Her muscles tightened.

'Relax my dear,' he said, 'let's just enjoy being close.'

She closed her eyes, but all she could see behind her eye-lids was a picture of Stanley thrusting and poking at an abandoned and squealing Gill, legs waving in the air, moaning and grunting as she surely would. Women like that were bound to be noisy. Suddenly the stroking hand became unbearable; why didn't he just get on with it? After the row this evening she did not dare tell him to leave her alone. She reached out and pulled him towards her. Stanley smiled.

Soon after, what Joan hoped was a convincing performance, she heard the front door being closed; Spencer must be back. Thank God Stanley had rolled off her, at least he was satisfied. They moved apart and now Joan did turn out the light. She lay back and was thankful for the dark which allowed her to separate herself from the evening's events. Her body felt bruised. Stanley had been rough, so unlike himself almost as if he wanted to hurt her. She felt a tremor of alarm but she knew what she had to say and say it she would.

'You will get rid of Gill, won't you?'

Stanley did not reply but Joan knew he was still awake.

Chapter 16

Joan sat in her dressing gown, cup of coffee in one hand, cigarette in the other. She watched Stanley as he ate his breakfast. He looked sad, defeated. It was his own fault; but if he had learned his lesson, so much the better. Joan smiled; everything would be so much better once Gill had gone. Joan shifted on her chair, aware of tenderness – the result of last night's sex. She could not regard it as lovemaking, it had been too violent for that. If it was the price she had to pay for a continuing marriage, she would pay.

'Are you telling her today?'

Stanley looked up. 'Probably.'

'You'll give her an excellent reference no doubt.'

Stanley stared at her. 'Of course, I'll give her a good reference, why wouldn't I?'

'Have you thought about Lillian's friend, Harry, couldn't he be your personal assistant or secretary?'

'You're assuming he can type.'

'I don't know; it's just an idea. You always complain I don't do enough for my sister. I should have thought offering some work to this fellow of hers, who turns up like a stray dog, would meet with your approval.'

Stanley sighed. 'I suppose I could find him something.'

'Hasn't Bergman got a P.A.?'

'Yes, and that reminds me he's coming over on Thursday so I must get Gill to arrange some accommodation.'

Joan broke the silence as she exhaled cigarette smoke. 'That's the sort of thing Harry could do.'

'That would work really well, a P.A. who knows bugger all about London hotels etc. etc. That would be really clever.'

'So, you're going back on your word, are you?'

'For Christ's sake, woman, give me a chance. I've a business to run, a son who couldn't sell snow in the desert and you on my back morning, noon and night.'

'So how is that Svenson or whatever his name is can manage to delegate? He's the owner but he can trust his manager to do the travelling around. That's what managers are for, or is it that you can't wait to get away from here?'

'When you behave like this can you blame me?'

Joan shuddered. The fear she felt last night, when she thought he might walk out, made her heart lurch.

'Don't you realise I'm lonely?' Her voice had lost its edge.

Stanley glanced at his watch and stood up.

'You'll never understand. I have to work to keep you in relative luxury. I've got to keep expanding, replace any customers we lose. It's a treadmill. If I stop, I'm dead; is that what you want?'

Joan looked away; she knew he was right.

'Have you thought about some sort of companion or a friend you could spend time with? I don't want you to be lonely.'

'Old women have companions.'

'What about Alice? She seems a nice enough girl and it must be pretty grim living in that hostel. Take her under your wing, help her to make the best of herself; you'd be good at that.'

Joan gave a tight smile.

'She works so when am I supposed to spend time with her, make her look as though she knows how to dress? That only leaves the weekends?'

'Well, think about it anyway.'

'Isn't that when I should be spending time with my husband?'

Stanley sighed, 'I must be off. There's been a problem with the over-locking machines and the maintenance men need a boot up their backsides. We've a big order to send off at the end of the week.'

'That's the sort of thing a personal assistant could sort out.'

Joan watched as Stanley opened his mouth to speak, changed his mind and leaned across to give her a perfunctory kiss. She listened as the front door closed behind him.

She lit another cigarette and stood in the middle of the kitchen. It was not a bad idea of Stanley's, but was Alice the sort of girl she would want to treat as a surrogate daughter? On the positive side, if Alice were to live under their roof, her relationship with Spencer could be closely watched. Yes, Joan thought, a most satisfactory suggestion.

They could all discuss it tonight when Spencer came home. If Stanley was going to send Spencer to Stockholm both she and Alice would be in need of companionship. The whole thing would have to be discussed with the girl and her parents, but from what Alice had said they were hardly doting. Probably welcome someone else being responsible for the girl.

Joan started to clear the breakfast things; as usual Spencer had left his. It amused her that Stanley insisted on Spencer making his own way to work as if it made any difference; everyone knew he was the boss's son. If you had privileges why not use them? She hummed to herself as she worked. Last night had cleared the air; she had done Stanley a favour and stopped him making a fool of himself.

Alice walked through the hospital's main entrance. Miss Pritchard had said

Susan was in Ward 3. It was Alice's first day back at work and she was exhausted, but still wanted to see Susan. She toiled up the three flights of stairs and once at the top held onto the rails while she got her breath back. She looked at the small bunch of violets, all she could afford. Still, they were better than nothing.

It was five minutes before visiting time and people were milling around the ward doors, waiting for the stampede to patients' beds. Alice wondered if any of these people were Susan's parents. Would they object to her being there since she knew the circumstances that led to Susan's brush with death? She decided she would not stay long, just long enough to assure herself that Susan was going to be all right.

The doors opened and the crowd of visitors streamed in. Alice hesitated; she didn't know where Susan's bed was.

'Who are you looking for, dear?'

'Susan Johnson.'

'Side ward 1, on the left, she's much better today.'

The nurse smiled encouragement and bustled off. Alice stood in the doorway, unsure of what to say. Susan was sitting up in bed reading a magazine; no other visitors had arrived yet. Alice didn't know what she had expected; surely such a trauma would leave its mark. Then Susan looked up and smiled.

'Hello, the nurse said you were better.'

'I didn't expect you, thanks for coming. Yes, I feel fine; I might even be able to go home tomorrow.'

'Home?'

'Yes, to Mum and Dad's.' She blushed and Alice wondered if she remembered all the uncharitable things she had said about her parents in the past.

'I don't want to go back to the hostel.'

'Oh.' Lucky Susan, she had a choice.

'We've had a long talk, you know, about everything. I'm going to try to make a go of it at home. I don't know if it will work, but I feel I have to give it a try.'

Alice nodded. 'I'm pleased for you.' She held out the violets which were looking tired. 'Shall I get something to put these in?'

Susan nodded and held the flowers close. 'They smell lovely.'

Alice felt her eyes fill. It must be because I'm overtired, she thought. I just wish one of my parents would ask me to give it a go. There was no point in travelling down that road, it was a dead end.

She found a small vase in the sluice room and placed it by Susan's bed.

The violets drooped a little but their heavy perfume filled the room. The two girls looked at each other, but recent events hung between them like a curtain.

'Does Miss Pritchard know you won't be coming back?'

'I don't think so; perhaps you would tell her.'

Alice stared out of the window. She would be on her own again, but it was wrong to think like that, she should be glad for Susan.

'But you might change your mind.'

Susan shook her head. 'I've changed, all this has been a nightmare and perhaps I'm beginning to grow up. I do owe Mum and Dad a lot so I must try to make it work.'

Alice wondered if the abortion would come back to haunt Susan in years to come. She had killed a child, her child. Perhaps shutting out what happened was the only way to cope.

'Are your parents coming tonight?'

Yes,' Susan glanced at her watch, 'they should be here any minute.'

'I don't think I'll stop then; you must be feeling tired. I'm just glad to see you looking so much better. You gave me a terrible fright.'

Susan gave a brittle laugh, 'You must come to see me once I'm settled in at home. I'm sure my parents would love to meet you. I have told them what you did.'

'Yes, that would be nice; you can always leave a message for me at the hostel.'

She stood, ready to leave. 'I'd better go. I've been poorly myself, had a bad dose of tonsillitis and I still feel a bit groggy.' She remained standing by the bed unsure whether to kiss, shake hands or hug. Susan held out her hands and gripped Alice's.

'Thanks for everything, I'll be in touch, honestly, I will.'

Alice nodded and waved when she got to the door. She wouldn't be in touch. They had a shared memory which had to be buried. It would be a constant reminder of Tony and what the relationship did to her life. This was goodbye.

Alice walked towards the stairs and noticed the couple coming towards her. The woman had the fluffy blonde, vulnerable look that Alice had so envied in Susan. Alice smiled as the couple passed her on the stairs. It must be Mr and Mrs Johnson anxious to see their daughter.

Joan rang the hostel; she couldn't wait until later tonight. She wanted to speak to Alice now, sound the girl out. If she didn't want to live with them Joan wanted to know before anything was said to Spencer. It took several minutes for Alice to come to the phone.

'Hello.'

'Hello, Alice, I was wondering how you got on at work.'

'Not bad, but I feel very tired. Had to call on a friend… she's in hospital, I went straight after work. Perhaps I've done a bit too much; I'll have an early night.'

'Very sensible. Actually, I wanted to make a suggestion to you. Stanley and I don't like the idea of one of our son's friends living in a hostel. We have a spare room and thought it would be nicer for you to live with us.'

Alice was stunned and clutching the phone took a deep breath.

'That would be very nice, Mrs Martin, you are so kind to me.

Are you sure I wouldn't be a nuisance?'

'We wouldn't have asked you if we thought that. Of course, we will have to have your parents' approval since you are underage.'

Alice felt perspiration break out on her forehead. She didn't want the Martins to meet either of her parents. After the business at Dad's flat, he had definite views on Spencer and none of them were flattering. Not only would he make his feelings clear he would interrogate the Martins in the process.

She knew she could predict how Dad would behave, but the same could not be said about Mum. On a good day, she was passable, but good days were few and far between. Her manic depression had blighted the family's life. If she were manic, she would be belligerent and argumentative. If she were depressed, she would neither speak nor acknowledge the world around her. What a dilemma; life was just too complicated.

'Alice, are you there?'

Alice started, 'Yes, sorry, I don't know what to say. I'm sure Mum and Dad would be quite happy with the arrangement.'

'Yes,' thought Joan, I'm sure they would be. After all, they are happy for their daughter to live in a hostel. What kind of parent does that? She felt virtuous and caring, a Good Samaritan in fact.

'Yes Alice, but Stanley and I do feel that the matter should be discussed with at least one of your parents.'

'I'll have a word with Mum, shall I?'

'A good idea, now will we be seeing you this weekend?'

'I think so. Spencer said he would call me tomorrow or on Wednesday.' She paused. 'I don't know how to thank you enough, Mrs. Martin.'

Joan laughed. 'Let us suggest Saturday to your mother, we could meet for a meal.'

'Yes, I'll call her tonight.'

Alice's hand was shaking and wet with sweat. Everything was

happening too fast. She slumped against the wall; she couldn't cope with it. She wanted to belong, have a family, but if they meet her Mum will they still want her?

Walking up the endless stairs, she listened to the thump of each footstep. She sat on her bed and glanced around the bare room. This couldn't be home because it would never be hers. She thought about all the material benefits of the Martins' house but what about the atmosphere? Could she cope with that? She would be near Spencer and that would be lovely, but he was going to Stockholm. She would be living with just Mr and Mrs Martin most of the time.

She sighed and rubbed her aching forehead then checked her purse for plenty of change and went downstairs to the phone to call her mother, Sheila.

The phone rang and rang and just as Alice was about to give up a breathless voice answered.

'Hello, who is it?' It sounded like Jane, Alice's younger half-sister.

'Jane, it's Alice is Mum there?' There was a pause then Alice heard Jane shouting.

'Mum, Mum it's Alice.'

There was a sudden piercing whistle down the receiver and as Alice took it away from her ear, she heard a boy's laughter. It was Anthony and just the sort of thing he would do. Never had his dislike and rejection of his older half-sister wavered; Alice knew it never would. She waited and thought she could hear footsteps.

'Darling, how are you?' The voice leapt out of the phone as though the disembodied voice had been made flesh.

Alice always found her mother's intensity of response, verging on the melodramatic and embarrassing.

'Hello Mum, I'm fine. How are you all?'

'Splendid, now when are you coming to see us?'

Alice heard a commotion in the background and then her

mother placed a hand over the receiver, but it didn't stop Alice from hearing the chorus of wails from Anthony and Jane. No, Alice thought, they don't want me to visit; they have never wanted that.

'We'd all love to see you, darling.'

Alice smiled to herself. Mum never would acknowledge the animosity between her children.

'That's why I'm ringing. You remember Spencer, my boyfriend.'

'You've mentioned him, now isn't it time I met him?'

'Yes, Mum, that's it, you see I want you to meet him and his parents.'

'Darling girl that would be wonderful, are you bringing them here?'

Alice gasped in horror. Mum's flat always looked as though a hurricane had blown through it. Alec was often drunk and always spent the weekends in bed and the kids were unspeakable. It had always amazed Alice that no matter what Mum's mood she seemed never to register the mayhem around her.

'They want us to go out for a meal with them, just you and me.'

'All a bit sudden, isn't it? You've not done anything silly, have you? You're not pregnant?'

Alice groaned. 'No Mum, I'm not pregnant. It's just that they want me to go to live with them. They don't like me living in a hostel.'

There was a pause and Alice waited for the storm to break.

'I see, I suppose you would rather live with strangers than with your own family. How long is it since I saw you?'

'Yes, but Mum, you know how Jane and Anthony are.'

'Don't be so silly, you imagine it, of course, they want to see you.'

Alice listened to the chorus of denial in the background. The receiver was put down and Alice could hear shouting and a general uproar. Mum must have placed her hand over the receiver while she shouted at the other two. Then there was a sudden bellow of rage and Alice recognised the sound of Alec, her stepfather. Once the noise diminished Mum came back.

'So, what are they like, darling, Spencer's parents?'

'They're all right. They were very kind to me when I was ill recently.'

'Ill, what do you mean you've been ill? Why wasn't I told?'

'I didn't want to worry you, anyway I'm better now. The point is they want to meet you. They don't think it's right for me to just move in unless you or Dad have met them and approved.'

'Your father, what's he got to do with it? What has he ever done for you? If he's there I shan't be coming, the bastard. And I'll never know why you went to live with him in the first place.'

Alice leaned back against the wall, closed her eyes and waited. It was always the same. Why didn't Mum realise how difficult it made things? If she can't say anything nice about Dad, why say anything at all?

'No, Dad won't be there. I think they want to take us out for a meal, somewhere nice, probably on Saturday, would Saturday be okay?'

'Yes, Alec can look after the kids.'

Thank goodness, at least Mum hadn't wanted Jane and Anthony to come too. That would have been more than flesh and blood could stand.

'I'll give you a ring later in the week to confirm arrangements. Bye

Mum.'

'Bye, bye darling.'

Mum was in her manic phase, Alice thought. Saturday, if that was to be when the meeting took place, was going to be tricky.

Axel Bergman, his wife Helga and Brigit Bjoerling had arrived in London on Thursday as planned. Stanley and his chauffeur met them and took them to the hotel in Hendon that Gill had booked for them. They were expected at the Martins for an evening meal. Joan had suggested Alice be invited too. If she was to be a member of the family, as seemed likely, she might as well start now.

An extra pair of hands in the kitchen would be useful. Besides she and Stanley would be taking Alice and her mother to lunch on Saturday as a treat. There was no reason why the girl should not earn the privilege of dining at the Dorchester. Joan wondered why Alice had been startled by the choice of restaurant. From what the girl had said her mother came from a wealthy and upper-middle-class family. Therefore, if Joan had to impress, impress she would.

Alice had set the table and folded napkins as Joan had shown her. She had changed into clean clothes and put her discarded ones in the bedroom that would soon be hers. Beneath her calm exterior, she was in turmoil and went through the conversation she had with her mother the previous evening. Once she explained they were to meet at the Dorchester, she suggested that Mum wear something nice. That had been a mistake.

Sheila had shouted down the phone that no one was going to tell her how to dress. It wasn't what people wore that mattered, it was what they were. And why should she dress up for people who were trying to take her daughter away? Alice could feel anxiety tighten in her stomach, by Saturday, she thought, she would be a gibbering idiot.

She checked the table and walked back into the kitchen where everything seemed to be under control. She was unsure of what to do next. Spencer had gone with his father to collect the dinner guests. She stood watching as Joan stirred sauces, basted meat, whipped cream and drank sherry. She looked flushed and Alice wasn't sure if it was heated from the stove or the effects of the alcohol. Still, Joan seemed in an amiable mood.

'Pour yourself a glass.'

Alice hesitated, would sherry on an empty stomach make things better or worse? Things could only improve so she poured a glass and sipped it slowly. Living here was going to be very different from anything she had experienced.

The front door opened and there was the sound of several voices. Joan wiped her hands, removed her apron, ready to greet her guests. Alice followed and stood on the periphery of the group while introductions were made. Mr and Mrs Bergman were in early middle age, prosperous and confident. Their clothes were expensive but understated, well-cut, elegant with no hint of flamboyance. Mrs Bergman wore enough jewellery to proclaim her husband was a good provider, but not enough to appear ostentatious. The personal assistant, Brigit Bjoerling, was young and dressed in a sombre, professional style. Alice had never mixed with people like this.

Spencer winked at Alice over the heads of the group, she smiled and felt herself relax. She wanted Spencer to be proud of her; she mustn't make a fool of herself. She would watch what everyone else did then there would be no mistakes. She realised with a start that Joan had spoken her name.

'This is Alice. She's a friend of the family and has been kind enough to help me in the kitchen.'

Alice felt a prickle of irritation. Why didn't she introduce her as Spencer's girlfriend? She said nothing, just smiled and shook hands. Everyone went into the living room where drinks were poured and the vagaries of the weather and air travel were discussed. Joan excused herself and gave Alice a look that indicated that she too was to go to the kitchen, in her role of chef's helper. As she walked past Spencer, he grabbed her hand. She felt the colour rise on her face and neck, her heart thumped and she hoped no one noticed.

Alice glowed with the effects of wine and good food. She felt lightheaded and found it difficult to follow the conversation, but that didn't matter, it was mostly concerned with business. She let her mind wander into a future that seemed rosy and it was so nice to have Spencer sitting opposite her his feet entwined with hers under the table. Provided Mum doesn't behave too badly I shall be able to move in and make a fresh start, like Susan.

Spencer was talking to his father and Axel Bergman about his wish to go to Stockholm. What a shame he wanted to do that, just as she was coming to live under the same roof. She mustn't be selfish, she thought, he has his career to think of.

'I think we can find plenty for this young man to do.' Bergman said. 'I know someone who will be pleased to see him again.'

'Oh?' said Joan.

'Ah yes, the lovely Berthe. Spencer made quite an impression on her.

She is a charming girl and acted as a guide when your husband and son visited before.' He beamed at Joan. 'She asked most especially to be remembered to you, Spencer.'

Alice felt a great weight press down on her chest. She looked across at Spencer, but he avoided her gaze.

'How kind,' Joan said.

Alice could feel Joan's eyes on her, looking for her reaction.

Chapter 17

Mark got off the train at Baron's Court and looked around. It was a dismal, depressing area and just to make everything look even more miserable, it was raining. Not for the first time, he wondered what on earth he was doing. He had been delegated to visit the Head Office for some kind of training seminar. At first, it had seemed a great opportunity to trace Alice. Now he felt stupid. He was chasing about trying to find a girl he had met once who might live in a hostel whose name he didn't know. He didn't even know Alice's other name.

He turned up the collar of his raincoat and started walking. He would just have to ask the first person he met. The rain was lashing down now and the streets were empty.

'This is hopeless,' he muttered and hurried back to the station. As he got nearer a flock of people surged past him all intent on getting home and out of the foul weather. At the entrance to the station, an elderly woman was struggling with her umbrella. Perfect, Mark thought, she's probably lived here all her life.

'Can I give you a hand with that?'

'Umbrellas are more trouble than they're worth, young man, see what you can do.'

Mark managed to loosen the jammed release button, opened the umbrella and handed it to the woman.

'Well, that's your good deed for the day, thank you so much.' She turned to leave.

'Actually, you might be able to help me. I'm looking for a hostel, round here, somewhere. You don't know it do you?'

The woman paused. 'Hostel? Yes, there is, let me just think.'

Mark crossed his fingers and waited.

'I know; it's Westbrook Grove. It's not far from here but it's for women I'm pretty sure of that.'

'Oh, I'm not looking for accommodation; I'm trying to trace someone.'

'I see,' the woman smiled, 'go out of here, straight on then turn left into Princess Avenue. I'm sure Westbrook Grove is the first on the right.'

'Thanks a lot, I didn't fancy wandering around in this.'

The woman gave Mark a knowing sidelong glance as she walked away.

'I hope you find her.'

'So do I,'

The rain had eased; at least it wasn't bouncing now. He smiled as he strode down the road, perhaps he was meant to find Alice.

He turned into Westbrook Grove and saw the hostel at once. It was a tall, imposing building, austere rather than cosy. He wondered if it had always been a hostel or if it had once been a workhouse, the kind of place that his grandmother had spoken of in hushed tones; a place to be dreaded. He opened the gate, walked to the front door and knocked. After a long wait, the door opened. Mark hadn't known what he was expecting, but the woman standing in the barely opened door was a surprise. She was dressed in a grubby overall and had a cap on her head.

Yes?'

Mark felt himself blush. 'I'm sorry to bother you but I'm trying to trace someone.'

'Miss Pritchard's out, been called away.'

'Miss Pritchard?'

'The warden.'

Rain was trickling down Mark's neck, but from the look on the woman's face he didn't think there was much point in asking to be allowed in.

'When will she be back?'

'How should I know, I'm in the kitchen, Cook told me to answer the door.'

'I'm trying to trace a girl called Alice.'

'Don't know nothing about that.'

'Do you know a Susan?'

'I told you I don't know nothing, I'm in the kitchen.'

'Can I write a letter then?'

The woman shrugged and went to close the door.

'Thank you so much you have been really helpful.'

His last few words were said to the closed door.

Mr and Mrs Martin, Spencer and Alice arrived at The Dorchester at twelve fifty. Stanley had ordered aperitifs while they waited for Alice's mother, Sheila, to arrive. At ten past one, Joan indicated her impatience by looking at her watch. Alice, crimson with embarrassment, said that her mother was not a very good timekeeper. She explained that there were two younger children and maybe there had been an emergency. Perhaps she had tried to ring the restaurant, maybe there had been a delay on the Tube. Stanley had patted Alice's hand.

'Don't worry, I've had a word with the Head Waiter; they will hold the table until half past one. She's bound to be here by then.'

Alice offered up a silent prayer that he would be proved right. She looked at Joan and looked away, her face was like thunder. She knew this would happen. Why didn't she tell Mum to meet them at twelve-thirty? Then they would have stood a chance. At half past one, Joan stood up.

'Well, I for one am not waiting any longer. Stanley, are we going through to our table now or I shall call a taxi and go home?'

The lump in Alice's throat threatened to choke her. She looked for support from Spencer who shrugged his shoulders and stood up. In desperation, Alice turned to Stanley.

'Shall I stay here and wait a little longer?'

'No, my dear, we had better go through and start to order before it's too late. I'll have a word with the receptionist; when your mother arrives, they will bring her through.'

Alice felt tears gather behind her eyes. She could cope with Joan being angry, but the combination of Stanley's kindness and Spencer's disinterest was unbearable. Things had not been the same with Spencer since the dinner party with the Bergmans.

He had denied anything untoward between him and this Berthe woman, but Alice was uneasy particularly as Spencer was leaving for Stockholm in two short weeks. Was it her imagination or was there coolness in his behaviour? She was too frightened to ask. She felt helpless, hurt and at a loss and now this; why couldn't Mum be like other mums?

They walked through to the restaurant with Joan leading the way. She reminded Alice of a ship's figurehead as she cleaved her way to the table indicated by an obsequious waiter. The Head Waiter hovered as menus were distributed and crisp white napkins were unfurled by an underling who then, with much bowing and scraping, placed one on each diner's lap

Alice was shaking so much she could scarcely hold the embossed cover which held the menu, a cornucopia of gastronomic delights. Alice's appetite had withered, but she knew she must make an effort or cause further insult to the already nettled Joan. She wanted to see if there was any sign of Mum, but as her back was to the door, this was impossible.

Her eyes skimmed the menu; it was in French. She blessed her GCE 'O' level which meant she did not have to ask what everything was. She chose melon followed by chicken in a cream sauce and having made her choice shut the menu and left it on the table in front of her. The Martins were arguing the relative merits of oysters and smoked salmon with shrimps. Alice prayed in silence for the ordeal to be over.

Alice noticed Joan looking past her as a frisson of surprise rippled through the restaurant. Alice sensed rather than saw the turning of heads. With a sickening lurch of her stomach, she assumed Mum had arrived. She watched as Joan's expression showed disdain, distaste and finally disbelief. She turned to Stanley who was ordering wine and whispered something that Alice could not hear. Stanley smiled and stood to greet his guest. Alice turned and swallowed hard. In this elegant room full of wealthy, well-dressed people her mother looked as though she was dressed for a hike across Hampstead Heath. Alice felt a surge of anger; why hadn't she made an effort? She had asked Mum to dress nicely, it wasn't fair. At that moment Sheila saw Alice.

'Hello, my darling,' her voice reverberated across the dining room, 'how lovely to see you. It has been far too long.' She bent and gave Alice an extravagant kiss on the cheek. She held out a hand to Stanley. 'You must be Mr Martin, so pleased to meet you. I'm not late, am I?'

Spencer choked on his bread roll and Alice cringed.

'I don't wear a watch, you see; why should I be governed by time?'

'As a courtesy to others.' Joan said.

'Of all God's creatures, only man straps a watch to his wrist so he can account for the passing of minutes and hours. All we need to know is that when it is light, we enjoy the beauty of our surroundings. We should live, love and create new life; when it is dark, we sleep to replenish our souls.'

Stanley broke the stunned silence. 'We are glad you were able to come.'

Sheila took the empty seat, removed her duffle coat and draped it over the back of her chair.

'Allow me, Madam.' The Head Waiter arrived, on silent feet, to stand behind Sheila's chair; he eased the coat away. His expression was unreadable as he held the garment between fastidious finger and thumb before handing it to one of the waiters. A menu was produced as Alice introduced everyone. It can't get any worse, could it?

Sheila glanced at the menu. "It's such a glorious day I thought a picnic would be nice. What do you think? I've just walked across the park; it was a delight. Couldn't it be arranged? It seems a shame to be stuck in a stuffy room when the sun is shining and good fresh air is just outside."

She beamed at everyone around the table. Joan took a cigarette from her case and lit it.

'I don't think we are dressed for such an arrangement.'

Alice felt the air chill.

'Would you like an aperitif while you decide what you are going to have?' Stanley asked.

'How nice but I rarely drink. Do you remember that holiday we had, in the caravan, Alice? I had a glass of cider and became quite tipsy. That was the year we ran out of money and we had to get on the train with no tickets.'

She smiled at Stanley.

'Alec, my husband had to rescue us at the station as the ticket collector wouldn't let us leave. So silly, I gave him my address. Alec had to bring enough money to pay all our fares. It was quite a hoot.'

Alice gave an inward groan; it could get worse.

'Sherry?' Stanley enquired.

'Yes please, not too dry.'

Sheila studied the menu.

'Can you read French? Or would you like me to translate?' Joan's tone implied she had little confidence in Sheila's ability to cope in any way with the social situation in which she now found herself.

'I speak and read French fluently. I lived in Paris for six months and taught English to anyone prepared to pay.'

'You didn't tell us you'd been to Paris, Alice.' Stanley said.

'I haven't.' Alice whispered.

'So where were you whilst your mother was on her travels?' Joan asked.

'She was with my ex-husband's parents, weren't you darling. I just took my son, Anthony. It was a wonderful experience for him and one that Alice would have shared if her wretched father hadn't done his best to keep this girl from me.'

The waiter came to take their orders and Alice blessed the intervention.

Once the waiter had gone Joan returned, like a bull terrier, to the kill.

So, you and your husband were in Paris for six months, on business I suppose. What is his line of work?'

'Oh no, I went on my own with Anthony.'

There was a pause while Joan digested the unexpected reply and the wine waiter gave Sheila her sherry.

'Didn't he mind you going off like that?'

'Why should he, he doesn't own me.'

Joan lit another cigarette. 'I imagine your son must have missed his father.'

'Oh, I don't know. Children are very resilient; they cope with most things.'

Sheila drank her sherry too fast for Alice's peace of mind. Please don't let Mum become argumentative.

'Has Alice told you of our suggestion?' Stanley said.

'About coming to live with you?'

'Yes.'

'Thank you for asking, but I would prefer Alice to live with me; I am her mother after all.' Sheila looked at each of the people around the table, daring anyone to object.

'But Mum you know it's difficult with Anthony and Jane and what would Alec say?'

The first courses arrived and conversation was stilled. The same old argument raced around Alice's brain, Mum would never accept that she could not live with Alec and the kids. It would be mayhem – particularly with Anthony.

Alice slowly picked at her melon which was splayed into a fan and garnished with jewel-like berries. The coolness of the fruit calmed her fevered mind as she let each spoonful rest on her tongue before chewing. She glanced at her mother who was spooning soup into her mouth; she was responsible for the slight slurping sound, Alice hoped she had imagined. What must Joan think?

'It's a long time since I ate out,' Sheila said between mouthfuls of soup, 'but the prices here are exorbitant. Do you realise a poor Indian family could live for a year on what this meal will cost?'

Spencer and Joan exchanged glances.

'I sponsor two Indian children you know. Most people in the western world eat far too much, pure gluttony most of it.' She spread her arms wide to encompass the whole restaurant. 'I don't suppose any of these people have ever known a single pang of hunger.'

There was a disapproving murmur from the nearest table and Alice realised that other diners were listening and hard glances were being directed towards them. Spencer choked on his spaghetti carbonara which was his substantial first course.

You seem to have a very healthy appetite, Spencer; you just hope it doesn't turn to fat.' Sheila smiled at him.

Joan put down her knife and fork and leaned forward. 'I believe that if one works hard, one is entitled to the fruits of that labour.'

'Yes Joan, may I call you Joan?'

Joan opened her mouth, but Sheila ploughed on.

'But if you were working in the fields, all day for the whole of your life, you would never be able to afford a meal like this in such a sumptuous setting.'

An elderly matron with blue-rinsed hair, in an extravagant bouffant style, was sitting at the nearest table. She gave a loud, disapproving tut.

'If I were such a person, would I want or even appreciate what you see before and around you?' Joan said.

'Are you equipped to judge what a poor person would want or appreciate? That seems condescending to me.' Sheila paused. 'I think I should tell you I am a fully paid-up member of the Communist Party. It is my belief all people should be given the same chance to have the best for themselves and their families.'

'I'm sure you are right.' Stanley said. 'In an ideal world we would all prosper and enjoy life however we chose. Unfortunately, it is not an ideal world so we must all do the best we can.'

'How many third-world children do you sponsor?'

'I must confess none at the moment so I am glad you have drawn my attention to such a grievous omission. We will have to do something about it won't we, my dear.' He smiled at Joan whose expression was icy.

Stanley continued, 'Of course, there are other ways of spreading the good things of life.' He smiled at Sheila. 'I like to think I do my bit by providing work for some fifty-odd people. That supports more than fifty when one includes their families. I believe I am a fair employer and pay the best wages the company can stand.'

'Do any of your employees eat here?'

'I doubt it, but if they didn't work for me, they might not eat at all.'

Stanley signalled to the waiters to clear the first course plates away.

While waiting for the main course Spencer talked about going to Stockholm and what he hoped to learn about the business. Alice tried to think of other safe topics, but when Mum was in her present, manic mood that was impossible. She did say a bit about her job, at the hospital, but avoided the subject of rats in case it upset Joan. After that conversation became more and more artificial and laboured.

'I think we should discuss the offer we have made to Alice regarding her coming to live with us.'

Stanley smiled at Sheila.

'I know you have not met us before and are bound to have reservations. Perhaps that is what we should talk about. As a mother who cares for Alice, I know you will want what is best for her. Although we love our two sons dearly, we would have loved a daughter.'

Joan stared at Sheila who had waltzed into a top-class restaurant looking like a bag lady with her hair dragged back into a rubber band for God's sake. And all she could do was sit in judgement on all that she and Stanley represented. How dare she? She indicated to Stanley that her wineglass was empty. She had suspected there was something odd about Alice which was hardly surprising when you met the mother. Who knew what other skeletons were in that family's cupboard?

'Perhaps we should ask Alice what she thinks.' Joan said.

Alice blushed, whatever she said was going to upset someone.

'Mum, I know you want me to live with you, but it wouldn't work. You know what it was like before; that was why I went to live with Dad.'

Sheila bristled.

'It would be worse now you know it would, Anthony and I have never got on.'

'Whose fault is that? If you hadn't gone to live with your father you and Anthony would have sorted out your differences.'

'Would we?'

'He's your brother.'

Alice looked in mute appeal to Stanley.

'There are always problems when families split up,' he said, 'but that is in the past and it is the future, Alice's future we are thinking about now. I promise you we will make sure Alice keeps in touch with you on a regular basis.'

Sheila looked at Stanley and smiled. Joan watched and was both startled and alarmed by the transformation of this strange woman who now looked beautiful. Too beautiful by half, Joan thought, Alice has inherited her mother's eyes and who knew what else.

Sheila placed her hand on top of Stanley's, 'You will look after her, won't you?'

'Of course, trust us.'

Alice's legs felt like jelly. She took a deep breath and felt dizzy with relief or was it the alcohol? The rest of the meal passed in a daze and she realised that she was more than a little tipsy. She concentrated on coping with the chicken without dropping cutlery or in any other way drawing anyone's attention Stanley kept the conversation going by encouraging Sheila to talk about herself.

Joan took great satisfaction in remembering how she had risen above her own very humble beginnings. She didn't have the benefit of an upper-class childhood. Yet this woman, so full of righteous indignation had squandered her chances of comfort – probably through wilful recklessness. Who was she to criticise? What hypocrisy.

At last, the meal was over and a silver tray with a folded bill was presented by the Head Waiter. Stanley, puffing on a large cigar, took the proffered pen and signed his name. Sheila looked puzzled.

Joan said, 'Expense account.'

'What does that mean?'

'It means that Stanley includes this meal as part of his business expenses which he is perfectly entitled to do.'

'How so? Surely this is a social occasion, shouldn't he pay himself?'

Spencer gave a nervous laugh and Joan glared at him.

'Of course, if you would like to pay for what you have had I'm sure that can be arranged.' Joan gave an anaconda smile as Stanley took her hand.

'I'm sure, my dear, Sheila would not want to cause any difficulties.' He turned to Sheila, 'We take this facility for granted. Please don't give the matter another thought; it is a perfectly acceptable method of payment. As long as you have enjoyed the meal and are prepared to lend us your daughter for as long as she cares to stay, we will be both happy and grateful.'

There was nothing more to say and the party stood and left the restaurant. Alice was aware that many eyes followed them as they threaded their way through the tables.

'Can I drop you anywhere?' Stanley asked.

'No thank you I will enjoy the sunshine and fresh air. So much nicer than being cooped up in a car, don't you think.' She smiled at Stanley, kissed Alice and with a cheery wave set off at speed up Park Lane.

Chapter 18

Barbara was tired. Everyone assumed that being a librarian was a peaceful occupation as books can't answer back, but borrowers can. I'm getting older, she thought as she ran a bath, adding a liberal sprinkling of bath salts to the steaming water. She stripped off her clothes and said to her reflection before condensation covered it, 'I deserve a drink.' She padded through to the kitchen and mixed a gin and tonic. Drinking alone was a bad sign according to her father.

'Sod it,' she said, as she took a large mouthful. Returning to the bathroom she balanced the glass on the side of the bath and stepped into the scented water. She lay back with the glass in her hand and felt the stress of a hectic day seep away. She closed her eyes and let her mind wander back to happier days when she and Paul married. That had been a glorious day. Then there was the day Richard was born. She sat up. Perhaps gin was not such a good idea, mother's ruin guaranteed to make you weep. She put the glass down and started washing.

She stopped scrubbing her feet and listened, it was the telephone. Why did people always ring when she was in the bath? She scrambled out, grabbed the towel and sprinted to the phone.

'Hello Barbara, it's Jeffrey.'

She laughed "Sorry I took so long to answer, I was in the bath. It's a good job you can't see me standing here dripping." She waited, expecting a comment, but there was silence.

'Hello Jeffrey, are you still there?'

'Yes, sorry to disturb you, I won't keep you long. I wondered if you would like to go out for a meal sometime, thought we might try the new Italian restaurant on the Kings Road.'

'That would be lovely, when had you in mind?'

'When are you free?'

'Tomorrow or one evening next week maybe.'

'Tomorrow it is. Will seven thirty be suitable?'

'Yes fine, I'll look forward to it.'

Barbara clutched the towel around her and went back to the bathroom, the water had cooled and she couldn't be bothered to get back in. Jeffrey was an enigma. On the surface he seemed confident, bossy in fact. But there was more to him, she felt sure. He was handsome, intelligent and good company yet he was burdened by a sack full of emotional baggage. She knew he was divorced and had a daughter because Gordon had told her, yet when he came for a meal his child was not mentioned. She pulled a comb through her damp hair. She would get him talking tomorrow.

'That woman is extremely odd.'

Stanley nodded his agreement, 'But that is hardly Alice's fault.'

'But it's in the blood; manic depression isn't that what Alice called it, that's a polite word for madness isn't it?'

'I really don't know, but does it alter your feelings about Alice coming here?' After all she seems normal enough.'

Joan thought for a moment. 'You're probably right, but I want it clear now, I'm not having that woman here.'

'I don't think it will be a problem. We'll give the girl plenty of encouragement to see her mother, in her own home. Stanley put his arms around Joan.

'I do think you'll enjoy having Alice here, particularly as Spencer is going away.'

'Have you spoken to Harry yet about working for you?'

'Briefly, he's coming in with me on Wednesday before Gill leaves.'

Joan raised her eyebrows. 'Leaving so soon?'

'Yes, my dear, so soon.'

Joan pulled away from Stanley's embrace. The 'my dear' had sounded

More like an insult than a term of endearment. 'I presume she's got a new job.'

'Apparently, her sister and brother-in-law run a hotel in Bournemouth. She's going down there to help out.'

Joan smiled. That was ideal; not only was Gill going but she was going soon and out of London. That was perfect. She decided to change the subject; it would not do to gloat too much.

'How do you think this thing between Lillian and Harry is going?'

'Very well I hope, I think they are good for each other.'

'But won't they want a place of their own? We've got to think about my parents; they can't be left. Mum isn't going to get any better.'

'We can't let that stand in the way, can we? After all, Lillian has done a hell of a lot over the years. She deserves her happiness.'

'So, what are you suggesting?'

'Nothing yet, it's early days and I can't see Lillian just walking away.'

'I suppose not. Now when is Alice bringing her stuff?'

'Friday.'

'Will she need our help or would it be easier if she gets a taxi?'

'I think she has a large trunk so a taxi would be best.'

Joan stood up; she had an empty brandy glass in her hand. 'I'm having a nightcap; shall I get you one?'

'No thanks.'

Joan knew Stanley was watching her as she walked from the room. She wondered if he was waiting for her to stagger, make a fool of herself, then he would be able to moan about her drinking. With care, she negotiated the coffee table and went through to the dining room. Her hand shook as she poured a generous measure of brandy. She put the stopper back in the decanter and retraced her steps.

'Here's to Gill's departure and Harry's arrival, cheers.' She saluted Stanley and drank.

Barbara checked she was ready for Jeffrey's arrival; he wasn't likely to approve if she kept him waiting. She smiled when she heard the bell and checked her watch, seven-thirty to the second. She hurried downstairs and beamed at Jeffrey as she opened the door. She had chosen a bronze-coloured silk shirt with a brown linen skirt. She had brushed her hair until it shone and used just a touch of makeup. Jeffrey looked startled.

'You look lovely, Barbara, truly lovely.'

Barbara enjoyed the pleasure that compliment gave her and realised she could not remember the last time she had been made to feel attractive, even desirable. She cocooned herself away for too long. She stood aside for him to enter.

'Do you want a drink before we go or have you booked a table?'

I've booked for eight so we'd better go, perhaps we can have a drink after.'

'Why not, I'll just get my jacket.'

She ran upstairs to get the brown linen jacket.

'Right, I'm all yours.' She linked her arm with his as they walked down the street.

The final flourish of summer was over. Window boxes and hanging baskets were past their best and encroaching autumn gave a slight chill to the evening air. Barbara shivered.

'Come here, woman, put that jacket on properly.' He lifted it from her shoulders and held it while she slipped her arms in. Then they walked in companionable silence picking their way through cheerful crowds all intent on enjoying a pleasant Sunday evening.

The Italian restaurant, with the obligatory red and green decor, was busy. Chianti bottles plus candles, encrusted with melted wax dribbles, were much in evidence. The clientele was young and noisy, so were the waiters. Jeffrey and Barbara were shown to the last empty table and decided on spaghetti and red wine. The clatter of plates and the animated chatter of the other diners made conversation difficult but there was ample opportunity for people watching.

Most of the diners were sitting in groups of six or eight. Waiters raced up and down the aisles bearing vast trays heavy with plates piled high with pasta and pizzas. The atmosphere was heady with good cheer, camaraderie and laughter.

'You look very serious.'

Jeffrey jumped as he realised Barbara had spoken.

'Just regret for lost years.' He squeezed her hand and smiled.

The waiter arrived and Barbara gasped at the quantity of spaghetti placed before her.

'If I get through this lot you will have to carry me home.'

'So, who's going to carry me?' They grinned at each other. 'We're just like a couple of kids,' Jeffrey said.

'And quite right too.'

The meal over, they sat back and gazed at each other. Barbara felt there was an intimacy in the look. Jeffrey signalled to the waiter, paid, left a tip and helped Barbara into her jacket. He grabbed her hand and almost dragged her into the street.

'It's a long time since I've felt like this,' he said as he put his arm around her waist. They walked along the road, the metallic click of his heels interspersed with the rapid tap, tap of her high heels. She giggled.

'Slow down, I've got little legs.'

Jeffrey stopped to stare at her. 'Someone else always used to say that.'

Barbara wanted to ask who, but looking at Jeffrey's face decided not to. Jeffrey offered his arm for her to link. She looked at him aware that something had changed his mood, everything was different.

'You'll come in for a coffee or a night cap, won't you?'

'Thank you that would be nice.'

There was a silence that created an uncomfortable void which Barbara tried to fill with talk of work, but the magic had gone and she didn't know why.

Alice had packed her trunk and was waiting for a taxi to arrive. This weekend was Spencer's last one for at least three months. What an irony. One week in the same house was all they would have. Alice checked again the cupboards and drawers, remembering how anxious she had felt when she arrived. It seemed so long ago yet it was only a few weeks. Now here she was embarking on a new life yet again, she felt nervous but for different reasons. Miss Pritchard had been kind and assured her that there would always be a bed available if she needed one. That was a comforting safety net which she hadn't had when she left Dad's. He hadn't replied to her recent letter informing him of her new address, she hadn't expected him to.

There were brisk footsteps in the corridor as well as the heavy tread of a man's feet. Miss Pritchard knocked and entered followed by the taxi driver. He viewed the trunk with disapproval and pursed his lips.

'I'll give you a hand with this,' Alice said grabbing a handle. They walked along the corridor and down the stairs with the trunk bumping against Alice's hip. She wondered how many more times she would have to lug the wretched thing around. Miss Pritchard followed carrying Alice's coat and handbag. While the taxi driver manhandled the trunk into the boot Alice said her last goodbye.

'Don't forget there's always a bed for you even if it's only a camp bed in the corridor.'

Alice grinned, it was a nicer goodbye that Dad had given her when he dumped her trunk and drove off without a word. She sat back in the taxi feeling quite grand. The last time she had been in one she had felt too ill to care about anything, this time she was going up in the world. To have a warm, comfortable bedroom with carpet and central heating would be a joy, no more bed socks and thick jumper in bed. She was contented with her lot even if Spencer would not be there.

By the time she reached Martin's family house in Golders Green, it was dusk. The house looked both grand and inviting. Stanley opened the door and together with the taxi driver lugged the trunk into the hallway. Stanley insisted on paying Alice's fare.

'Welcome to your new home.'

'Leave the unpacking until after we have eaten.' Joan called from the kitchen.

Spencer bounded downstairs, gave Alice a hug and kissed her cheek.

'Hi, good to see you.'

How silly to think he was getting tired of her; it was going to be fine.

Barbara sat drinking her coffee and wondered what it was about Jeffrey that was so intriguing. She had felt sure they would end up in bed after their Italian meal. She wouldn't have objected; she had few hang-ups about sex. It was an expression of feelings, sometimes love, sometimes not but she could not regard it as a sin when two unattached adults chose to indulge their passions. What went wrong? One minute he was dragging her out of the restaurant and the next it was like being walked home by a vicar. He had come in for coffee, but chose to sit in an armchair not the settee. They had made polite conversation and then he left.

She could not recall what had been said before he switched off his feelings. There had been nothing of significance only that he was walking too fast. Was he still screwed up about his ex-wife and there was his daughter too? 'I'm going to find out more about you, Mr Ward, you see if I don't.' She got paper and an envelope.

Dear Jeffrey

Thanks for the meal, your turn to come to me next.

I'm free next Saturday, are you? Give me a ring to confirm arrangements.

Yours Barbara.

It was a nuisance he wasn't on the phone. She looked outside, it was a pleasant evening and not quite dark. She'd walk around and maybe pop in for a drink with Gordon and Anne on the way back.

What is it about council flats, she wondered, they always seem to have a desolate, rundown appearancd. Her footsteps echoed on the concrete stairway. There was a light on in Jeffrey's flat, she hesitated, not sure whether to knock or just push her note through the letter box. The decision was made for her when Jeffrey opened the door.

'What a surprise; what are you doing here?'

'Just delivering your mail,' she handed him the note.

'Come in a moment, I was only going for a walk.'

'I'll come with you if you like or are you the cat that walks by itself?'

He smiled. Oh, I think I could cope with your company.'

She looked around the room while he read her note; everything was tidy but nothing personal like family photos.

He read the note, 'Saturday will be fine. Shall we walk down to the river then along the Embankment and I'll drop you off on the way back.'

'Sounds good.'

They clattered downstairs and linking arms walked in the now deepening dusk. The Albert Bridge was festooned with lights like sparkling diamonds on fine silver chains.

'I love the river at night. Just look at the Moon, I could reach out and touch it.'

Jeffrey stopped. 'Men will go there one day; I wish I could go with them.'

'Why?'

'I would look down on Earth and all mankind's problems would look small and insignificant.'

Barbara squeezed his arm, 'That sounds sad, are you sad, Jeffrey?'

He shrugged and started walking again. Barbara took a deep breath.

'I know you have been married, Gordon and Anne told me, and that you have a daughter. Tell me about her.'

'Not much to tell. She's eighteen and went to live in a hostel after she left me. Now she has moved in with her boyfriend's family. Can't say I approve, but she isn't likely to take much notice of what I say.'

'Why not?'

'Wilful, undisciplined, like her mother.'

'She must have missed you, away in the army. How long was it?'

'Fourteen years.'

'I suppose she was with your ex-wife.'

'Good God no, I got custody. No way was Sheila a fit mother.'

'So where did she go?'

'She lived with my parents for four years, but then Dad died and I had to make other arrangements. Not easy I can tell you.'

'Couldn't have been easy for her, she must have felt like an orphan.'

'I always did my best you know.'

'I'm sure you did but children need stability.'

'That's my point, Sheila was far from stable and that's why the whole burden fell on my shoulders.'

They walked in silence. Barbara considered his last statement. Burden was such a strange word to use, had he thought of his only child as a burden? If so, no wonder the girl had left, a child is for loving. The old familiar pang of loss squeezed her heart; it was not like the first sharp agony but it was still there. She could live with it and accept it without it destroying her peace of mind. We remember the past, she thought, and learn from it but we must not live in it.

'I'd like to meet your girl; does she have a name?'

'Oh,' Jeffrey sounded surprised, 'Alice.'

'I bet she could tell me a thing or two about you, you're such a mystery.'

'Yes, but she wouldn't say anything flattering.'

'Does that worry you?'

'Of course not, she's only a child."

'At eighteen she's nearer to being an adult than a child.'

'You don't understand. My ex. did the dirty on me. She had a child with another man while I was fighting in North Africa. I came back to find her gone. Not only that, she took everything, my furniture, everything and of course Alice as well. Is it any wonder I'm bitter?'

'But Jeffrey it happens all the time. Of course, it must have been dreadful, but you have to go on, make a new life, put the past where it belongs, behind you.'

It was on the tip of her tongue to tell him about her child, but somehow now was not the time. Jeffrey's bitterness would despoil the purity of her memories. She didn't want to be bitter; she wanted to protect those golden days when the two people she had loved most had been her family.

'She made a fool of me.' The anguish made Jeffrey's voice rasp as the words were torn from him, 'I can never forgive that.'

'But my dear Jeffrey, none of that is Alice's fault.'

'No but she looks just like her bloody mother. If she were not my daughter, I would fall in love with her.'

They stopped. Barbara turned towards him and spoke very quietly.

'That is the way to madness and destruction for both of you.'

'I know,' he whispered.

'I think it's time we got back.' In silence they returned to Barbara's flat then Jeffrey walked home alone.

Chapter 19

Tonight, Alice wanted to look her best; Spencer was taking her out for a meal. It was their last evening together as he was off to Stockholm in a few days. She wished she didn't feel so sad; she must put on a brave face and make sure the evening went well. She could do no more. She put on her best skirt and her shantung blouse aware that she had nothing that was fashionable. Her best shoes were low-heeled but, as Spencer said they were walking to the restaurant, they would seem a sensible choice. He had promised a taxi back.

She reflected on this, her first week living in luxury, so different from all she was used to. At first, the heating overpowered her forcing her to open her bedroom window wide or swelter in bed. Spencer had been attentive, too much so, he had crept into her bedroom once Stanley and Joan were in bed. She was frightened by her feelings and terrified that Joan or Stanley would hear them then she would be thrown out in disgrace.

She was in turmoil; her body was taking control. She only had to look at him to feel the heat of desire, the situation was getting out of hand and she didn't feel she could cope much longer. Was this how Susan had felt? Perhaps it was a good thing Spencer was going away it would give them both a chance to cool down.

She went down to the living room where Spencer was waiting.

'You do look nice,' Stanley said.

Joan looked her up and down. He was right she was a very attractive girl when she made the effort. Joan recalled how Sheila had looked when she smiled at Stanley in the Dorchester. Neither mother nor daughter could be called conventionally pretty but there was good bone structure and of course both Sheila and Alice had such beguiling eyes.

'Do you want me to drive you to the restaurant?'

'I don't mind walking, Mr Martin'

'You can if you like Dad.'

'My son is becoming an idle toad, but we can't have your hair ruined by the wind.' Stanley patted Alice on the shoulder. 'Come on it's your last night for a while.'

Joan watched in silence as they left the room.

Susan stretched out on the settee; it was good to be home. Mum and Dad had made such a fuss of her that the pain of the abortion was receding with every day. After long discussions about her future, it had been decided she should enrol at the local college and try to get some qualifications in child care. With some luck she might get in at the start of the September term. At times she wondered if it was a wise choice after all she had destroyed a life; was she a fit person to work with children?

She sighed and had another look at the letter from Mark, which she had received that morning. It had been enclosed with a letter from Miss Pritchard which explained that it had not been possible for her to pass on Susan's address to him, only Susan could do that. On the back of the letter from Mark had put his name and address, somewhere in Manchester. Susan was not sure what she wanted to do. The first time she read Mark's letter she, screwed it up and threw it in the waste bin. She didn't want to be reminded of what she had been through.

Miss Pritchard's letter explained why Mark had called at the hostel. He wanted to trace her and another girl. He had been turned away by one of the kitchen hands who had only remembered Susan's name. Before she even read Mark's letter, she knew it was Alice he wanted to contact, not her. She unfolded the letter and reread it.

Mark had got a new job near his home in the North West. He hoped Susan was fully recovered. If she had left the hostel, his letter would be forwarded. Then it came to the important bit. Had Alice been a resident at the hostel? He was unsure. Was Susan still in contact with her, if so, would she forward Alice's address? He explained about the meeting that didn't take place. Susan had been surprised, as Alice had claimed she always arrived early for a date. What had happened? He must be keen to go to so much trouble.

'You're looking very serious, poppet.' Mr. Johnson sat down on the settee with a groan. 'Not as young as I used to be.' He put his arm around his daughter, 'Nothing wrong?'

Susan folded the letters quickly and smiled at him. 'No everything's fine.'

He looked at her. 'I wonder if we only appreciate what we have when we come close to losing it?'

Susan wondered if her dad realised what he had said. She did lose it, her baby, by her own actions. Silence clogged the air, poor old Dad, he didn't mean any harm. She must tell him about the letters, maybe ask his advice.

After the taxi driver was paid Spencer and Alice ambled up the path. Her feet didn't seem to be in contact with the ground, it had been a relaxed, intimate, romantic evening. If she didn't think about Friday, maybe it wouldn't come. They walked into the living room where Joan and Stanley were sitting.

'Had a good time, kids?' Stanley asked.

'Oh yes, it was wonderful.' Alice sat down, her body was boneless, she was floating. It was difficult to make her eyes focus so she closed them. It was a mistake as the room started to swirl and lurch from side to side. She felt the colour drain from her face and perspiration beaded her forehead. Joan watched her.

'I think I'd better go upstairs,' Alice said.

Joan saw Stanley give Spencer a knowing wink as Alice struggled to her feet.

'Take her up, lad, she might lose her way.'

Spencer grasped Alice's elbow and steered her around the furniture. So, it's amusing for Alice to come back sloshed, Joan thought, she clicked her tongue in annoyance.

'I suppose she's not used to alcohol; she'll be all right.'

Joan didn't bother to reply.

Upstairs Spencer helped Alice into her room. She clung to him fearful she might fall.

'Shall I help you get undressed?'

Alice opened her eyes wide with alarm and clamped a hand over her mouth. 'What would your mother say?' she whispered.

Spencer shrugged, 'I'd better go down.' He turned then came back, put his arms round her. 'Am I going to get a good night kiss?'

She pursed her lips and closed her eyes, clung to him as the room started to spin again.

'No,' he whispered, 'I want a proper kiss, later.'

She opened her eyes and looked into his. What could she say, was this the right time? He was going away and there was the Berthe woman in Stockholm. She thought again of Susan and what had happened to her; it was a sobering thought.

'I don't know, Spencer, I just don't know.'

'I've got some Durex, please Alice.'

He put his arms around her, his grip even tighter and kissed her hard. She heard footsteps coming up the stairs and pulled away.

'You must go,' she whispered.

Spencer turned to leave as Joan walked past on her way to her bedroom.

'Off to bed, Mum?'

'No, just getting my book.'

'Isn't it downstairs, on the settee?'

'Perhaps it is.'

Alice lay on her bed, this was awful, what was she going to do? She listened as Spencer and Joan walked downstairs. Perhaps it was all her fault and it would have been better if she had stayed at the hostel. Everyone knew that young men put pressure on girls, Spencer couldn't help it and he was going away. But men didn't want to marry easy girls and if she did what Spencer suggested, she would be easy, wouldn't she?

She decided to get undressed, clean her teeth and go to bed. She would feel better after a good night's sleep. As she walked across the landing and heard Joan's voice.

'Don't forget, Spencer, while that girl is in our house, we are responsible for her.'

Alice stood and listened to a low buzz of conversation between Spencer and Stanley, something about work and Stockholm. Feeling guilty at eavesdropping she scuttled into the bathroom, soaped her face, did her teeth and hurried back to her room. She heard footsteps and felt her body tense, it was Spencer.

'See you in the morning, Mum, Dad, goodnight.'

Alice clenched her fists and hoped hard that Spencer would not come in; she was not ready. Minutes passed and the noise of people moving about got quieter. Alice relaxed. She heard Stanley call downstairs something about locking up so Joan was not going to bed yet. Alice felt glad. Spencer wouldn't do anything with his mother still awake.

Joan looked at her watch, twelve o'clock and her eyes were closing. Perhaps the last brandy, after Stanley went upstairs, had not been such a good idea. She wanted to be alert. It didn't matter if she were late to bed as she could always lie in when the others went to work. Spencer was so obvious. Did he really think she didn't know what he was up to? She was sure she had heard moving about on a couple of occasions, but it might have been someone in the bathroom. She wondered what she would do if she heard noises coming from Alice's bedroom. She hoped she had spiked

Spencer's guns and he would accept seduction was not on the menu tonight.

She closed her book. All things considered, it was as well Spencer was going away. She and Alice would have to do some very serious talking. She turned out the lights and went upstairs; she paused at her bedroom door. There was nothing to stop her from checking on her own son, she peered around his bedroom door. Moonlight was streaming through a gap between the curtains. She tip-toed to the window and pulled the curtains together. The heavy breathing suggested that Spencer was deeply asleep.

Alice jumped with alarm and Spencer clapped his hand over her mouth before she could make a sound. She stared at the clock, on her bedside table, it was three o'clock in the morning.

'What are you doing?'

'Ssh,' he whispered, 'move over, let me get in.'

'Your Mum and Dad might hear.'

'Not at this time. Mum will be dead to the world and Dad wouldn't say anything.'

Her sleep had been so deep, she now felt drugged and stupid. Her head was throbbing and she had a stale, unpleasant taste in her mouth. This was like the repulsive business with Jim. Love was supposed to be hearts and flowers and gentleness, not all this grunting and hot breath. Spencer was trying to devour her, his tongue invading her mouth like a surgeon's swab cleaning a wound, pressing, probing until she felt she would choke. His body was heavy against hers and then he was on top of her pressing her down. She felt his penis, hard and hot, pulsating against her abdomen.

'Please, Spencer,' she whispered, 'please don't. I'm frightened.'

'What is there to be frightened of, I love you don't I? And I'm going away; you'd do it if you loved me.' His whisper was harsh and hot in her ear. 'Show me that you love me, come on, Alice, please.'

She felt her body go rigid with terror. All she could see, behind closed eyelids, was blood, oceans of blood and Susan slumped, ashen-faced, on the floor. The butcher's shop smell of congealed blood which swamped Susan's hostel bedroom filled Alice's nostrils again. Nausea pushed against her throat and she retched.

Spencer stopped. In the gloom, she could see his face, his eyes and mouth dark holes, like a death mask. She felt tears on her cheeks.

'What's the matter?'

'I told you I'm frightened.'

He clicked his tongue and Alice felt like a stupid child who had annoyed a grown-up. He lay beside her and she felt his hand moving up and down. He groaned and grabbed her hand. 'Just hold it; you're driving me crazy.'

She placed her fingers around the stiff, hot, hateful thing. How can women want this inside them, letting it thrust deep into their most secret, delicate place?

'Quick, help me with this.' He held the sheath and pushed it on. 'Roll it down quickly, you'll be all right. I promise I'll be gentle and I won't hurt you.'

Alice felt paralysed; she could not escape, there was nowhere to go. He guided her hand and clasped it onto the rolled sheath.

'Roll it down for God's sake.'

Terrified, she rolled the rubber down until she felt coarse, harsh, pubic hair against her hand. He checked it was in place and groaned as he rolled on top of her. He tried to force her legs apart but she could not, dare not relax. He thrust against her, his breath rasping in her ear.

'Please, Alice.'

'I can't,' she sobbed, 'I can't, it's wrong.'

Without warning, he rolled off her and though he lay beside her he was no longer with her. Without a word, he sat up and fumbled with his pyjamas. He walked on silent feet from her room leaving her limp with despair. Tears coursed down her face. Was it always like this, she wondered, was romantic love just make-believe?

She lay listening for any sounds. She thought Spencer had gone into the bathroom and then she heard the toilet flushing. There was the sound of footsteps going past her room and into Spencer's then a conclusive click of his bedroom door. She pulled the covers over and turned to the wall using her pillows to stifle her sobs.

Chapter 20

'I meant what I said you know.'

'What about?'

'Meeting Alice.'

Barbara watched as Jeffrey squirmed. She had been shocked by what he said last week and wondered if she should cancel the invitation for him to come for a meal. But what had he confessed to? He hadn't actually done anything; he only said how desirable he would find Alice if she were not his child. He wasn't the first man to feel like that.

'Why the interest in my daughter?'

'I'm not sure, but she sounds to have had quite a lonely time; maybe I could be a friend. If Sheila is so unreliable perhaps the girl needs an older woman to confide in. Women and girls do that.'

'Apparently, she's got her boyfriend's mother. Do you realise I haven't even met the people she's living with? Met the boyfriend and can't say I was impressed.'

'What father is impressed with his daughter's choice of mate? Isn't it a case of poacher turned gamekeeper?'

'Perhaps so.'

'My parents were less than impressed with Paul.'

'Who's he?'

'Who was he, he was my husband.'

'I didn't know you had been married.'

'You haven't given me much chance to tell you a lot about myself.'

'I hope my disclosures haven't been a burden for you.'

Barbara laughed.

'I'm sorry; I didn't mean it like that.'

'What a prickly person you are, I can see I'm really going to have my work cut out with you.' She smiled as she stood up. 'Better check it isn't going to be burnt offerings to go with your sackcloth and ashes.'

Jeffrey followed her to the kitchen. 'I'm sorry. You know I don't mean to be a pompous ass, perhaps living on my own is to blame.'

He watched her for a moment. 'Anything I can do?'

'Open the wine, food won't be long.'

'I'm not very good at this.'

'What opening wine bottles?' Barbara raised her eyebrows.

'No, offering a sympathetic ear. You know you can always talk to me about…well…you know…your past, if you want to.'

'The past is a funny thing, you can't get rid of it and, if you let it, it can bugger up your future. I'm selective about my past. I want to cherish the good times and push the pain and grief into a corner of my mind where it will do no harm.'

'Did you have good times with Paul?'

'Oh yes.'

'So, what went wrong?'

Barbara watched as Jeffrey's face flushed with embarrassment.

'You don't have to say if you don't want to,' he said.

She looked at him and wondered how often in the past he had expressed an interest in another person's life.

'Let's eat first and I'll bare my soul afterwards.'

Jeffrey smiled and carried the wine through to the table.

The television murmured quietly in the corner and Joan sighed, another evening with little conversation, but plenty of time to think. She had said nothing about her suspicions regarding Spencer's intentions on Thursday night. She did notice how subdued both he and Alice had been on Friday. Stanley had noticed nothing, but then he never did. Now Spencer was in Stockholm she could breathe a sigh of relief.

She wondered how much company Alice would prove to be; she had hardly spoken all evening. She spent far too much time in her room or, when she was downstairs, had her head in a book; it wouldn't do at all. Perhaps the girl was overawed by the improvement in her lifestyle. Having seen most of Alice's belongings it was clear not much was spent on clothes. It would have to change if Alice was to be one of the family, she would have to look the part. They would go shopping together and have lunch afterwards. She glanced across at Stanley who was sprawled in his armchair, asleep

'Alice,' she said quietly, 'get me a brandy, it's in the dining room.' She held out her empty glass.

Alice put her book down and also glanced at Stanley, she wondered if Joan would have made the request if he had been awake. In the short time she had lived with the Martins, she had observed the constant battle of wills between Stanley and Joan, a battle centred on her drinking. Alice was in a difficult position; her accommodation was of the grace and favour variety and depended on her not upsetting anyone.

In order to please Joan, she would cause Stanley concern. She did not want to upset Stanley, she liked him, but she feared Joan more. Very quietly she left the room and poured what she hoped was an acceptable measure of Courvoisier.

Returning to her seat she faced the television, but her thoughts were elsewhere. Neither she nor Spencer had made any reference to his failed seduction. It was so unfair; he was behaving like a spoilt brat. If only she had someone to talk to. Everyone knew men didn't marry girls they slept with so that must mean he had no intention of marrying her. She was all right to be used and then discarded when a suitable virgin came along; she wondered if the dreaded Berthe was a virgin. He didn't respect her feelings therefore he didn't love her, Alice's heart ached.

Stanley stirred and sat up. Joan watched as his eyes went to her glass. She smiled at him and knew he would say nothing.

'I've been thinking Stanley, Alice says she has a day's holiday owing to her. I think I should take her shopping to pick out some suitable clothes.'

'That seems a good idea, what do you think, Alice?'

'I do need some new things.' There's only one problem, she had very little money and Joan was bound to take her to expensive shops.

'You could do with a decent suit and a few dresses.'

Alice looked at Joan in alarm. She was saving money now she didn't have to pay her hostel rent, but she didn't have enough to buy all the things Joan was suggesting.

Stanley laughed. 'Don't worry. We'll give you an early Christmas present, some money to help with the shopping expedition.'

Alice grinned. Joan watched, that smile would get Alice a long way.

Barbara and Jeffrey were sitting on the settee, one at each end. Barbara had removed her shoes and lounged against the cushions. Despite the space between them, the atmosphere was relaxed if not intimate. Mellowed by wine and good food, Barbara watched and waited to see if Jeffrey was prepared to probe a little into her past.

'You know I said to Gordon that I couldn't understand why you had never married; does he know about Paul?'

'Oh yes, but he's very discreet. Perhaps he thought I might not want to tell you but there's no secret about it.'

'I think Paul must have been a very foolish man,' Jeffrey stopped for a moment, 'to allow himself to lose you.'

Barbara smiled, 'Maybe, maybe not, anyway he's happy now.'

'How do you know that?'

'Perhaps I'm just assuming, but he looked happy the last time I saw him. He's remarried and his wife's expecting a baby.'

Barbara swallowed hard; this was always the difficult bit. 'You see our child died.'

She heard Jeffrey gasp, but he didn't speak.

'I had a very bad time having Richard and I was told I should not attempt to become pregnant again.'

'My dear Barbara I am so sorry. I've blathered on about myself; I had no idea.'

Barbara went to her bedroom returning with the silver photograph frame. Jeffrey drained his glass and stood.

'I'm imposing on your grief and that is unforgivable.'

Barbara turned the frame to show a chubby-faced, smiling child with golden hair.

'This is Richard. The picture was taken when he was three, just before the accident.'

'What happened?'

'It was a road accident.' Barbara worked at keeping her voice flat and even, all feelings squashed out.

'He'd gone to the park with his father and it was on their way back. They'd been playing football and Richard was bouncing the ball on the pavement, but it rolled into the road.' She paused. 'The driver didn't see him.' She drank some wine and heard the glass clink against her teeth.

'When did it happen?'

'Seven years ago, he'd have been eleven now.'

Jeffrey put his glass down and took Barbara's hands in his. She noticed his face was drained of colour. Perhaps he is not as tough as he would have her believe.

'Paul was distraught, we both were. But he could not deal with his feelings of guilt and my grief. You see my tears were like daggers in his soul. He blamed himself and went over and over it, if only, if only.'

'But it was his fault.'

'Jeffrey, what has fault got to do with it? Would it have given Richard an extra day of life? It happened. Wishing and hoping will not change that.'

'Is that why you divorced him?'

'Because of the accident? No. We realised we would destroy each other if we didn't separate, that was the only way. So, we parted and waited the appropriate length of time and divorced each other.'

'And now he's married again, another child on the way. It's wicked for him to get away scot-free.'

'Has he? He still has to live with himself.'

'What has he left you with?'

'Memories, happy memories, I wanted to be a mother and I was. For me, it was only a short time, but they were golden days. Now I have a different life, I'm not unhappy it's just different from what I expected.' She shrugged and stood up. 'That's quite enough of me let's get this table cleared.'

Alice tore open the envelope, it was a letter from her father and as always it was to the point. He expected her to go to his flat for lunch on Sunday in two weeks. They would be eating at one o'clock. She had not expected to hear from him never mind be asked to visit. She must reply, by letter, and tell Stanley and Joan.

Today was the day Joan was taking her shopping and Alice

viewed the expedition with trepidation. Supposing Joan suggested things she didn't like; would she dare to make alternative suggestions? She checked her Post Office Savings Book. She had twenty-seven pounds which was hardly a fortune. Stanley had given her another twenty, what a nice man he was.

She pondered on how different life would have been if Dad had been more like Stanley maybe Mum and Dad would not have divorced. She reflected on the relative difficulties of being a husband to Joan or Mum, in their different ways there was not much to choose between them.

Joan was calling so Alice quickly gathered her savings book and purse and hurried downstairs.

'We'll go to Oxford Street there's so much choice there then we'll have some lunch.'

Once in Joan's car, they headed for town. Alice wondered if it would have been easier to go by Tube then there would have been no problem with parking. She suspected Joan found public transport beneath her.

Alice found being driven by Joan an alarming experience; at best her driving was flamboyant. The Ford Anglia swept in and out of the traffic and Joan's patience evaporated as they cruised around trying to park. With an air of triumph, Joan careered into a space in a back street just off Oxford Street.

'Will it be all right here?'

'Of course, we're off the main road.' Joan slammed the door shut and locked it.

'Now you have Selfridges, John Lewis, then Dickens and Jones. We'll go to a nice restaurant for lunch; might as well make a day of it.'

Alice was overwhelmed; the big department stores had a magic about them associated with wealth and privilege to which she had no access in her own right. For entirely different reasons neither of her parents would consider entering places like this. Yet for Joan it was a normal part of life.

The morning passed in a flurry of dressing, undressing and staring at herself in mirrors. Agreeing with Joan when she wasn't sure, sounding unsure when she didn't like the garment under appraisal. I should be enjoying this, she thought, if I can't choose what I like what's the point? After traipsing up and down from one store to another, they agreed enough was enough.

Alice now had a dark blue suit with a straight skirt and a shawl collar, a pink tweedy, short-sleeved dress and a full-skirted dress in dark green with a wide belt. Joan had treated her to a pair of plain black, court shoes with slender, high heels – higher than Alice had ever had before. Joan had bought herself an elegant maroon dress and jacket with a turban-style hat and gloves to match. Those items were put in Stanley's account. Poor Stanley, Alice thought.

They walked back to the car to find a parking ticket under the windscreen wiper. Alice said nothing while Joan ranted and raved and strode up and down wanting to know who had done such a monstrous thing. In the end, she accepted the inevitable with very bad grace indeed, wrenched the ticket from the windscreen and flung it on the back seat of the car.

'What are these fools trying to do? They'll kill the trade in the West End if people can't drive in to shop. It's an absolute disgrace, how dare they?'

Alice slid into her seat and clutched her carrier bags. If only she could disappear. People passing had watched Joan's initial outburst and now with an ear-splitting crunch of gears, the car shot backwards and stopped with a jolt. There was a tinkle of broken glass and Joan swore as she yanked the wheel around, crashed into first gear and shot forward to pass the car in front. People stared and gesticulated while Alice stared out of the window – not daring to catch anyone's eye.

'Get me a cigarette, they are in my bag on the back seat.'

Alice leaned across got a cigarette from the silver case and lit it with the matching silver lighter. Her hands were shaking. They crawled down Oxford Street, turned into North Audley Street, past Grosvenor Square and Brook Street to arrive at an Italian restaurant.

Joan seemed unperturbed by the incident which had left Alice mortified. She wondered how much damage Joan had done to the car she hit and how could she just drive off. Suppose someone had taken her registration number, supposing the police were told a younger woman had been in the car with her. Would she be regarded as an accessory to a traffic offence, should she tell Stanley? She felt sick.

'Come on girl, get a move on.' Joan was waiting to lock the car door. Having secured the car Joan set off at speed towards the hotel entrance and Alice had to run to keep up with her.

Once inside Joan accosted the first waiter she saw. 'A large brandy, please then a table for two.

'I'm sorry, Madam, the restaurant has stopped taking luncheon orders.

It's after two p.m.'

'Just get me a brandy then.'

'Are you a resident, Madam?'

Joan swelled with rage. 'I am Mrs Martin and my husband and I regularly use this hotel for meals and accommodation for our business colleagues when they visit London. We have recommended your restaurant many times however that can be changed, get me the manager.'

The waiter rolled his eyes and scuttled off. Alice stood still and gazed into the distance aware of people in the foyer, staring and talking behind their hands. Joan lit another cigarette from the stub of her last.

A large, genial-looking gentleman approached with the frightened waiter in tow.

My dear Mrs Martin so good to see you, I believe we have a

slight difficulty, but nothing that we cannot sort out,' he glanced at Alice, 'for you and your young friend.'

Joan nodded and waited.

'Now if you would like to follow me, we can take you to a private room where we will provide a light luncheon, a selection of sandwiches followed by gateau and coffee.'

He bowed and smiled as he clasped and unclasped his hands, he reminded Alice of Uriah Heap. They were taken to a room with comfortable chairs and low coffee tables.

'I'll have a large brandy,' Joan said and turned to Alice, 'what do you want?'

'A lime and lemonade, please.'

The manager and waiter departed at speed leaving Joan and Alice in a heavy silence. Alice waited for Joan to speak, to explain or justify what she had done to someone's car. Joan drew hard on her cigarette. When the waiter appeared with drinks, she took a large mouthful of brandy.

'You have to let these people know you won't be messed about.'

Alice nodded, sipped her drink and waited.

'Do you like the things you've bought?'

'Oh yes, they're lovely and I am so grateful you helped me choose. I couldn't have managed on my own. And the shoes, they will go with everything. Thank you ever so much.'

'Don't say 'ever so' it sounds common.'

Alice blushed and stared into her glass. She remembered Grandma Cardew correcting the way she spoke; that had been years ago. She'd been a lady but Joan wasn't a lady, she was horrible. She didn't think she would ever like Joan.

The food arrived, a plate ladened with dainty, triangular sandwiches, minus crusts. Alice realised she was very hungry.

'Another brandy, please waiter.'

He took the glass and left. Alice glanced at Joan and felt a quiver of anxiety, she was being driven home by this woman and surely it could not be wise to drive after so much alcohol. She dared not say anything and picked up the plate of sandwiches. Perhaps it would make things better if she could encourage Joan to eat something, to soak up the brandy, but Joan wrinkled her nose.

'They do look nice,' Alice said.

Joan took two but lit another cigarette. Alice sighed and started eating as there was no point in wasting them. The waiter reappeared with the brandy, bowed and shuffled away.

'Has your mother always been so strange?'

Alice swallowed hard.

'Stanley said he thought her very odd.'

Remembering the meal at the Dorchester, it struck Alice that Stanley had accepted Mum with less difficulty than Joan, but there was no point in saying so.

'She was very ill some years ago and had to have brain surgery. I think it was called a lobotomy. I don't think they do it anymore; it changes people's personalities too much. She used to be all right.' She couldn't tell Joan that Mum had always been alarming.

Joan nodded and ate one of the sandwiches. So far so good, Alice thought, eat the other and she'd offer the plate again.

'These are good, smoked salmon I think.'

'Are you hoping to marry my son?'

Alice felt her face redden. 'I don't know; we haven't talked about it. Perhaps we are a bit young yet.'

'You have to be so careful with mental problems.'

Alice stared at Joan. There could only be one explanation for that remark, hands off my son because your Mum's barmy. What had kids yelled at her and Anthony as they walked to school? 'Your

Mum's in the loony bin'. The sandwich she was eating turned to sawdust in her mouth and she blinked back tears.

Joan tapped a cigarette on her case and watched Alice's reaction. She lit the cigarette and smiled.

'Have some gateau,' she said.

But Alice was no longer hungry, she shook her head. What did anything matter when she had her mother, like an albatross, around her neck?

'Coffee?' asked Joan.

'Yes please, shall I pour you a cup?'

If Joan wouldn't eat, perhaps coffee would ensure that they both got home in one piece. Alice watched as Joan drained her brandy glass and hoped she would not order another.

The manager appeared. 'I hope everything is satisfactory, Madam.'

Joan gave a brief nod, 'Would you bring the bill, please.' The manager turned, clicked his fingers and the waiter appeared on cue. Placing the silver tray plus bill on the coffee table he dipped his head low to Joan and waited.

Joan glanced at the bill and extracted a note from her wallet. 'Keep the change.'

'Thank you, Madam. We hope to see you and Mr Martin again soon.' He bowed low and left. Joan drained her coffee cup and stood. She stared at her reflection in the large, gilt-framed mirror; she patted her hair and smoothed her skirt. Alice scrambled to her feet and followed as Joan swept out.

Back in the car park Alice saw that the car's rear lights were broken and there was a nasty dent in the bumper. She didn't tell Joan. They set off and were soon in heavy traffic on Edgware Road. At least when it's this busy they had to go slowly.

Once past Lords' Cricket Ground and on to the Finchley Road the traffic thinned and Joan gained speed. Alice could not believe how close Joan got to other cars without touching them and seemed oblivious to hooting horns and irate drivers who caught up with her at lights and gesticulated their annoyance. Any conversation could cause a life-threatening distraction so Alice closed her eyes and said nothing.

As they turned into the Martins' drive Alice wondered if her legs could still hold her upright. She struggled out of the car with her shopping.

'Let me carry yours in,' Alice said as Joan scrabbled in her bag for the front door keys. She had left the driver's door open and the keys in the ignition. With a sigh, Alice went in and closed the door.

Chapter 21

Susan showed her father the letters from Miss Pritchard and Mark. He scowled.

'Is this the man responsible for…'

'Oh no, Dad, he was really good he contacted Tony and told him that he must help me.'

'I'd like to meet that young man.'

'Who, Mark?'

'Well yes, he sounds a decent bloke. No, it's Tony I'd like to meet; I'd knock his bloody block off.'

'I was the fool, Dad; Tony just took advantage of my stupidity.'

Yes, well…' Mr Johnson put his arm around Susan and hugged her. She felt safe and loved. All the irritation that used to explode in her head whenever her parents told her anything had vanished.

'So, Mark wants to contact this girl, Alice, wasn't she the one who found you?'

'Yes, I should have written to her, I said I would.'

'Then do it, she's at the hostel isn't she?'

'As far as I know.'

'Why not give her a ring now.'

Susan dialled the number and listened as the phone rang and rang. She liked Mark and felt jealous of Alice, so plain and ordinary, with rubbish clothes and no money. Why couldn't Mark have liked me, she thought? At first, she had thought she would not bother to contact Alice or pass on Mark's letter, but now she had confided in Dad, she had no choice. Just as she was about to ring off, she heard a voice.

'Baron's Court Hostel, Miss Pritchard speaking.'

'Hello, Miss Pritchard it's Susan, Susan Johnson. Thank you for the letter, but it isn't me Mark Ogden wanted to contact it is Alice, Alice Ward.'

'I see. There's a slight problem as Alice has moved out. But I do have her address. As you know Hostel Trust rules do not permit me to pass on any resident's new address.'

'If I write to Alice and enclose Mark's letter with it, would you pass on both?'

'Of course, my dear, all part of the service. And by the way, are you fully recovered from your ordeal?'

'Yes, Miss Pritchard, and I'm going to enrol at college.'

'Quite right too, I'm pleased to hear it, I wish you every success.'

Susan sat in the living room; she would write to Alice that evening. Her father smiled and suggested going to the post box when she'd finished.

Stanley walked into the kitchen, 'What's happened to your car?'

'Some stupid sod boxed me in, had the devil's own job to get out.'

'You do realise the bumper is going to have to be replaced and you'll need a new off-side light.'

Oh.' Joan continued preparing the evening meal.

'You'd better not drive it again until it's fixed.'

'How long will that take?'

'I'll ring the garage first thing; they'll probably come to collect it.'

Alice heard Stanley's heavy footsteps on the stairs; she was sitting on her bed writing a note to her father accepting his invitation for a meal. Stanley tapped on her door.

'Can I come in?'

'Yes, of course.'

'Must have been a nasty bump you had.'

Alice knew Stanley was watching her, she wondered how much Joan had told him.

'It was a bit difficult for Mrs. Martin to get out and I think she was annoyed about the parking ticket.' From his reaction, she knew he hadn't been told about that.

'What did the other driver say?'

'The car was just parked, there was no-one in it.'

Stanley loosened his tie and leaned against the chest of drawers. 'This is awkward but I must ask; had she been drinking?'

'No,' Alice paused. 'Not then…'

'I see.' Stanley turned and went downstairs.

Alice remained in her room; she didn't want to be with Joan. She shouldn't have come here; it has all been a dreadful mistake. The awful night with Spencer wouldn't have happened if she had stayed at the hostel. Now she would be piggy in the middle between Stanley and Joan, she could not face food; she felt sick. She listened to voices downstairs in the kitchen, the conversation sounded tense though she could not make out exactly what was being said.

'Your meal's ready,' Joan shouted.

'I'm sorry,' Alice called down the stairs, 'but I don't feel very well, I don't think I could eat anything.'

There was no reply from Joan and Alice lay on her bed and stared at the ceiling. Perhaps she should write to Spencer. He had already sent a letter to his parents perhaps he was waiting for her to make the first move. Perhaps she should apologise and tell him she really did love him and would prove it when he came home at Christmas. She became aware that now there was a row going on downstairs. She heard her name among a stream of otherwise unintelligible invective. In the brief pauses, she caught the lower tones of Stanley trying to placate his incandescent wife. She heard the kitchen door bang followed by the clanging of saucepans. What should she do? She didn't want to be dragged into a screaming match.

There were footsteps on the stairs and Alice prayed it wasn't Joan. For the second time, Stanley tapped on her door.

'You'll gather from the racket that Joan isn't in a good mood.'

'I'm sorry; I suppose it's my fault.'

'Not entirely although she's taken exception to your refusing to eat.'

'I didn't know what to do; she just crashed into the car and drove off. Supposing someone reports her to the police. I was so frightened and she wouldn't eat anything and she had two large brandies and I kept offering her sandwiches and things, coffee, you know to soak up the alcohol. I didn't want her to have another accident. What could I do?' Alice drew a shuddering breath.

Stanley sighed. 'I'm so sorry, but do you think you could manage a little? I know Joan can be difficult, but from her point of view she's taken you shopping and she's tired; she's cooked a meal but you don't want it.'

He paused. 'Will you come down and try to eat something; will you do it for me?'

'I'll try.'

Stanley smiled, put his arm around and gave her a quick hug. 'Go wash your face and try to look cheerful, please.'

The atmosphere in the dining room crackled with tension. Stanley complimented Joan on the meal, Alice apologised for causing a delay but Joan said nothing and pushed her food around the plate.

'When am I going to see what you girls have bought?'

'Shall I bring them down after the meal?' Alice looked at Joan.

'And what did you get, dear,' Stanley said, 'I hope something nice caught your eye.'

The tension eased and Alice continued to force down food, swallowing was the problem.

'I managed to pick out some lovely things for Alice and I treated her to a pair of shoes.'

'That was very kind.' Stanley said.

'I've never had such nice clothes.' Alice replied.

'Well, I think a fashion show is in order, don't you?' Stanley beamed first at Joan then Alice.

After the meal Alice offered to clear the table and do the washing up. Standing at the sink she let her mind drift away from the tension that seemed to be a permanent feature of life with the Martins. She must write to Spencer, but somehow her feelings for him had changed. He hadn't written to her yet although he was the one who had behaved badly. She wondered if he was copying his mother.

She thought of Mark and sighed, was it fated that they should not meet again? Was there anything she could do about it, at least say sorry for not keeping the date, would that look too forward, pushy? Perhaps she could call as she knew where he lived. If she just put a note through the door, that way she could write her new address on the note then it would be up to him.

'Is the model girl ready?' Stanley stood in the doorway and winked.

'Two minutes,' she replied.

As she left the kitchen, she watched Joan walk downstairs in her new clothes. Alice smiled. 'Gosh, that looks lovely.'

'Of course, I've got an eye for fashion. Now hurry up and get changed.'

Alice scuttled upstairs, scrambled into the pink dress, turned to hurry back to her bedroom, put on the black high-heeled shoes

Joan bought her. In the seconds it took her to change her clothes she had decided what she would do about Mark. She would go to his house.

She slid her feet into the elegant black shoes and realised it would take time and practice to get used to such high heels; she walked, with great care, downstairs.

'Well, my dear,' Stanley said to Joan, 'you have made an excellent choice, as always. I can see you two girls are going to have lots of fun shopping.'

Joan smiled but Alice felt uneasy for although she smiled, the smile didn't reach her eyes. After several changes of clothes and an avalanche of thanks and appreciation for all that Joan had done for her, Alice felt drained. She tottered upstairs certain she would be expected to wear her new shoes when she went to Dad's for lunch. She would have to spend some time each evening getting used to them.

She lay down on her bed and wondered how Stanley had stuck it for so long. With Mum it was like treading on eggshells and coping with Joan wasn't much different. Alice sighed, she must be positive; she would go to Mark's flat and leave a note. Better do it after work one evening, before Mr Martin went on his next business trip. She would tell them tonight that she had to work late, it would give her an opportunity to deliver the note without any awkward questions from Joan.

Mrs. Ogden collected the post; there was a letter with a London postmark, it was addressed to Mark. She went to the stairs and shouted.

'Letter for you, son, I think it's from that young lady you are trying to find.'

After a thudding of bare feet down the stairs, Mark appeared.

'Don't let this sweetheart of yours see you like this she'd run a mile.'

Mark gave his mother a loud kiss on the cheek and took the letter. It wasn't from Alice.

'It's from Susan.'

'Who's she?'

'The one who had the abortion, remember; I helped her with some money.'

'And what's she got to say for herself?'

'Oh, you know, just saying thank you again and how I would always be welcome, and her parents would like to meet me.'

'That's nice.'

'You don't know her; spoilt rotten she is.'

'What like you?' Mrs. Ogden ruffled Mark's already dishevelled hair.

'She'd better have passed on my letter to Alice otherwise I'll go down all right, to give her a piece of my mind.'

'I'm getting worried about you. This girl is becoming an obsession and that isn't healthy.'

'I know, but I've just got this feeling.'

'Which Alice might not share.'

'Then let her tell me herself, I don't want someone else deciding for her.'

'Fair enough now don't you think you should get ready for work; I don't think turning up in your pyjamas would go down well.'

Alice arrived outside the house, note in hand. She pressed the bell for the top flat and waited; it was cold and dark; she was scared. She decided they must all be out, so she would push her note through the letter box. Then the door opened.

'Well, well, well if it isn't Susan's frigid friend.'

Alice stared. It was the repulsive Jim who lounged against the door frame and leered at her. 'Is Mark in?'

Jim laughed, 'He's left.'

'Have you got his new address?'

'Suppose I have, why should I give it to you? Mark wouldn't like that.'

Alice paused; Mark must be very angry because she didn't turn up. But would he have confided in Jim?

'I don't think he would mind, I was ill you see, so I couldn't meet him.'

Jim watched her.

'I just want to say sorry and explain why I wasn't there.'

Jim straightened up and grasped the door latch. 'Well tough luck because I don't know where the hell he is and do you know what, I don't bloody care.' He closed the door in her face.

Alice stood for a moment, it was fate, they would not meet again. She tore the note into small pieces and pushed them through the letter box; let Jim clear up the mess.

The journey home to Golders Green was horrible, as usual, and when she arrived, she found Joan on her own.

'Letter for you and it isn't from Spencer.'

Joan passed the envelope over, obviously expecting to be told who it was from. Alice checked the postmark, Baron's Court.

'It's from the hostel, probably from one of my friends there.'

Joan arched her eyebrows. 'By the way, what have you got on my husband?'

Alice felt the breath catch in her throat.

'What do you mean?'

'The other night, after we went shopping; I'm not your servant you know. Cooking a meal for you, only to be told you didn't want it. How did my husband persuade you to come downstairs?'

Alice felt her face flush, she had no idea what she should say so said nothing.

'I took you shopping, I chose things for you, I even spent my own money on you.'

'It was just the the car and everything,' Alice paused.

'But it only took a word from my husband and suddenly you were happy to join us. I repeat what have you got on my husband?'

'I don't know what you mean?'

'Are you trying to get off with him? You wouldn't be the first little minx who has tried to ensnare an older man.'

Alice gasped.

'I notice Spencer hasn't written to you yet.'

Alice felt her heart thudding, the woman must be mad.

'I'm very sorry you think I would do such an awful thing. I'm not like that.' She was so angry she was trembling as she went upstairs.

'But I bet your mother is,' Joan shouted after her.

Chapter 22

Alice was pleased to hear from Miss Pritchard, but there were two other letters enclosed one from Mark and one from Susan. After reading both Alice's spirits rose, Mark had been trying to contact her. She sat very still and remembered their one and only meeting, it had seemed so right although she could not say why. He wanted to see her, he isn't angry because she didn't turn up for their date and now, she thought, I have his address. She must write to thank Susan, but she'd write to Mark first.

Her delight at hearing from Mark confirmed she was not in love with Spencer, perhaps she had been in love with the idea of love. Of course, she might not fall in love with Mark either, but she knew he would be a friend and at the moment, perhaps it was all she wanted. She had already written a chatty, sisterly letter to Spencer and wouldn't mind if he didn't reply. At least Joan would be relieved that the romance with her son was over. Alice wondered if she should say so, but with Joan the less said the better.

Alice re-read Mark's letter and smiled, although Manchester was a long way away, they would manage to meet somehow. They would take one step at a time, there was no rush. She wrote to say how much she wanted to meet him and explained about being ill last time. She gave her address but decided not to include the telephone number. She thought it would be best if he didn't phone her.

Stanley had been away for three days and the evenings with Joan had been an ordeal. Twice Alice had been sent to the local off-licence for bottles of brandy. It was fortunate Joan liked watching the television because after the third drink she was not only incoherent she was also confrontational. This was the last evening they would spend alone and Alice breathed a sigh of relief as she walked down stairs.

'When do you go to see your father?'

It was a safe topic; Alice would ask Joan for some advice which was bound to please her.

'On Sunday, I was going to ask you what I should wear.'

Joan smiled and put her cigarette and brandy glass down.

'The suit might be a bit formal.'

Alice nodded.

'But have you got a decent coat? It won't be warm enough to go in just a dress.'

'I've only got the navy one. It's very straight, I'm not sure the green dress would go underneath it, the skirt's so full."

'Wear the pink then, pink goes well with navy. What about shoes?'

'Oh, I must wear the lovely black ones you bought me.'

'Have you a black handbag?'

'Yes.'

'That will be fine.'

'Thank you so much. I do appreciate all that you've done.'

Joan held out her empty glass and Alice went to the decanter for a refill.

Barbara was not sure whether to arrive at the time Jeffrey had given or whether to go early and offer to help. He might view such an offer as a reflection on his ability to cope alone. Sod it, she thought, this is ridiculous. Besides, he was probably feeling nervous and Alice would be too. It would be easier for both of them if there was a third person present. She put on her jacket, picked up her handbag, bottle of wine and the potted plant she had bought. She glanced at her watch; she'd be there by twelve twenty, if nothing else she could set the table.

Barbara knocked at the door of Jeffrey's flat and heard a loud crash and then an exclamation of anger. Seconds later the door was flung open.

'Don't look so harassed, I'll keep out of the way.'

'No, no, come in, it's just that everything's at the critical stage!'

'Well, have a glass of that, to calm you down,' she handed him the wine.

'Then go back to your kitchen, slave!'

He smiled, took the wine and her jacket. She walked into the living room and noticed, with amusement, that the table had been set; she should have known.

'It looks very nice, shall I put this,' indicating the pot plant, 'in the middle?'

'Why not, thanks, it's kind of you.'

He disappeared into the kitchen.

'I hope Alice isn't going to be late.'

'If she's her father's daughter, she would rather die than be late.'

'Well, her mother could never manage it, always late she was, be late for her own funeral, I expect.'

Barbara pulled a face; it was like living with a ghost. He must think about Sheila all the time; an obsession that's what it was. She walked to the window and gazed out, at nothing in particular. It certainly wasn't an inspiring view. Dust-bin sheds, neat and well painted but hardly aesthetically pleasing and a central yard, with washing lines, for the tenants. One or two children were tearing round on home-made carts. They reminded her of Andrew; she turned away and went into the kitchen.

There was a knock at the door.

'Must be Alice,' Barbara said.

'Will you go?'

'I think you should, after all she hasn't met me, it could be a bit of a shock. You go.'

He shot out of the kitchen, muttering. Barbara sighed, how sad to feel like that about your own daughter.

Alice took a deep breath as the door opened. 'Hello, Dad.'

'Good heavens girl, you've grown.'

She blushed, 'I think it's the shoes.'

He had never allowed her to wear high heels, wouldn't have expected it, probably wouldn't approve.

'Come in, child,' he took her coat.

Barbara came to meet her; she held out both hands.

'I'm Barbara, a friend of your father's; I hope we will be friends too.'

Alice felt a great surge of relief; it was going to be all right.

'You must excuse me; I need to go back to the kitchen.'

Barbara rolled her eyes to the ceiling, in mock despair, Alice giggled.

'Now you tell me about yourself. Are you working or still at college?'

'I work at the Middlesex Hospital, I'm a lab technician.'

'That must be interesting.'

'It is, if you don't mind rats!'

'Do you, mind them?'

'They're not my favourite animal and you have to be careful you don't get bitten. The professors I work for are very nice, though.'

'I'm a librarian, at the local library, at least books don't bite.'

'Have you known Dad long? He's never mentioned you.'

'Three or four months, that's all.'

'Come along, food's ready.' Jeffrey raced in with two plates, piled high and dashed back for the third and a gravy jug. He opened the wine and poured two glasses.

'Now, are you going to be able to cope with those stilts you're wearing, if I give you some wine?'

Alice blushed as she walked to the table.

'Don't be an old grouch, Jeffrey. I think she looks very smart indeed. You didn't tell me you had such an elegant daughter.'

Jeffrey frowned and poured out a third glass.

'Come on now, eat up, you don't want it to get cold.'

Barbara's light touch with the conversation made a relaxed atmosphere inevitable. She made them laugh and she encouraged Alice to talk and would not allowing Jeffrey to dominate the conversation. She very gently poked fun at the slightest hint of pomposity. Alice felt more relaxed in the company of her father than she could ever remember. Barbara really was wonderful, she thought, she knows exactly how to handle Dad. I'll have to take lessons.

Barbara and Alice remained seated after their meal as Jeffrey insisted on doing all the washing up. Alice was amazed to see that it was three o'clock. Usually, her father's meals were over in a flash, army training he had always insisted. Alice had always assumed, that if that were the case, the entire British Army must be martyrs to indigestion.

'Once your dad has finished crashing about in the kitchen,' Barbara said, 'we could have a little stroll. I'll show you where I live, it is quite near here. I know your dad's not on the phone, but you could have my number if you like, should you ever needed to contact, him in a hurry.'

'Thank you that would be great.'

She leaned back in the armchair feeling relaxed; she could easily go to sleep. She had been anxious about today yet it had gone like a dream.

'Now then,' Jeffrey said as he wiped his hands on a tea towel, 'how about some fresh air and exercise.' He pointed a finger at Alice. 'You'll get fat, my girl, if you're not careful.'

Well, you shouldn't feed her so well,' Barbara replied. 'In any case we've already decided what we're doing, if you promise to behave yourself, we might ask you to come along too!'

Jeffrey looked at Barbara, about to say something then changed his mind.

'Come on you old bear, get your jacket on.'

Jeffrey did as he was told.

They strolled down the road, Jeffrey in the middle, Barbara on one arm, and Alice on the other.

'This has been good,' he said.

Susan watched her father, such a kind man why had she been so ungrateful?

'Dad.'

Mr Johnson put down his Sunday paper, 'Yes?'

'You know that man who helped me… you know.'

'The one who wrote?'

'Yes, Mark.'

'What about him?'

'I thought it would be nice to invite him here, he wants to meet you and Mum.'

'I can't imagine why he would want to do that.'

'Well, I think he likes me, he must do, to have helped me like he did.

I've got his telephone number, perhaps he could come here next weekend.'

'Ask your mother.'

'But you wouldn't mind?'

'No, can I read my paper now?'

Susan hurried to the kitchen where her mother was cooking the Sunday roast.

'Dad says he thinks it would be a good idea to ask Mark here next weekend.'

'Mark? Oh, he's the one who gave you money; where did you say he lived, Fulham was it?'

'He did, but he's moved to Manchester.'

'Why on earth would he want to come all this way?'

'I just think it would be good to say thank you properly and he's very nice.'

'You can ask if he wants to come for a meal on Sunday though how he'll get here I don't know. Has he got a car?'

Susan didn't bother to answer she rushed upstairs and found her address book. He gave his telephone number as well as his address in the letter. She hurried downstairs and dialled.

'Hello.'

'Mark, is that you?'

'Yes.'

'It's Susan, Susan Johnson; I forwarded your letter to Alice.'

'Thanks.'

'Mum and Dad thought it would be nice if you came down for a meal.'

'That's very kind but it's a long way for a meal. Thank them anyway.'

Susan bit her lip. 'I'm asking Alice too.'

'Oh,' Mark paused, 'it all depends on the trains. I'll have to get back to you.'

'Have you heard from Alice?'

'Not yet.' Mark replied.

Susan didn't really want Alice to come for a meal, but she must ask her now. She paused, she didn't have Alice's address, she would have to write to Miss Pritchard and ask her to send the letter on. If she left it until Wednesday to write, Alice might not receive it until it was too late. It wasn't her fault; Alice should have replied to her letter sooner.

Chapter 23

Jeffrey and Barbara said goodbye to Alice and watched her go down the escalator.

'She's a nice girl,' Barbara said.

'She's got a lot to learn.'

'Haven't we all,' Barbara replied as they strolled away from the station, 'let's walk through St. Luke's gardens.'

'St. Luke's is where I got married.'

As no appropriate comment sprang to mind, Barbara said nothing.

'Her mother and stepfather opposed the marriage. I wasn't good enough, only a working-class boy.'

'That must have made things difficult for you both.'

'They disinherited her.'

'She must have loved you a lot to go against them.'

Jeffrey snorted, 'She had a funny way of showing it. It would have been better for me if she had listened to them and the whole thing had been called off.'

Barbara stopped dead. 'But then you wouldn't have had Alice.'

'Well, she's going to turn out just like her mother. Look at her, no more than a child, tottering along in those ridiculous high heels, waggling her backside in that tight skirt, for all to see.'

He tried to link his arm through Barbara's but she pulled away.

'You really are a sanctimonious, judgmental prig! If this is how you treated Sheila, I am not surprised she sought comfort elsewhere.'

Without a word he walked away, but she grabbed his arm, forcing him to stand still.

'You have a delightful daughter who, I suspect, has had a thoroughly nasty time because you and maybe Sheila as well, have indulged in monumental self-pity.'

'Do you think it's been easy for me?'

'Probably not but you were an adult making your own decisions. What about her? She didn't ask to be born.'

'What can you know about it? I came back after the war to nothing…'

'Yes, Jeffrey, you've told me, but what support have you offered to Alice during the painful transition from child to being a woman? What comfort, understanding and love, for God's sake, have you given her? She's your flesh and blood, Jeffrey.'

'What could I do? I don't know how to deal with a girl.'

'Do you know, the one deep impression she left on me? A gut-wrenching loneliness, coupled with a desperate desire to please, so what do you do, Jeffrey? You criticize.'

'She did look like a tart in those shoes. Am I not allowed to have an opinion?'

'Yes, you are, but you must temper those opinions with love and kindness.'

'So, what did I say that was so awful?'

'If you don't know there is no point in my trying to tell you. But comments that ridicule someone are wrong. She looked lovely and you should have told her so.'

'You mean tell her lies.'

'Jeffrey, you are driving her away. There is only so much any human being can stand. If she finds someone who can appreciate her, love her for what she is, not criticize her for who her mother is, then good luck to her.'

'Have you quite finished?'

'For the time being, yes, I can only hope some of what I said has sunk into that brain of yours; otherwise, my dear, there is no hope for you.'

This time as he turned, she made no attempt to stop him. He strode away, head erect, stiff-legged with impotent rage. He walked past Sydney Street, which would have led to the gardens; he took instead the next turning. She watched as she walked slowly behind him.

'Don't think I will follow you,' she said quietly, 'you have a lot to learn and you will have to learn it on your own.' She wondered how an obviously intelligent man could be so blind. She felt a great weariness as she turned down Sydney Street and entered the gardens. She watched some children in the playground, as she walked past, found a seat facing the massive, austere church. This was where it all began.

Stanley took Joan out for a meal. It had been a pleasant evening; Joan had shown she was glad to have him back. They discussed plans for her sister's wedding, which she would sort out as she was good at such things.

'That will keep you busy, my dear.'

Alice returned at seven looking happy and relaxed.

'Had a good time?' Stanley asked.

'Yes, Dad seemed pleased to see me and I met his new girlfriend. She was great, really great,' she smiled.

'Did he like your new dress and shoes?' Joan asked.

Alice hesitated; it would not be tactful to pass on what he really said.

'He thought I looked very grown up.'

Joan nodded and, not for the first time, wished she were young again.

The telephone rang; it was a call for Stanley from one of his suppliers.

'It's too bad having business calls even on a Sunday,' Joan sighed.

Stanley shook his head, 'Can't make it before Wednesday or Thursday, Eric, only just got back, I'll have to go into the office tomorrow and Tuesday to sort things out. Then I'll get back to you.'

'Good God, he's hardly here before he's off again.' Joan stomped into the sitting room.

Alice decided to put the kettle on, and make coffee for them all. She heard Stanley go into the sitting room and waited for the explosion. She was sick of having to keep out of the way. While she waited for the kettle to boil, she thought about the meeting with Dad. Barbara was so nice and now she had her address and phone number. Alice smiled, she'd call Barbara soon, once all the fuss died down. She wanted to say how pleased she was to have met her. Dad seemed better as well; perhaps that was Barbara's influence. Alice set the tray and carried in the coffee.

'Since you two girls are going to have the house to yourselves on Wednesday and maybe Thursday, why don't I book a table for you, for one of those nights at the new restaurant on Golders Green Road? You know, the French one. After all I'm going to be wined and dined in Manchester. Which would you prefer, Wednesday or Thursday?'

Alice looked at Joan, the decision must be hers. That would mean being in the car after Joan had been drinking. Alice felt a tremor of concern but what could she do?

'Thursday, I think, Stanley.' Joan said without reference to Alice.

'Fine, you might as well go there and back by taxi. Then you can relax and have some wine and even a brandy or two with your coffee. Be better than taking the car.'

Alice flicked her gaze from one to the other, fearful that Joan might interpret the suggestion as a reflection on her driving ability, but there was no adverse reaction. That would make life a lot safer.

The only problem was how on earth was she going to find things to talk about during a whole evening with Joan?

The letter arrived by first post on Wednesday. Stanley had already left to catch an early train to Manchester. Alice had taken the post and a cup of coffee to Joan before she finished getting ready for work. She was startled to hear Joan cry out and wondered if she had spilt her drink. Alice rushed into the bedroom.

'Are you okay?'

Joan was sitting bolt upright in bed, ashen faced.

'He's definitely going into the Army after all I said. He's all I've got and now even he's leaving me.' She started to cry.

Alice rushed to the bathroom for tissues. A letter from Malcolm, he'd done it, he told her he would. Although Alice had little opportunity to get to know him, she had been struck by his quiet determination. This was going to make things difficult. Joan would rant and rave and carry on of course and Stanley would not be back until Friday.

She stood by the bed not sure what she could say without making matters worse. Joan needed to speak to Stanley, but he would be somewhere between London and Manchester by now.

'Could you leave a message for Mr Martin at the hotel? It's the Midland, isn't it?'

'How could he do it? I thought I'd persuaded him when he was home last time.'

No, thought Alice, he just went along with what you said for the sake of peace and quiet. Having made the only sensible suggestion she could think of and have it ignored it seemed there was nothing more she could do. She glanced at her watch. If she didn't hurry, she would be late for work.

'I really should go now so will you be all right?'

'Go, what do you mean go?' Joan leapt out of bed and grabbed

Alice by the shoulders.

'You can't go. How can you leave me now? We must go to Malcolm's school before it's too late; I've got to stop this.'

'I can't miss work.'

'I've always had to manage without my husband; it's always been the same. I've had to deal with everything while Stanley has swanned around having business lunches.'

'But wouldn't it be better to talk to Mr. Martin first?'

'I've done everything for him and the boys and what thanks do I get? We even take you in; it was my idea you know, felt sorry for you. And all you can think of is some tuppenny half-penny job.'

Alice tried to pull away. Joan's nails were digging into her flesh; it was like being in a vice. What was more alarming was the expression in the woman's eyes. She's mad; she had the same expression as Mum had when she was really manic. Alice felt afraid of what Joan might do to her; she couldn't stay and struggled to get free.

'Please let go of my arm because you are hurting me. Please ring the hotel then you can leave a message; that's the best thing.'

As Joan loosened her grip her face seemed to crumple. Alice hesitated, unsure whether to put an arm around the woman or escape whilst she could.

'Sit down; you've had a nasty shock, drink your coffee. Mr Martin left the hotel's phone number in case you needed to get in touch. It's on the notice board in the kitchen, isn't it, I'll get it.' She rushed downstairs, grabbed the piece of paper and ran back.

'Leave a message; ask him to 'phone as soon as he arrives. I'm sure everything will be sorted out.' She paused, should she point out how successful Dad's career in the Army had been? To do so would suggest that she approved of Malcolm's plan. Deciding that discretion was most definitely the better part of valour, she said nothing.

Joan started to dial the number as Alice finished getting ready.

'I'm sure it will all be sorted, see you tonight.' She hurried downstairs.

'Don't leave me, take the day off. I need you here, don't leave, please.'

Alice ran across the hall; she must get away. She opened the front door and as she glanced back, saw Joan was following her. Surely, she wouldn't come out in just her nightdress. Alice ran up the path and turned left, towards the station. She could hear Joan screaming after her.

'You bitch, you selfish little bitch, all you think about is yourself.'

Alice glanced back; Joan was still standing in the doorway. She was yelling, but a brisk morning breeze carried her words away. Alice feared she would faint; her legs were shaking and her heart thumped. She had got away but it was only a temporary reprieve. She would have to go back tonight; she had nowhere else to go.

Joan slammed the door and stormed into the kitchen. There were Alice's breakfast things left for her to clear.

'The slut, the lazy little slut.' With a single sweep of her arm, Joan cleared everything. A plate broke with a satisfying crash as it hit the floor and marmalade oozed from its smashed jar.

'You can clear this lot up when you get back, you ungrateful little bitch.' She had better leave the kitchen, the broken glass and plate would cut her bare feet to ribbons. She went to the sitting room to get a cigarette. She fumbled with the packet, but her hands were shaking so much, she dropped it. The cigarettes spewed in a cascade across the floor. She clutched at her chest and wondered if she was having a heart attack.

What she needed was a drink to steady her nerves, she got the brandy and a glass from the dining room. The brandy would do her good, everyone knew brandy was good for shock. She drained the glass and poured another hefty measure. She dared not go for a shower; it was bound to be when Stanley would ring.

She wandered through to the living room and stared out of the window at the garden. The last of the summer's roses were turning brown at the tips.

She remembered how she had put roses in Malcolm's bedroom to welcome him home. He'd scoffed at her because she had shown how much she loved him, but he didn't care, no one cared. She started to cry; how much longer would she have to wait for Stanley? All her life was spent waiting, waiting for other people. She sat down on the settee and let her head rest against the cushions. The brandy was helping; the ache in her heart had eased. Stanley even begrudged her that consolation, always going on about her and her drinking. If he were a better husband she wouldn't need to drink. He's the one driving the boys away; it's his fault she ended up on her own all the time.

The 'phone rang and she glanced at her watch, it was ten thirty. She had been waiting for hours. She walked to the 'phone with a languorous step, let it ring, let him worry about her for a change. She lifted the receiver.

'Midland Hotel, Manchester, call for Mrs Martin,' said a young cheerful voice, putting you through now.'

'Hello, Stanley, Stanley. You've got to come back at once, I've had a letter from Malcolm, he's going into the Army. You've got to stop him.'

Her lips felt thick and the words seemed to jostle together.

'Listen, Joan, I can't come back. For God's sake don't be so dramatic. Nobody is going to press gang him between now and Friday. We'll talk about it when I get back.'

'Friday, you expect me to wait until Friday. Don't you care?'

'Yes, my darling, you know I care, but I can't do anything right now. We can speak to Malcolm; we can even go up to see him, if you like, at the weekend. But there is nothing I can do today.'

'Bastard.'

'Joan, listen to me please, I know you're upset. Wait until I get back then we can decide on the best thing to do.'

'You're all the same, no one cares about me. Even Alice, after all the things I've done for her. She went off to work, and left me; she knew I was upset.'

'Look, I've got to go. I'll ring you at lunchtime and we can have a proper talk. Now promise you'll have something to eat and some strong coffee. You've got to keep your strength up.'

Joan slammed the 'phone down.

Stanley had been right about one thing. They must go to the school, speak to Malcolm in person, point out that he had responsibilities towards his parents. He had no right to just walk away, that was selfish. He must be told. She walked into the bedroom; the coffee Alice had made was still there. Perhaps Stanley was right. She drank the cold coffee in quick gulps, but almost immediately her stomach seemed to be clenched in an unrelenting knot; she was going to be sick. She just got to the bathroom in time.

On hands and knees, she retched and gulped as the brandy burned her throat. She slumped sideways; perspiration beaded her face. She shivered and pulling herself to her feet staggered to the hand basin and splashed her face with cold water. She felt dreadful but must speak to Malcolm. She turned on the shower, and under the blessed stream of hot water; she let the warmth comfort her shivering limbs. As the water cascaded over her head and shoulders, she lifted her face and revelled in the beat of it on her face. This will cleanse my soul, and take away the pain. Everything will be all right once I've explained to Malcolm then he won't leave me.

Slowly she dried her limbs, taking infinite care, just as she had for Malcolm when he was a baby, her baby; he'd always been hers. She dragged a comb through her, still wet, hair. Didn't bothered drying it. She'd wear the turban she bought when she took Alice shopping. Just wait until she gets back. If she was going to stay, she'll have to learn how to behave herself. Joan walked back to her bedroom.

Dress to kill, she thought, she knew how to put on the style, and arrive looking like a duchess. Tell Malcolm his father would not allow him to join the Army. That's it, his father was furious. She would warn him to change his mind while his father was away. Doing him a service, saving him from his father's rage.

She looked at her reflection in the mirror, not bad, not bad at all. Malcolm would be proud of her; he won't want to let her down. She walked downstairs. She had a terrible taste in her mouth even though she had cleaned her teeth. She paused in the hall; perhaps she should just have a cup of coffee to settle her stomach. After all, she had been upset and who would wonder at it? She looked at the mess in the kitchen. She could pick her way through the debris, and might as well have a piece of toast with the coffee, perhaps Stanley was right.

She sat in her hat and coat, sipping coffee and slowly eating the toast. She had to admit the hot drink was soothing. When she drank the cup Alice made it had been cold, that was probably why it made her sick. She talked through what she would say to Malcolm, reminding him of how pleased he had been when he heard he would miss National Service. Why was he even contemplating joining up?

She thought about the other young men she knew of, the sons of acquaintances and business colleagues of Stanley's, just a bit older than Malcolm. They had seen fighting in Suez and Cyprus. Her hand began to shake; Spencer had been so lucky not to have been posted abroad, but would Malcolm have the same luck?

She stood up and took a few deep breaths. She tried to remember the route Stanley usually took to Mentmore School, just south of Dunstable. He always drove; insisted he was not a good passenger and claimed he got bored. Joan wondered if he did not trust her driving, but that was nonsense; she was an excellent driver. She tried to picture, in her mind's eye, the way they went.

She was sure they picked up the North Circular and then headed towards Watford. From there it was through Hemel Hempstead and on, North West, through the Chiltern Hills.

The countryside would be ablaze with autumn colours, she smiled, this was going to be her adventure. She'd show Stanley she could stop this stupid nonsense. Wait until Friday, indeed she would not.

Chapter 24

Although the day was cold, the sun shone in a clear blue sky. It was a day to lift the spirits and Mark whistled as he walked down the street. It was Wednesday and the weekend would soon be here. He had checked the train times and realised that the Sunday service would not enable him to get to London and back while leaving enough time, between journeys, to have a meal with Susan, her parents and Alice.

He decided he would have to travel down on Saturday, he could call at his old workplace, it would be good to see his ex-colleagues again. He glanced at his watch, there was enough left of his lunch hour to call them, when he got back to the office, to tell them his plans. One of them might offer him a bed for the night, if not he would find a bed and breakfast.

Once back at the office Mark was told Mr Jones, the branch manager, wanted a word with him. Although it was not Mark's Saturday to work, would he be able to come in? Mr Jones had a family crisis which he would have to deal with over the weekend. He was sorry and hoped it would not interfere with Mark's plans and pointed out that everyone had to make sacrifices. He for one would far rather be at work than dealing with his cantankerous mother-in-law. Mark would be left in charge and this would be valuable experience and stand him in good stead in the future.

Mark managed to retain a fixed smile throughout the fulsome excuses and did not comment on the telephone conversation he had overheard. Mr Jones had been enquiring about the possibility of getting a ticket for Saturday's rugby match.

'Of course, I'll come in, Mr Jones,' he said.

'Good lad, remind me to give you the keys on Friday night, keep them over the weekend and make sure you're in early on Monday morning.'

Mark walked out of Mr Jones's office and thought how

fortunate it was that people couldn't read each other's thoughts. There was no point in ringing his mates in London he would have to travel down on Saturday evening after he had locked up the office. Another visit to the station was needed so he could see what later trains were available. He didn't fancy arriving in London late on Saturday night with nowhere to sleep and wondered if he could crash out at his old flat. The thought of having to ask Jim for a favour made him dismiss that idea.

As he had a driving licence perhaps, he could borrow a friend's car, just for Sunday, and set off early. Why was life so complicated? If he couldn't borrow a car, he would catch the earliest train on Sunday and thumb a lift back. But what if he didn't get a lift? If he didn't get to the office by half past eight, quarter to nine at the latest, no one would be able to get in. The phone rang and with great difficulty Mark managed to put on his best office voice.

Alice felt dreadful when she got to work and Professor Walker suggested that she should go home if she wasn't well. That was the last thing Alice wanted to do. She was sent to the hospital canteen and had a cup of tea after which she felt calmer. She wondered what time Stanley would be home and if she dared to stay out until she was sure he was back. But he might not come back tonight, hadn't he planned to be away until Friday? How could she wander the streets for hours or days even in this cold winter weather?

The paper with Barbara's address and phone number was in her purse. She yearned to speak to someone who would be sympathetic; Barbara was just the person, but she would be at work. Alice didn't know what time Barbara's library shut. Perhaps she could go over to see her but, if she didn't go home, Joan would be even angrier than she had been this morning. Alice sighed. She would just have to confront Joan; there was no point in getting worked up about it yet. However, she thought, it would be a good plan to 'phone Joan at lunch time to show she cared.

Joan arrived in a flurry at Mentmore School; she had no time to waste.

Perhaps she should ask the Headteacher for permission to take Malcolm out to lunch or afternoon tea. She rehearsed what she would say, there was nothing to fear; she would make Malcolm see sense. Some half-witted careers teacher had put the lunatic idea into Malcolm's head and the dear boy didn't want to hurt his teacher's feelings.

The approach to Mentmore was up a long tree-lined gravel driveway. The school was housed in a large stone mansion, surrounded by acres of parkland where the boys were encouraged to take part in a wide variety of sports. This was why Stanley and Joan choose the school. Malcolm was a keen sportsman and clearly enjoyed the school's facilities.

As her car crunched up the drive, Joan wondered if she should have rung to make an appointment. Surely not, this was a family crisis, besides they were paying handsomely for Mr Brownlow and his staff to have the privilege of educating their son.

She stopped outside the main entrance, locked the car and walked up the porticoed entrance. The entrance hall was cool and imposing, with large plaques on every wall, in celebration of past pupils' successes. She noticed another more sombre plaque that listed past pupils who had died serving their country in the two World Wars. A cold finger of fear ran up and down her back.

No one was about as she walked through the hallway, her high heels clacked on the polished floor. There was a sign on the left, 'Reception', with an arrow pointing down another corridor. She could hear a typewriter chattering as she knocked on a glass window. After a moment, the glass window slid open and an earnest-looking woman, in late middle age, smiled at Joan.

'Can I help you?'

'Yes, I've come to see my son, Malcolm Martin.'

'Is the Head Master expecting you?'

Joan paused; she should have rung first.

'No, there's been a family crisis and under the circumstances, I thought it best to come straight here.'

The woman stared at Joan. 'Mr Brownlow is a stickler for the school rules, I'm sorry but he takes exception to parents arriving unexpectedly without an appointment. He believes the school does its best to provide a good education and parents must abide by his rules with the same rigour as he demanded from his pupils.'

'So, I'm not allowed to see my own son.'

'I didn't say that but you had better see Mr. Brownlow first and I believe he is in a meeting at the moment with another parent, who did make an appointment.'

'How long will he be?'

'It's difficult to say, would you care to wait? There is a waiting room just down the corridor, on the right. Can I get you a cup of tea or coffee?'

Joan sighed, 'Yes, I suppose so, coffee please.'

She turned and walked down the corridor as instructed and, feeling thoroughly exasperated, sat in one of the overstuffed tweed-covered chairs. Must have a cigarette, she thought. After a few minutes, the woman appeared with a tray holding a coffee jug, cup and saucer, milk, sugar and biscuits. She placed the tray on the low table, in front of Joan.

'There is no smoking allowed, Mrs Martin, I'm sorry. It is one of Mr Brownlow's very strict rules. We want our boys to be healthy in body as well as mind.'

Joan felt she had had her legs slapped and anger bubbled in her head as she ground out the cigarette in the saucer and poured herself some coffee.

She sat, with increasing impatience, waiting for Mr Brownlow to appear. After half an hour she started pacing up and down. This was ridiculous; she couldn't see her own son. She wondered if she should go back to that po-faced secretary to remind the woman she was still waiting. After three quarters of an hour the door opened and Mr. Brownlow walked in.

'Mrs Martin, sorry to have kept you waiting, but it is usual for parents to make an appointment.'

He walked towards her. After a perfunctory touching of hands, he suggested they go to his office. He showed her to a seat and went behind a huge desk which dominated the room. Once seated, he clasped his hands on the blotter in front of him.

'Now, Mrs Martin, what seems to be the problem?'

'I need to speak to my son.'

He waited, smiling.

'It's a personal matter.'

'I see. We do like to know if there are family problems. We don't like our students to have worries or concerns. After all, we are in loco parentis and wish to support our students in times of trouble.'

Joan took a deep breath, 'I received a letter from him this morning which caused me considerable concern.'

She paused while Mr Brownlow nodded and smiled in encouragement.

'I understand, from that letter, that he has decided to join the Army,' she paused again and Mr Brownlow waited.

'His father and I are vehemently opposed to any such idea.'

'I see.' Mr Brownlow stood up. 'I do interview all my six formers, about their future plans. I saw Frederick quite recently but…' he smiled, 'I will get his file, just to refresh my memory.'

He left the room via the side door and Joan heard him open a filing cabinet. He returned, sat down and flicked through Martin, M's file.

'Ah, yes, I saw him three weeks ago. Now he did talk about

your husband's business, he is determined that he will not join it,' he paused, 'is that what you and your husband had hoped for?'

'Not necessarily, but not the armed forces, we had all agreed on that.'

'All?'

'Yes, we had discussed it with Malcolm and he agreed.'

'He's a very keen member of our cadet corps you know; he has always enjoyed the structure and discipline.'

Joan wanted to scream. It was this stupid man who had put pressure on her son, how dare he? She swallowed hard and took a deep breath.

'Maybe, but do parents and their wishes count for nothing? Is it not possible that we might know best?'

'Of course, parents have a considerable part to play in helping their children fly the nest and choose a career that is suited to their talents and inclinations. But, Mrs. Martin, I do think we sometimes have to accept that our children may want to do something that we would not choose for them. Is it not a matter of letting go and accepting, with love and understanding, their choice for their future?'

Joan realised the interview was a complete waste of time. They were all in it together; colluding to distance her from the one person she loved above all others.

'Can I see Malcolm, please?'

Mr Brownlow glanced at his watch.

'I'm sorry, but the sixth-form boys are out of school on an activity day. They left an hour ago. We do not expect them back until six this evening.'

He sat with his hands resting on Malcolm's file.

Joan leapt to her feet she must have only just missed him!

'I am so sorry to have wasted your precious time, please have the decency to tell my son I have been here. I presume that is allowed.'

Mr Brownlow stood and extended his hand. 'I'm sorry I could not be of greater assistance.'

Ignoring the proffered hand, Joan strode to the door, snatched it open and turned, 'I bet you are!' She slammed out, banging the door behind her.

Joan was shaking with rage as she drove away. When she reached the end of the drive she stopped for a much-needed cigarette. She had a good mind to take Malcolm away from Mentmore, how dare that man be so condescending? He had behaved as though he knew Malcolm better than she did. After that she needed a drink, her nerves were in tatters. She'd look for a nice country pub, one that will make her a sandwich. Once she engaged first gear, she set off with a screech of tyres.

Alice walked from the canteen and went to the public phone. Her stomach was knotted with tension. After this morning Joan was hardly likely to be sweetness and light now. Alice dialled the number. Her throat was dry and she cleared it several times as she tried to sort out what she would say when Joan answered. The 'phone rang on and on and a wave of relief flooded through Alice. Joan wasn't in. She could tell Joan she called, to apologise; it was always best to say sorry even when it wasn't her fault. Alice had learned that lesson quickly. She'd take her a bunch of flowers, buy some up at the station, on her way home.

Chapter 25

The Blue Boar public house looked pleasant. Joan drove into the car park, locked the door and walked into the lounge bar. It was very quiet with just a few customers sitting in dark corners. There was a faint hum of conversation and the smell of wood smoke which came from the huge fireplace, piled high with crackling logs. She went to the bar.

'A large brandy, please.'

The well-built, middle-aged barman finished polishing a glass, smiled and turned to the appropriate optic.

'Do you have sandwiches or anything?'

'Yes, Madam, cheese or ham? The ham's home-cooked.'

'Yes, that would be fine thank you.'

She picked up her glass and walked to an empty table by the window. The brandy made her stomach glow and she felt very hungry. She lit a cigarette while she waited for the food. After ten minutes a comfortably rounded, middle-aged woman, in an apron, appeared with a plate of sandwiches.

Joan smiled and turned to the barman, 'Another brandy, please.'

'Double, Madam?'

'Yes, please.'

She thought about the morning's events; she would just have to put her foot down. She would not be treated so casually. She glanced at her watch, by now Stanley should be wondering where she was, maybe even worrying about her for a change. As for Alice, if she didn't buck her ideas up, she could go; let her find someone else to wait on her hand and foot.

Glowing with righteous indignation, Joan finished her meal. She stood, relaxed. She felt comfortable with herself, all the anger had gone; she was in charge now. She could sort things out. She settled her bill, waved a cheery goodbye and walked with studied care to her car.

She sat thinking for a moment. If she went back the way she had come there would be lots of traffic. She could go on the new motorway down to Watford then she would miss Hemel Hempstead. She had never been on the M1; Stanley always took what he called the scenic route. It would be fun on a motorway, she could put her foot down, it would be like the highways in the States. She started the engine, reversed and drove out of the car park keeping her eyes open for the motorway signs.

She drove with exaggerated care; demonstrating to herself what a fine and competent driver she was. Every gear change was executed with precision; she imagined she was taking the Advanced Driving Test. She might do that one day, that would be one in the eye for Stanley. So deep in thought, she realized, too late, she had missed the motorway. She slammed on her brakes and glanced in her mirror, there was a lorry behind her. She wound down the window and waved the driver on. A spotty-faced youth, in the passenger seat, pulled a face and indicated, in a surly manner, that she needed to go to an optician. She ignored him, probably couldn't even drive, who was he to try to lord it over her, the stupid little runt?

Now she needed somewhere to turn around, but there were no obvious turnings nearby. She'd do a three-point turn, that would be best and she started to manoeuvre. The deserted road suddenly become crowded with cars and lorries, but Joan's car was straddled across the road. She felt flustered; she had been doing so well, why were these people harassing her?

In her haste, she stalled the engine. She jammed her foot hard down on the accelerator and tried the starter, now she could smell petrol. She must have flooded the engine. She could see there was a long queue of traffic in both directions and horns were blaring. The driver of the nearest car was getting out.

'What the hell are you doing trying to turn here?'

The sharp retort on her lips evaporated, a bit of charm might be better. She smiled in, what she hoped was, an alluring way.

'I'm lost, I need to get to the motorway, it's urgent. Please help me.'

The man pulled a face, 'Bloody women drivers,' he muttered loudly enough for Joan to hear, 'smells as though you've flooded it. Get out I'll see what I can do.'

Another driver came to offer assistance.

'Want a push, mate?'

'She's flooded it.'

Joan stood on the roadway and shivered; the euphoria had gone. The car was manhandled into the side of the road and after two attempts the engine started.

'Thank you so much,' she said as the two men returned to their respective vehicles. She got back in her car, engaged gear and letting the clutch out too fast, jolted and jerked her way up the road. She could not control the shivering; she must be in a state of shock. How could she get warm? She pulled into the first lay-by she saw and turned up the heater. She lit a cigarette but after a few drags threw it away, she felt sick, she must get home.

She saw the motorway sign ahead, her plan to go that way home was the best, she would get there quicker and be able to have a good hot bath. Perhaps she was sickening for something. She would go to bed after her bath and let Alice find her there. As Stanley had said he would ring, he was bound to ring again. Joan hoped he was worried that he had not been able to make contact with her earlier.

The heater was doing its job, she felt better and the shivering had stopped. The thought of sinking into a steaming bath spurred her on. She engaged first gear and drove down the slip road to join the M.1. She got to the start of the carriageway and saw streams of traffic thundering past. It was really shifting. She wondered if she was doing the right thing after all, but there was no turning back.

She couldn't do a three-point turn now.

She eased forward, waiting for a gap, hesitated then lost patience and flooring the accelerator shot into the nearside lane. She saw a car coming up fast behind her. Just keep going, she thought, as she pressed her foot down harder. The gap between her car and the one behind increased. She was all right now; she could ease up a little. She fumbled for her cigarettes on the front passenger seat. This was fun. She glanced at the speedo, eighty miles an hour; she laughed out loud. She imagined the look of horror Stanley would have on his face if he had been beside her.

She lit a cigarette and sat back; she would soon be home. It was a good little car, bouncing along so happily, she should do this more often. She was lulled by the regular sound from the wheels as they rode over the concrete slabs that made up the motorway surface. It was a bit like being on a train, clackety-clack, clackety-clack. She yawned and wriggled a little in her seat; she must not get too comfortable. She could go a bit faster and get home sooner. She glanced in her mirror and with nothing behind her, she pulled out into the middle lane and put her foot down.

She was beginning to feel sleepy. Open the windows a little, and get some fresh air, she took several deep breaths and her head felt better. As she started to close the window the front offside tyre exploded. She had only one hand on the steering wheel which bucked and jerked out of her hand as the car careered towards the central reservation. Confused, Joan pressed her foot down hard on what she thought was the brake as the car lurched onto the wheel's metal rim. She tried to grab the steering wheel with both hands and turn it. She could hear the screeching of brakes, it must be her brakes, but the car wasn't slowing down, what was happening?

The wheel would not turn, she was being forced into oncoming traffic. It was then she saw the bridge, it seemed to leap towards her, squat, ugly, menacing, grey concrete. It loomed over her and suddenly it was all she could see in front of her, blocking out everything else; this monster would crush her. She opened her mouth to scream, but blood thudding in her ears obliterated the sound.

The Anglia hit the bridge at forty-five degrees. The sharp edge of the central support held fast and the bonnet of the car was crumpled down the whole of its length, dividing the front of the car into two equal but compressed halves. Joan watched as the front of the car seemed to disappear beneath her. There was terrible pressure on her legs and she heard a strange crunching sound, her legs were being squeezed, tighter and tighter. She supposed the sound must be her bones breaking. She looked down, in surprise, the steering wheel was coming up to meet her, it too was crushing her; it was crushing her chest.

The windscreen shattered. Her eyes were open wide as glass flew towards her; she gasped when a long sliver penetrated her right eye. It didn't hurt, but she was puzzled that she could not close her eyelid. She tried to lift her hand to brush whatever it was away, but her arms were pinned down by the steering wheel which came closer and closer. There would be no room for her soon, no space left in her dear little car. The pain in her chest was becoming unbearable. She heard that strange, crunching sound again; her ribs could withstand the pressure no longer. One by one they crumpled into razor-sharp splinters, waiting to deliver the coup de grace. Must breathe, must get air, she can't stand this pressure any more.

In one, last, desperate effort she tried to expand her lungs and the slivers of bone slid, effortlessly into the quivering tissue and both lungs collapsed with a soundless sigh. Her head slumped forward, she needed to rest. The last sound she heard was the wailing of the car horn as the weight of her head depressed it.

Chapter 26

Alice stood for most of her train journey home. The butterflies in her stomach felt as though they had clogs on. She checked her purse as she left the station. She had just enough money for a reasonable bunch of flowers. The chrysanthemums looked lovely with their russet shades echoing the trees' autumnal foliage. She walked slowly down the street, her feet dragging her nearer to the inevitable scene with Joan.

If Spencer had been serious about her, it would have been worthwhile to continue making an effort to get on with the woman. What was the point now? Increasingly she accepted that her relationship with Spencer was over, there was no reason for her to stay with the Martins.

As she approached the house, she was surprised to see Joan's car was not there, she was usually at home when Alice returned from work. She let herself into a house that was silent and clearly empty. The car wasn't due at the garage for repairs; Mr Martin had sorted that out already. She stood in the hall not sure what she should do. Perhaps the best thing was to get a vase and put the flowers in water. She could point them out when Joan returned. Perhaps should she leave them wrapped and present them and grovel a bit. Joan liked arranging flowers.

She walked into the kitchen and stared at the wreckage. Of course, in the morning's furore, she had forgotten to clear her breakfast things. Considering the mood, she had been in, Joan had obviously taken exception to Alice's oversight.

Alice sighed as she draped her coat on the back of a chair, stuck flowers in the sink and went for the dustpan and brush. She swept up the fragments of the smashed plate and gingerly picked up the marmalade-encrusted pieces of glass, shovelling the lot into the bin. The floor was sticky and streaked with coffee. She took the bin outside, emptied it and grabbed the mop and bucket on the way back. She had just finished when she heard the sound of a key in the front-door lock. She raced to replace the mop and bucket outside the back door, grabbed the flowers and went to meet Joan.

To her amazement, it was Stanley standing in the hall. He had removed his overcoat and was just standing there. The expression on his face made Alice's heart lurch, something dreadful had happened.

'You haven't heard yet, have you?' His voice was barely a whisper.

'Heard what?'

'There's been an accident,' he paused, 'Joan is dead.'

Alice collapsed; the flowers were crushed by the weight of her body; their petals scattered on the black and white tiled floor, like droplets of blood.

Stanley contacted Mentmore School later that day and then drove up to collect Malcolm. Spencer had been contacted in Stockholm and returned by 'plane the following afternoon. Alice had stayed in her room most of the time, unable to sleep, and eating little. There had been much coming and going as the funeral was arranged. The three remaining members of the Martin family spoke in low voices which drifted upstairs to remind Alice of her isolation. She was ashamed; she could not leave them to their grief, but where could she go?

Stanley knocked on her bedroom door, came in and sat beside her. His worried look made her tears flow again.

'Is there no one you can talk to? I hate to see you like this.'

She had shaken her head.

'You must stop blaming yourself, it could have happened at any time.'

She had sat very still, eyes so swollen with crying she looked as though she had been beaten up.

'Let me at least get you a cup of tea or coffee, you can't go on like this.'

He was right, she felt drained.

'Shall I 'phone your parents?'

'I'm so sorry, she asked me to stay with her. but I went to work.'

'I will not let you blame yourself. Are you listening, my dear? It was not your fault.'

'I was totally selfish and thought only of myself, I was so frightened, I didn't know what to do."

'We both knew Joan had a problem. You witnessed that first hand, didn't you?'

Alice nodded.

'It seems Joan had been drinking, that was her decision. She took an awful risk with her life, but it could have happened anywhere. It had nothing to do with you. If anyone is to blame, I am.'

'But you were so good to her.'

'Maybe not; I should have listened to her more, understood how unhappy she was.'

Stanley hugged Alice and gave her his handkerchief to wipe away tears.

'Now if you continue to blame yourself, I shall be very upset and you don't want that, do you?'

Alice nodded.

'I'd rather not upset you, not tonight anyway.'

Stanley patted her shoulder and went back downstairs where Spencer and Malcolm were finishing a meal their father had cooked.

Alice lay on her bed, in the dark, listening to the steady hum of traffic on the main road. She had tried to imagine how Joan must have felt when she knew she was going to hit the bridge. The police had reassured Stanley that Joan would not have suffered; it had been over in a split second. Despite all Stanley had said, Alice could not stop her tears.

Again, he asked if he should contact her parents, but Mum and Dad were the last people Alice wanted to speak to. In their different ways, neither would have understood how she felt. She would have to leave here, that she knew, but it would not be to go to either of them. Of course, there was Barbara, dare she phone her? Did she have the right to burden someone she had only met once?

Although Stanley had been so kind surely, he would prefer not to have a lodger at such a difficult time. Alice went downstairs to speak to him and found him slumped in an armchair. Spencer and Malcolm were in the kitchen.

'May I use the 'phone?'

'Of course, my dear, do you want to use the one in our room?'

They exchanged glances, acknowledged his error, it was his room now.

'Thank you.'

She went back to her room and searched for Barbara's number.

Spencer and Malcolm were washing up, talking quietly when Stanley joined them; he put the kettle on the stove, glad his sons seemed comfortable in each other's company.

'I'm making a cup of tea for Alice; she's blaming herself.'

'That's stupid,' Malcolm said, 'if anyone's to blame, it's me. I sent the letter that started it all off.'

Stanley sat down, at the kitchen table. 'I think it's time we laid that particular ghost to rest once and for all, neither one of you is to blame. Your mother had a serious drinking problem, you both knew that. You could say I'm to blame for buying her a car. What's happened cannot be undone; blame won't make any difference. Will you take the tea upstairs, Spencer? Try to comfort the poor girl.'

Spencer looked uneasy. 'I'd rather not, Dad. You see I should have written and told her.'

'Told her what?'

'Berthe told me to write, but I kept putting it off, what can I do now when she's so upset?'

Stanley watched him but said nothing.

'Will Alice go on living here, after what's happened?'

'I don't know, I have asked her to contact her parents but she doesn't want to.'

'It's a bit awkward really.'

Stanley raised his eyebrows.

'I don't think Alice and I will be seeing much of each other in the future…' Spencer's voice trailed away.

'I presume she doesn't know that yet?'

'It didn't seem the right time. Alice's all right, but she's just a kid, Dad.'

'You may not feel like saying anything over the next few days, but I do expect you to do the decent thing before you go back. Now take this tea up and at least try to be kind to the poor girl.'

As well as tea Spencer took biscuits, he tapped on the door and walked in.

'Dad said you are blaming yourself. You shouldn't, you know; it wasn't your fault.'

He stood by the bed but Alice knew he wanted to go downstairs. She would have to talk for him; it was obvious he didn't want her.

'It's not going to work, is it?'

'What?'

'Us.'

'Is that why you are so upset?'

Alice looked at him, how arrogant when his mother had just died.

'Us being apart made me see that we aren't really suited.'

His look of relief told Alice everything, no matter how much her heart may ache at the moment, he was really a weak man. She would probably have come to despise him

'Thank you for the tea,' she said, 'I have a phone call to make.'

Spencer left without a backward glance.

Alice took a deep breath and dialled Barbara's number. She tried to keep calm, but the need to explain everything would make her cry. Although she had not liked Joan, she had never wanted this. Perhaps it had been unhappiness that made Joan behave as she did. How sad.

Barbara had not recognised Alice's voice at first, but as she listened it was clear something dreadful had happened. Alice kept saying it was all her fault and someone had been killed. Had Jeffrey had an accident? Had he been injured, or was it he who had been killed? Surely, she would have heard. She waited for the avalanche of words to slow and finally stutter to a halt. She heard Alice crying quietly.

'Alice, Alice can you hear me?'

'Yes.'

'Listen, my dear, I realize you are dreadfully upset, but I couldn't make out what you were saying. Does it involve your dad?'

'No, no it's Mrs. Martin.'

Who the hell was Mrs Martin?

'You know, Spencer's mother.'

'I see. I am so sorry, you poor thing.'

'But it was all my fault, you see she wanted me to take the day off work, but I wouldn't, because I was frightened and she had this dreadful accident and if I'd been at home it wouldn't have happened…'

'Hush child, hush, of course, it wasn't your fault.'

'But it was, she'd been drinking, that's what the post-mortem showed. If

I had been with her she might not have had a drink. She just needed someone to talk to and I didn't listen, I just went to work and I bought some flowers to give to her, to say sorry, but she was already dead.'

Barbara waited. 'Do you want me to tell your father?'

'No, no he'll say it was my fault too.'

'I'm sure he wouldn't.' But perhaps he would, Jeffrey did have a facility for offloading blame. 'What would you like me to do?'

'I don't know. I need to talk to someone; Spencer and Malcolm have come home and I just feel I'm in the way. They must hate me.'

'Of course, they don't." Barbara decided that a little briskness was needed, "Now first of all, what's your 'phone number? Secondly, when is the funeral?'

'Next week I think.'

'Would it help if you came over to see me? Go to work tomorrow, that will stop you brooding, then come straight over. Tell Mr Martin you think it best to leave them to grieve on their own. You can give my phone number if you like, should they need to contact you."

Alice sighed. Her anguish seemed to melt away; at last, she had someone who wanted to take care of her.

'That would be so good,' she said, 'are you sure I won't be a nuisance?'

'Of course, you're bound to be a terrible nuisance, but don't worry, my dear, I can cope.'

Susan looked at the contents of her wardrobe; she needed to look her best on

Sunday. She had already booked a hair appointment for Saturday morning and after that, she would go shopping for something new. Part of her felt guilty; she had sent the letter to Alice, but not until Wednesday evening. If it didn't arrive in time, she would have Mark to herself. But these two people had been good friends to her; they were more than she deserved. There was only one thing to do, she took a deep breath, went to the phone and dialled the hostel's number.

'Hello, Miss Pritchard? It's Susan, I'm sorry to bother you again but have you received a letter from me today?'

'Yes, I sent it on.'

'Oh, it's rather important and I didn't post it as soon as I should. It probably won't arrive until Monday and that will be too late. Can you contact Alice and ask her to phone me?"

Miss Pritchard laughed, 'Leave it with me.'

Susan stood for a while and knew that she had, for once, done the right thing.

Alice walked downstairs. She had slept deeply and felt quite light-headed. The house was very still. Now she had decided her time in this house was coming to an end, it was like being in a hotel. She was transient, just visiting, so she must behave with care, and take nothing for granted. She presumed everyone was still asleep. She stood in the doorway of the kitchen and saw Stanley at the kitchen table; she wondered if walking in on him would be an intrusion. He became aware of her presence.

'Come in, dear, have you managed to get some rest?'

'Yes, thank you. I'm going to get off to work soon unless there is anything I can do.'

'You go, it will do you good. I'll see you tonight.'

'Do you mind if I don't come back, Barbara, that's Dad's friend, has asked me to go to her place after work and stay the night. I can give you her number if you like, in case anyone calls.'

'I think that's a good idea; we are not ourselves, at the moment. Now you must have some breakfast before you go.'

Alice knocked at Barbara's door, she felt surprisingly nervous. She heard footsteps coming down the stairs and when the door opened, there she was arms wide, smiling, a glorious welcome; Alice could feel her eyes filling.

'Come in, my dear, it is so good to see you.'

They walked upstairs together and Alice felt the warmth of belonging.

'You've had a horrible experience and if you want to have a damned good cry, I don't mind, I've got plenty of handkerchiefs.'

Being given not just permission to cry, but positive encouragement made it unnecessary. Alice sat down on the settee and felt tension recede. The table was set, just because she was expected. It had been set beautifully with flowers and wine glasses, just for her. She sighed and let her head sink back into the cushions. Barbara sat beside her. There was no pressure, no recrimination; everything would sort itself out somehow.

'Do you think it would have made any difference if I had stayed with Mrs Martin if I hadn't gone to work?'

'I honestly don't know. Did she drink much as a rule?'

'Yes, she and Mr Martin were always at loggerheads about it.'

'So, what could you have done?'

'I don't know. I suppose it's because I was the last person she saw before she went off to Malcolm's school.'

Barbara pulled a face, 'I think you are punishing yourself needlessly. I doubt Mr Martin thinks you could have done anything. I should imagine he's just sad.' He paused, 'No, relieved that you are here.'

Alice opened her eyes wide; it had not occurred to her. Of course, if she had stayed at home, she would almost certainly have been dragged to Mentmore School too! And yes, she would have either been killed or very seriously injured.

'You see, my dear, then it would have been a double tragedy; it would have made everything even worse. You have your life ahead of you. I don't know why Mrs Martin had a problem with drink; her husband might not be able to answer that one either. What I do know is that she effectively took her own life, by accident or design; that was her choice. She must not be allowed to do the same to you and thank God, she didn't.'

Alice was too stunned to reply.

Barbara patted her knee, 'I think it's time we had something to eat; you are looking decidedly peaky.'

After their meal, it was Barbara who brought up the subject of where Alice was going to live.

'I assume you don't intend to go back to Dad.'

'It wouldn't work. Does he know what happened?'

'Actually, I haven't seen him for a while.'

Alice looked up. She had such an anxious expression Barbara could not help but laugh at her.

'My dear girl, don't look so worried. Our friendship does not depend on your father, I like you for yourself. As I'm sure you know, he is an obstinate old cuss and I told him so. At the moment, he is stewing in his own juice. It will do him good; in the end, he'll be a lot more tender.'

Alice giggled. She had an absurd image of her father wedged into a large casserole dish.

'So, what will you do? I suspect Mum's out too.'

Alice nodded, 'My stepbrother and sister would see to that.'

'What about the hostel, if only as a temporary measure?'

'Of course, yes, Miss Pritchard said she could always find a bed for me.'

'That's it then. You won't have to stay there forever and when you are here on a visit, I can always put you up, as long as you don't mind the settee.'

'Why are you so nice to me?'

'I've told you I like you.'

'I'm glad.'

'Right, down to business; I'm going to clear the table, you are going to 'phone this Pritchard person and then we are going to confront the dragon in his lair.'

'What do you think he will say?'

'Haven't a clue, but I'm not worried and you mustn't be either.'

While Barbara washed up Alice phoned the hostel.

'Miss Pritchard speaking.'

'It's Alice Ward, Miss Pritchard, I wonder if you can help me. You did say that you would always be able to find a bed for me if I needed one and if it's possible, I would like to move back.'

'I'll just check.'

Alice heard the rustling of papers and kept her fingers crossed.

'There will be a vacancy in ten days, can you manage until then?'

'Yes, that will be fine, thank you so much.'

'Before you go have you heard from Susan Johnson?'

'No, not recently.'

'You had better phone her; do you have her number?'

'No, I don't.'

'Now I do not usually give out personal information, but I understand from Susan that she wants to invite you to her house, this Sunday. Therefore, I feel I can break the rules just this once.'

With the number provided, Alice went to the kitchen to help.

Alice's head was spinning, everything was happening too fast. She took Susan's address and said she would call back to confirm arrangements.

'Guess what?' she said to Barbara and recounted the tale of the party that wasn't, the repulsive Jim, Mark's lunch date that wasn't and Spencer and Berthe.

'Good Lord, it's a wonder you've time to breathe. I presume you would like to see Mark again.'

'Yes, he was so kind and I think we could be good friends.'

'What a very sensible young woman you are. Friends are so important; romance can come later if it's right.'

'Susan lives in Elstree, I'm not sure how I'll get there.'

'We'll let your father sort that out; he can make himself useful.'

Alice giggled.

'He can take me to lunch after he's dropped you at Susan's and we will pick you up afterwards.'

They walked to the flats, armed with paper and pencil to leave a note if Jeffrey wasn't in. Once at the front door, Barbara made sure that they were standing level if not exactly shoulder to shoulder. Alice knocked and they heard his footsteps coming up the hallway. Alice looked at Barbara. The door was opened and Jeffrey stared at them both for a second, taken aback, but it was only for a second before he gave a welcoming smile.

'What a lovely surprise, come in my dears, come in. I'll put the kettle on.'

Chapter 27

Saturday was busier than usual and Mark had little time to think about plans for his journey south. He had been unable to borrow a car so would have to rely on getting the earliest train on Sunday. He had phoned Susan to find out how he would get to her house from the station. She had assured him that her father would be happy to pick him up once he got to Euston. She also said she had spoken to Alice and she would be able to come for lunch too. Apparently, her father would drop her at Susan's.

If, as his mother claimed, he was in the throes of obsession, only seeing Alice again would sort out his feelings. He could not make any plans for the future until then. Part of him wanted to write to Alice to make his own arrangements to meet; he wasn't sure how wise it was to involve Susan. And there were so many other difficulties, was it all worth it? Perhaps I'm scared, he thought, scared that he would make a fool of himself.

Quite apart from the problems of getting to Elstree, there was also the worry he might not be able to thumb a lift home. The manager, Mr Jones, would hit the roof if the office was locked and there was no one to open up on time. There must be another set of keys somewhere, so Mark would have to hope for the best.

Alice had breakfast with Barbara before she set off for work.

'I've decided I will go to the Martin's after work and collect some clothes for tomorrow; I can't go in this lot.'

'Shall I ask your dad round tonight?'

Alice hesitated. 'Would you mind if I asked you not to, it's just that I can't talk about it all yet, I couldn't bear it if he said I told you so.'

Barbara patted Alice's arm, 'Don't worry, we'll have a girl's night in. After all, we'll both see him on Sunday. I must dash, but

I'll leave you a key.'

Alice cleared up and wondered if she should phone before she left for the Martins' house. If she did, it would give Spencer a chance to avoid meeting her. After some thought, she decided he didn't deserve such consideration and set off to catch the Tube.

When she arrived the house was empty, perhaps they had gone to the undertakers. She ran upstairs and put the clothes she wanted and, of course, the shoes Joan had bought her into a large carrier bag. She hurried back downstairs and decided to leave a short note explaining she had been invited out by a friend and would return on Sunday, for the last time.

Sitting in the train she had time to think about all that had happened. She knew people didn't, as a rule, change much as they got older but yesterday's meeting with Dad had been strange. He seemed softer, kinder and had, without hesitation, said he would be pleased to take her to Susan's. It could only be Barbara's influence, perhaps stewing in his own juice had done the trick. Alice smiled and then saw that the man opposite her was smiling back. She blushed and looked away.

It would be nice seeing Susan again after the horrors of the abortion. Perhaps it had made Susan nicer too but, what a terrible way to learn. Was that why Susan had invited her for a meal? Maybe she accepted that she hadn't behaved well and wanted to make amends. It was curious that Mark had been invited too although Susan had said several times that she liked him. Was the meal an opportunity to show that she, Susan, was staking her claim to him?

Alice sighed, Mark the enigma, Mark who had been such good company. It all seemed so long ago now. She recalled how upset she had been over Jim's attempted rape. Mark had soothed her and she had relaxed, felt so comfortable in his presence. Supposing when they met, he just thought she was not interesting or pretty enough. Susan was pretty. Perhaps she was making too much of it; after all, that experience with Jim had been enough to make anyone's judgement dodgy.

She walked from the station and debated with herself whether or not she should have her hair done. She had not given the Martins her board and lodging money. Most of the cash she had was not strictly speaking hers. She hesitated outside a hair salon took a deep breath and walked in.

Mark rose early on Sunday morning, but his mother was up before him.

'You don't think I'd let you go off without a decent breakfast, do you?'

Mark smiled, 'Good old Mum, what would I do without you?'

'Get into a terrible mess, I don't doubt.'

Mark watched as she bustled about boiling eggs, making toast and brewing a large pot of tea. She was beginning to look old; she hasn't had it easy with Dad dying before his time yet she never complained. He glanced at his watch he would have to be off soon. He had such mixed feelings about the whole thing, perhaps he was just being a romantic fool.

He rushed out of the house and caught the Manchester bus. He would have to get a car; he couldn't go on like this. Besides with a car, he would be able to take prospective buyers to view properties instead of always being stuck in the office. It would make travelling to London easier too because he would be travelling there, wouldn't he?

Worried that he would miss the train, he ran up the approach to Piccadilly rail station ticket office.

'London Euston, please, a return.'

The man behind the grille smirked. 'Not running, mate.'

'What?'

'Been cancelled, leaves on the line.'

Damn, damn, damn,' Mark said, 'leaves on the bloody line.'

'Here mate, not having any of that,' and with a crash, the booking clerk closed the ticket office window.

Mark turned away and walked back to the bus stop for his return journey. Now what? He'd better get home and call Susan to make his apologies.

Alice was wearing her full-skirted green dress but hadn't brought a coat.

'I shan't need a coat as Dad's chauffeuring me,' she told Barbara who had lent her some pretty gold earrings.

Jeffrey arrived on time, as expected, and this time did not make any derogatory remarks. He had a route planned having gone to the nearest phone box and called the A. A. for some advice. Barbara sat in the front and read instructions from the sheet of directions he had given her. Watching them from the back seat, Alice hoped that Dad would have the sense to keep hold of Barbara who had already made such a difference to both their lives.

They arrived and, once Johnson's front door opened, drove off with

Barbara giving a cheery wave.

'Who was that?' Susan asked.

'My Dad and his girlfriend.'

'Thought you didn't get on with him.'

'Well, I do now, sort of.'

'I'd better introduce you to Mum and Dad,'

Susan took Alice through to the kitchen where Mrs. Johnson was preparing vegetables.

'Now, is there anything you don't like?' Mrs Johnson asked.

'No, it all looks lovely, thank you for inviting me.'

Mr Johnson walked in from the sitting room, 'Thought I heard voices, you must be Alice.'

Once introductions were over, Susan took Alice upstairs.

'This is my bedroom.'

Alice gasped, 'It's lovely,' and remembered the stark, cold room she had at Dad's.

'Mark called about an hour ago,' Susan said, 'he can't make it. He was coming down on the train, but it's been cancelled. He left his number if you want to call him.'

Alice felt herself blush, 'Yes, please, if you don't mind.'

'Phone's downstairs, in the hall.'

Susan listened as Alice hurried downstairs then firmly closed her bedroom door.

Alice stood with the receiver in her hand, what should she say to him? She dialled and waited as the phone rang. A woman answered, Mark's mother, Alice assumed.

'May I speak to Mark, please?'

'You must be Alice; I've heard a lot about you.'

Alice felt herself blush.

'I'll just get him.'

'Would you believe it, leaves on the line the ticket clerk said.'

Alice started to laugh and heard Mark, at the other end, join in.

'Shall we call it quits? I couldn't help being ill, and you can't help leaves on the line.'

'So do we give up on the grounds the fates are against us?'

Alice paused, 'Oh no, don't let's do that.'

'I'm glad that's how you feel.'

Alice felt her heart thumping, he really does like me, she thought, and I'm so pleased. Now I've got his number we can keep in touch that way until we can arrange to meet.

'What are you doing next weekend?'

'Nothing,' Alice said.

Right, I will get a train down on Saturday and book a B&B for the night and go back Sunday, leaves on the line permitting.'

He was so easy to talk to, she told him about Joan and Spencer and Barbara and her decision to return to the hostel for a while. He told her about the job and his mum and going walking in the hills and having to work yesterday when it was really his Saturday off. It was all wonderful, she thought, and well worth waiting for. She gave him Barbara's number and the Martin's too so he could contact her wherever she was.

'I will see you next week, my girl, even if I have to walk.'

'I'll hold you to that.'

She went back to Susan's room grinning. 'Sorry I was so long.'

Susan knew she must forget Mark and be glad for Alice.

During the drive back to London, Alice talked about the meal and meeting Susan's parents, but didn't mention speaking to Mark. She would tell Barbara another time when they were on their own. After collecting her things from Barbara's flat, Jeffrey drove Alice back to the Martins'. On the way there, they chatted about what a nice pub he and Barbara had visited for lunch. Alice told Jeffrey of her decision to move back to the hostel for a while.

'I never did like…' Jeffrey stopped. 'Glad you had a good time today, my dear,' he said as he pulled into the kerb.

'Thanks, Dad, I'm so grateful for the lift and everything.'

Jeffrey smiled. 'I think I'll pop in on Barbara on the way home, she promised me a nightcap once I'd seen you safely here.'

He leaned over and kissed her. 'Take care, my dear, keep in touch.'

This had been the lovely end to an almost perfect day, and next weekend she would meet Mark. She had so much to look forward to.

Available worldwide from Amazon

Michael Terence
Publishing

www.mtp.agency

mtp.agency

@mtp_agency

Printed in Great Britain
by Amazon

24560278R00148